EVIL IN DISGUISE

Simon Pack Novel # 4

John M. Vermillion

PART ONE

DEATH TRAIN

CHAPTER ONE

Before it left our solar system, from six billion kilometers away, the spacecraft Voyager 1 turned its camera back in the direction of planet Earth one last time. The resulting shot was immortalized in the words of astronomer Carl Sagan, who called it 'the pale blue dot.' It humbles us, that photo, reminding us of our puniness in the vast universe. It reminds us that the wisest among us, for practical purposes, knows nothing on the cosmic scale. That the distance of six billion kilometers is, for practical purposes, infinite. And yet, this Earth is what we have and where we are. Some of our human inhabitants, the only life forms of such a type yet known to exist in this universe, do their best to prevent it from working. Others do their best to make it work. The cosmos remains a mystery, or so it seems to the smallness of our minds.

Thomas Edison, George Westinghouse, and Nikola Tesla all reached a point where they had to throw up their hands and rest in the mystery. Brilliant scientists all, they could explain the equipment required to generate electricity, and describe the physics, but when asked to state what exactly this electricity was, they were left slack-jawed, having to say 'it just is.' But what marvelous things they could make this electricity do: produce light, produce heat, spark an engine to life. But still, in the end, electricity is so much a mystery.

Simon Pack, former Marine General and former Governor of Montana, was one of the ones who tried hard to make his speck of the cosmos work. By any reasonable standard of morality, he was a good man. He attempted to help others pave their own roads to a successful life. He respected the boundaries of his fellow citizens. He fought on behalf of causes he believed in.

But Simon Pack had his own close-to-home mystery in which he had to rest. It was simultaneously curse and blessing. Trouble found him or he found it, a formulation that to Pack was a distinction without a difference. Maybe Tesla could examine Pack and discover there actually exists a magnetic force that without surcease (as a practical matter) has beset him his entire adult life. Said force permits Pack little rest between episodes of violence.

Now, somewhere just beyond the middle point of his years, we find the General like a ball no longer in motion (at rest) at his cabin in rural northwestern Montana. Not far from the Upper Yaak River Valley, where mere months earlier he had some considerable set-to's that brought him national attention (one more time, glommed onto many previous times). As this story thus opens, Simon Pack cannot fathom the circuitous path he will follow to encounter one Bad Man (who does his best on our little speck of the cosmos to make it worse). A Bad Man whose name is Blaise Paschal.

But the author is getting ahead of himself. Looking down from a pedestrian terrestrial distance, we would see Simon Pack today just taking it easy. A domesticated cat who has found his comfortable spot in the sunbeam through a window on a cold winter day. A lioness swatting playfully, but almost lazily, at her newborn cubs.

We suppose Pack is sufficiently aware to recognize this 'taking it easy' will not pertain for long. Because it never has. Trouble visits him. Soon enough Simon Pack will encounter Blaise Paschal, but before he does more misery awaits. Misery perpetually is part of the mystery for Simon.

Blaise Paschal: An Introduction

Far as Blaise Paschal knew, he was the only member of his line still alive. This was good. There could never be a reporter doing a human-interest story about how the young boy had survived a rough past.

He'd hated his family, if you could call a callous mother and abusive brother a family. Not because they were poor. More because they were shiftless. The mother was content to let them subsist on welfare. She never held a job, never tried to get one.

The brother was six years older, and beat on Blaise remorselessly since the younger one could remember. Real beatings. At twelve the older brother was a drunk, the mother apparently oblivious to it. By fourteen, he'd been a corner boy in Dayton, Ohio. By seventeen, he'd been shot to death in some drug feud that police didn't care to dissect to a level of detail that would explain what happened. Blaise didn't miss his brother. A detective came to take 11-year-old Blaise to the Montgomery County morgue to identify his brother's body. He could feel the detective's eyes on him as the morgue attendant slid the corpse out of the cold chamber. Blaise's demeanor, the detective saw, registered nothing…no sadness or pain…the detective, a veteran of the streets, couldn't stop himself from suspecting this lad—

who should've been playing a Little League sport—would end up on such a slab himself in not many years.

They lived in a trailer park, but that was too splendid a name for it. Its unofficial but fitting name was The Rathole. It was a place where trailers were butted up against one another in all kinds of ways, making for a disharmonious and confusing display. It was as if someone had been assigned the task of jamming as many trailers into x space as he could, the result being a foul overcrowded rat maze mishmash. No self-respecting Health Department could have allowed such a rathole to exist, but it did. Rats literally were everywhere. All day long Blaise heard raised voices and cursing and the plaints of females of all ages. Rapes happened routinely but no one cared. Police didn't come into The Rathole. Probably the police didn't get summoned to come, either. Fights occurred daily, and it was not uncommon for gangs to brutalize just one boy or girl, regardless of their ages. Meanwhile, his shiftless mother lay out, sprawled on a sofa looking at inane television shows day and night. On the typical day, Blaise ate corn and beans directly from the cans.

He hated elementary school too. The school nurse sent a note home asking the mother to pay more attention to her son's dental hygiene. Get him to a dentist, she said. All his teeth are rotted out. It might've been medicine mouth or Mountain Dew mouth, the not uncommon affliction of poor children, the nurse couldn't tell. Blaise held his mother responsible for ruining his teeth. Blaise didn't smile from that point forward. He wouldn't allow his schoolmates to stare at the little brown nubs inside his mouth. Shame became his middle name.

His clothes came from Goodwill and other relief agencies, courtesy of a couple of teachers. All through the lower grades, he was the top student. Learning was effortless. If he saw books lying around the school unused, he'd take them home and have read them in short order. He especially liked almanacs and books with maps. He possessed a near-photographic memory for facts. He knew populations of most major cities of the world, as well as rivers and mountains and deserts. And most of the time, after his brother's death, he dreamed of killing his mother. He averted his eyes when he came inside the trailer. Blaise couldn't bear to see her. How could he love a person who showed no love, none at all, for him?

He had never known his father, never saw him, never heard his name in conversation, so he had no curiosity about the man. He dreamed of killing him too.

By twelve he got jobs here and there, all of them outside The Rathole. He tried to stay away from that toxic waste dump. He went there only to sleep. He hated the dirty tiny cot and the hazy overhead lighting. By thirteen he was tall and skinny, and the junior high coach asked him to come out for the basketball team. He declined. With the money from his jobs he enrolled in mixed martial arts (MMA) classes. At first he was awkward and unskilled and got pulverized with regularity. But he saw MMA required brains as well as brawn, and he took to it as well as he did to classes in school. He bought protein drinks and started paying attention to his diet. Within a year he went from beaten to beater. By seventeen he could defeat everyone in the gym.

He took care of his teeth. His permanent teeth had grown in white and straight, and received his daily attention. Never again, he said to himself, will anyone mock me for my teeth.

As a high school senior he was tall and trim and sinewy. Lots of girls turned coy, demure, and fawning around him. The Homecoming King typically came from the football or basketball team, but at some kind of assembly he didn't attend, a panel of girls chose him. They also accorded him the title, "Handsomest Boy." For two years, girls had asked him to the prom, but each time he'd made up an excuse that sounded reasonable to him. He didn't have a suit, and didn't want to buy one on his limited budget.

His academic record was excellent. A guidance counselor told him scholarships were available for students like him. Blaise, though, had a different plan. He went down to a Marine recruiting office. The Sergeant there knew immediately he had filled a quota before he asked Blaise a question or administered an exam. On the way out, Blaise looked again at the sign that had arrested his attention before he walked into the recruiting station: "*It wasn't willed to you; it isn't a gift...few can claim the title; no one may take it away.*" MSgt Thomas P. Bartlett

The day before using the bus ticket that would transport him to boot camp, he walked into the cramped, untidy trailer for a final look around. He wouldn't ever have to live like this again. Maybe in a combat zone, but that wouldn't be by choice. His mother lay in her usual position watching a stupid program. He told her he had enlisted in the Marine Corps, and if he made it out of boot camp, he'd stay for five years. She grunted. She didn't look up. They didn't kiss, didn't hug.

She was in poor health, wheezing and coughing and spitting up vile green mucus the day long. When he went out the trailer door for the final time, he knew that was the last time he'd see her. Dead or alive. When the Red Cross next-of-kin notification reached him sometime down the line, he would ignore it. The Rathole and everyone in it could rot to hell.

+++

His only minor curiosity about his family involved his given name. A little touch of cleverness was required to name him Blaise. Blaise himself had learned a little about Blaise Pascal, but who in his family likely had the education to give him the name? The only blaze his mother could've identified was, maybe, one that erupted in The Rathole. Maybe the name came from his biological father, but that seemed dubious also. More likely, it was someone at the office where they signed birth certificates, or perhaps a doctor. In any event, that was one mystery in which he was content to rest.

Early April, approximately 9:30 P.M.

The Amtrak <u>Empire Builder</u> had made perfect time until this after-dark pause in a small Montana town. The smell of the brake pads remained pronounced in the still mountain air. Some of the passengers who'd *boarded much farther east were starting to take notice of the unexpected delay. In each of the six passenger cars, conductors and assistant conductors moved slowly through the aisles explaining in comforting tones that the train would soon be underway again. Maintenance crews, they said, were responding to a not-uncommon boom heard underneath one of the cars just before they entered the town's train station. Such things happened almost routinely; the train might have run over a bucket, barrel, wheelbarrow, or untold other items. A couple of maintenance men left the train, floodlights in tow, to inspect for possible damage. Another rail worker took advantage of the delay to repair an uncomplicated problem with the heating system. The conductors stressed that the repairs in no way affected either the extensive primary or backup safety systems. Not more than 30 minutes later, the Super Liner double-decker gathered power and recommenced its westward journey.*

Shortly after 11 P.M. in the lounge car a middle-aged fellow from Minnesota announced to his wife and three children he reckoned it was time for them to retire to accommodations in their sleeper car. A sleeping car attendant by this time had readied their beds. A newlywed couple from Chicago a couple of tables removed overheard him and grinned at one another as if to say, "the night's young, babe, but the oldsters just can't hang." A lady from Montana traveling alone appeared serene as she sat by herself at a table reading <u>The Things Our Fathers Saw</u>. A farmer from North Dakota grunted cheerily every now and then as he came across a funny passage in his book about Will Rogers. A prim old lady from Wyoming had her face burrowed at close *range as she squinted into a book of Sudoku puzzles. At this point their coastal destination lay between eight and nine hours ahead, if all went on schedule.*

Two mighty General Electric 65' locomotives pulled ten other cars. In order, they followed the typical consist (a railroad specialty word pronounced KON-sist) for this route: a baggage car, four sleeper cars, a dining car, a lounge, two passenger cars, and a dormitory car for the train crew.

At 12:27 A.M., one of the heaviest barges operating in the deep waters of Lake Pend Oreille, Idaho, rammed the nearly mile-wide bridge that crosses over toward Sandpoint on the western side. The collision had occurred roughly four hundred feet from the eastern bank of the lake. The fog hung thick over the lake, making for patchy visibility. The Captain of the vessel had felt too ill to man the helm and went below to try to recover. His replacement had gotten thrown into the breech at the worst of times. His navigation system wasn't responding and he was not certified in reading water charts. He was lost and in the fog did not see the pilings in his path. To complicate things, his comms were on the fritz. After the violent collision, he was unable to raise anyone. Upon feeling and hearing the mighty crash, the sick captain rose from his cot and vomited. It was a series of Murphy's Law events concatenated in the worst way.

The rails on the bridge above the barge crash site had become displaced and deformed. The ribbon, or continuous welded rail, construction did not, however, break. Had the rail fractured evenly, it would have given the engineer a stop signal in advance of the bridge.

Similarly, if track inspectors had identified the deformity soon enough, the engineers (because this run was greater than six hours in duration, the train carried an engineer and assistant engineer) would know it and have stopped the train. Or, if another train had crossed before this Empire Builder, the engineers would have had foreknowledge and taken appropriate actions. So lacking the danger signal, the engineer approached the bridge at a speed five mph above the limit at that point, in an effort to make up some of the time lost from the inspection of the undercarriage. Although the engineer could see 500 feet ahead with headlights under good conditions, on this misty evening he was unable to see well enough to identify the distorted track through the fog. Even if the engineer had spotted the damaged rail, he could not have prevented what happened; he would have had insufficient time to react, not enough time to activate emergency brakes and other systems. At 12:54 A.M. the lead locomotive struck the deformed rail and essentially flipped, its torque flipping the second locomotive as well, which in turn cast the following four cars off the rails, plunging them into the cold waters of Lake Pend Oreille. Three of those were sleeper cars. The pilings at this section of the bridge rested 90'-100' beneath the surface. The remaining six cars flipped as well, but on land on the east side of the lake. Fortunately, the knuckles that coupled the sixth and seventh cars had sheared cleanly. Most of those who survived incurred severe injuries.

Serendipity. If the inspection and small fixes back in Montana had not delayed the train by 30 minutes, the Empire Builder would have crossed the span three minutes before the barge inflicted its lethal damage. *Now, 120 people were lost to the gelid waters, and many others were struggling for their lives. Small things accumulated over time can become a big thing, and they had in this case.*

+++

Mid-March, two weeks before the train derailment

Keeley Eliopoulos called downstairs toward Simon Pack's basement office: "Simon, it's Wilkie Buffer for you."

"Be right up. Two minutes," Pack called back.

There was another small office off the dining room, where Pack settled into a reading chair to take the call. "Hey, Wilk, haven't heard from you in a while, which is just fine by me," Pack joked. "Was hoping never to hear from you again. Look at how you've wrecked our Treasure State."

"Don't forget who you're on the line with, Simon Pack. There aren't many guys anywhere know you better than I do," Buffer said.

Not many years ago both Pack and Buffer had had run-ins with the President, whose defeat their personal popularity had probably helped insure. Pack had been a US Marine General who had been called back to Active Duty at the behest of the Army Chief of Staff, a man who saw foundational problems at West Point, the United States Military Academy, and who further saw General Simon Pack as the one person capable of refocusing the Military Academy onto its original mission. At the same time, Wilkie Buffer was serving as the Secretary

of Defense. In the most technical terms, Buffer was Pack's superior.
But the President, Keith Rozan, on the cusp of canning both Buffer and
Pack, instead received their resignations within a week of one another.
Pressed to run for Governor of Montana, Pack grudgingly acceded. The
selfless Buffer offered his services to Pack, who made Buffer his
campaign chairman. After Pack's gubernatorial win, he asked Buffer to
take over as Chancellor of Montana's university system. Buffer
accepted, making Pack his boss. Theirs had indeed been an interesting,
amiable relationship. Neither was hung up on rank or its privileges.

Quite a number who followed what was really happening in
America regarded Wilkie Buffer as the country's premier living
intellectual, the one they turned to first to make sense of the nonsense
being parroted on every street corner and on every TV screen. Perhaps
someone somewhere possessed an intellect as capacious as Buffer's,
but Pack knew no one who could so deftly tie the lessons of the past to
the exigencies of the moment. Give him two threads, he could tie them
coherently. Give him ten thousand threads, he could tie them
coherently. Both were champion dot collectors, but both also were in
the elite dot connector category. Call Wilkie Marine (as he once had
been, leaving as a Sergeant), call him Professor (as he was at Stanford),
call him Secretary (as he was of Health and Human Services, then
Defense), or call him Director (as he was of the Central Intelligence
Agency)—he was a broadly talented man, and had published about
three dozen books with perspicuous prose. If a modern American man
had any right to exude froideur, it was Wilkie Buffer, yet he remained
as humble as his piney Georgia roots.

"I'd like to sit down with you, Simon. I had a brainstorm the other day, and would appreciate an invitation to your cabin to bat it around with you. At your convenience, of course, preferably sometime within a week. Can you give me some time?"

During the early days of Pack's gubernatorial campaign, all the political planning was done in Pack's cabin in northwestern Montana. The four principals had been Pack; Buffer; Pack's Man Friday, Tetu Palaita; and James Dahl, who replaced Pack as Governor. Pack's cabin was remote, but Buffer knew the location so well he could sleepwalk to it. Five months ago Pack concluded the single term of office he had committed to, but Buffer remained in his position as head of the state university system. Pack hoped Buffer would stay in place a lot longer, considering the good he'd already accomplished.

"Sure, Wilk. Keeley's here visiting, but I guess you know that. She'll enjoy your visit as much as I will. Bring Cissy if you want. I'm not pressed for time right now, got nothing planned, so heck, if tomorrow's not too soon, come on over. We can make a weekend of it—or not, if you need to get back."

"I'll be there, and I'm bringing Cissy too, even if she doesn't know it yet. We'll leave the cabin Saturday. See you then."

***

Spring had officially arrived days ago, but it showed itself slowly in this part of the country. Pack had a fire going in the living room; it did its job in taking the cool bite out of the air. He sat before the fire, gazing contentedly at the flames, wondering what Wilkie wanted to talk about. He could think of many things happening around the state Wilk might like to discuss, notably the huge, expensive fight against the devastating mollusk infestation of Montana's lakes and streams, then he reminded himself he wasn't the Governor anymore. Buffer could discuss any of those matters with his successor, Jim Dahl.

Pack's girlfriend was Keeley Eliopoulous. After five years of courtship, they had reached the decision to marry. Pack wasn't the sort of man who shacked up with a woman, and she wasn't the type woman to shack up with a man. He loved her company and she his. They didn't decide not to live together. They simply never accepted that arrangement as a possibility. Their respect for one another was mutual and ironclad. It was a principle they held true to, this fastidious protection of their reputations. As a lady with almost limitless financial resources, Keeley bought a modest home a few miles down the hill from Pack. They saw each other every day. Typically, she came up to Pack's cabin around nine in the morning and used her key to enter. She'd say hi and leave him to work on whatever occupied him that day. It was a relationship that had worked. It would stay that way until they officially became man and wife.

Pack crept up behind Keeley at the front of the cabin; most times he was cool and calm, stolid and solid, but he could get pleasure from being frivolous and funny too. She was nurturing a garden outside his cabin that she hoped would take bloom in summer. She had excitedly described its explosion of color. There would be golden daffodils, yellow roses, and sprays of colorful wildflowers. She caught

Simon just before he was about to grasp her shoulders. She spoke first: "What're you thinking about? Bad news from Wilkie? I love the smell of that wood smoke, don't you?"

"Which of those questions you want me to answer first?" Pack asked. "No, Wilk didn't have bad news, at least none he apprised me of just now. No news at all. All I know is he wants to talk, and he and Cissy will be here tomorrow afternoon, and leave the next morning. I'm not concerned…if something big is on his mind, he would've already said so. You know them well, so I'd like you to be here when they come, eat with us, and so on. I'll take you home whenever you feel like it.

"I'll go into town tomorrow morning to order some meals for dinner. I already have enough fixings for a big breakfast Saturday. I figure after dinner Wilkie and I will go to the basement, sit around the fireplace, and shoot the breeze about what they've been up to. I'm not planning any activities." Pack didn't say, what *we've* been up to. What *he* had been up to was the stuff of a novel. Stated most briefly, he had spent lots of time in the remote wilderness of Montana's Upper Yaak Valley, where he made enemies of rough criminals, one faction of which took him hostage. In the end Pack and Palaita Tetu and a posse of reclusive Yaak men shot it out with the bad guys, and almost unwittingly stymied a major mass terror plot against innocents in the four corners of America.

Keeley said, "I think you're getting tame, Pack. Last weekend you vegged out, and you plan to do the same this weekend. Maybe I'm not marrying the man I thought I was, the big brave man of action.

Maybe I ought to just go back to Greece and pick up one of those beach Adonises." At that, she stood and gave him a loving hug, reaching around his waist to scramble her hands up and down his lower back. "I love you, buddy," she added, "and only you."

"Love you too, Keel. I don't regret giving Chesty to Tetu, but it'd be nice to have him here now to complete this picture of domestic serenity. You know, have him saunter up, all tuckered out, after futilely chasing some varmint down the hill....Then I'd go find the nearest soft spot to rack out for a long nap," one of those facetious comments he couldn't resist tacking on. Pack's true idea of relaxing was manual labor, not snoozing on a sofa. He was a man scornful of timidity and weakness.

***

What Pack and Keeley had done last weekend was attend Tetu's wedding up in Yaak. Yaak, a tiny hamlet whose school the state listed in the "small" category. Small indeed. The little wooden house that served as the school contained eight students, four boys and four girls. The permanent residents in the area numbered around 100 in a vast territory. The gargantuan Samoan Tetu had been Pack's right-hand man for more than five years. During those years, there were a half-dozen occasions in which they might as well have been back in the combat forces of the US military from which they had come; Pack was a target often attacked in civilian life and the ever-loyal Tetu was always at his side to help in the fights. Tetu was an essentially gentle man who turned brutal when his Matai (as he called Pack) was threatened. Tetu was also as smart as he was ferocious. As Governor of Montana, Pack had employed and deployed his friend in myriad necessary capacities. Pack never regarded, or treated, Tetu Palaita as superfluous or in any way a payroll straphanger. They were about as tight as two men could be.

Tetu had bought a rustic Sportsman's Lodge and was settling down with his new wife, the former Swan Threemoons of the Blackfoot tribe. Although the year-round population of the Yaak River Valley was tiny, Tetu's Lodge would operate at near full occupancy all year. The Yaak, the name given to the entire region, was a sportsman's paradise, an ecosystem teeming with countless game animals large and small, and trout streams overflowing with their bounty in season. Because Tetu's new acquisition was the only lodging for many miles around, reservation requests from all around the US flowed in incessantly. He had rued the parting with Pack, but knew he would be happy with his lovely bride.

At the time of his marriage proposal to Swan, Tetu foresaw Swan working side by side with him helping engineer the full scope of Lodge operations, from cooking and cleaning to maintaining all their equipment, to running reception and restaurant. That was until Swan broke into tears while divulging her master plan of working with Native American youth and women of the local Yaak tribes, if they would accept her. She had seen too many injuries inflicted upon females at the hands of despairing drunken braves. Swan believed her duty lay in working to clean up that mess so prevalent in most American Indian tribes. Then something else unexpected also happened. Led by the efforts of General Pack, some members of the community tried to rouse a listless, pantophobic minister named Dar Castor into breathing life into a church in a ramshackle building donated by the Kootenai. Dar Castor failed, and Swan Threemoons stepped in to lead services on an interim basis. Under Swan the congregation was growing, and the small community of believers urged her to stay on as their leader. Despite her obligations to the community, Swan strove to return home by mid-afternoon most days to spend time working with Tetu.

It had been a magnificent ceremony, a night wedding with elements of Samoan and Blackfoot practices. Lodge guests eating dinner and drinking stopped and came outside to observe respectfully. A series of firepits lighted the path to the front door of the Lodge where a minister from down in Libby administered the nuptials. Swan was resplendent in her native garb, her many beads reflecting the firelight. The ring bearer was Tommy, an 11-year-old lad for whom Tetu was a demigod.

Simon Pack was not indisposed to appreciating beauty, but the pomp of this wedding, or any wedding, did nothing for him. He detested every formal function he had to attend as a senior military officer. He had had more control as Governor, and minimized such events. Yep, he loved Tetu like a son, and fate had thrown him into dire circumstances right here in the Upper Yaak, thereby causing him to develop lasting relationships with most of the folks at this wedding, but in truth he was more interested in watching these people.

There weren't many people left like these Yaakers. They weren't socializers or clubbers. A Rotary Club around here?...forget it.

They lived far apart, trapped and hunted and fished and fashioned their own clothes, and wanted nothing more than to be left alone. Tetu had helped them through a recent crisis, earning their respect, which they showed by appearing here now. They were content to run into one another at church or at Georgeann's General Store, but that was about all the company they could take. Pack wondered if he would ever see most of these people again, outside of Tetu and Swan, of course. Penetrating into this society was difficult, almost undoable, and Pack found the thought baleful.

Nonetheless, Tetu was more than a friend. He was his sidekick. So even though he felt a tinge of sadness at the possibility of losing contact with these good people of the Upper Yaak, his sacred friendship with Tetu caused him to view the wedding ceremony as a sparkling happy gathering. In fact, it ignited his own desire to get moving on making Keeley his betrothed. They hadn't set a date yet, but very likely it would happen amid a small gathering in late summer. He intended to leave details to Keeley.

***

The next morning saw Professor Wilkie Buffer turn his new Lariat 4x4 off the dirt road onto the gravel surface leading down to Pack's cabin. Pack had seen the truck coming from a mile away. He and Keeley were waiting for Wilk and Cissy. Hugs got exchanged all around. Pack popped off with, "Sorry to see you haven't gotten any whiter, Wilk. If you'd get about a dozen shades whiter, President Rozan wouldn't be able to call you the Black Pack any longer." This was true. The former President reviled Pack and thought about the same of Buffer.

"And I regret to report you haven't gotten any blacker, Simon. I'm tired of hearing the media refer to you as the White Buffer." That wasn't true, but it didn't matter, because skin pigmentation meant nothing to either man. They were sufficiently close friends they could joke any way they wanted.

"Wish I could afford a tricked-out Lariat like that," Pack said.

Buffer laughed, because that's exactly what Pack drove. They were even the same color, Ford's fancy name for some shade of black. "Honest, man, I know you used to have a regular 150, but I didn't know you had a new Lariat. Honest."

"Naw, I'm flattered," Pack said, "that our tastes coincide. I had that 150 for 10 years. 'Course I also had the Jeep, but sold it to help pay for this one." Pack had lied. Truth was, he had donated that Jeep to an Old Soldier's Home not far away. The administrator there was making good use of it.

Following a simple meat-and-potatoes kind of meal, the four of them split into male-female pairs. The women stayed upstairs. From downstairs, Wilkie and Simon could hear Cissy yelp with glee at something Keeley told her. Simon had no doubt he knew what Keel had said: "We're getting married, and you're invited to our small gathering."

At that, Simon told Wilkie what he suspected was an open secret. Buffer's reaction was unlike his wife's. He simply locked eyes with Pack, got out of his chair and walked to Pack with his hand outthrust. "Congratulations, my friend. You deserve the constant companionship of a good woman. I'm deeply happy for you. You can't find a more decent, more intelligent, more caring companion." Then Buffer relaxed, smiled, and said, "And she's gorgeous and rich to boot, you damned lucky dog."

Keeley Eliopoulos was a centi-millionaire, one in close company with billionaire, a minor factoid Pack had only recently learned. The absolute truth was Pack hadn't cared, and he didn't care. He would not change his style of living, and he let Keeley know that. Her money would be her money. He was a frugal man, and would continue to be. If others wanted to be impressed by her wealth, when they learned of it, Pack's feeling was neutral. If anyone believed he was marrying for money, he wouldn't bother to dispute it.

"OK, Wilk, let's get down to bidness, you don't mind. Why did you drive over from Helena?"

Buffer held high his glass of Blanton's, noting its cat's-eye chatoyance in the flicker of the fire, which was the only source of illumination in the basement room. "Well, General Pack, in short, I would like to make you Professor Pack. You know better than anyone the agent of change I've tried to be in Montana education. You know the specifics of the changes I've tried to institute. The fact remains, though, that I can't say with certainty the degree of success I've achieved. I'd like to have someone on the inside, someone really wise, someone I trust, give a first-hand assessment.

"We've had discussions before about the ways in which Napoleon deployed a cadre of 12 to 15 adjutants to assess various issues in his Corps'. The Israelis call their modern version the 'directed telescope,' meaning they've developed interrogatories designed to elicit accurate, actionable information about, say, the condition of soldier health in a given subordinate unit. I'm thinking much the same way. You go into a teaching position in the largest university in the state and find out whether we're getting the results we want." He paused, peering again into his tumbler. Pack didn't interject, just sat placid and motionless, letting Buffer have his say.

Buffer continued. "Or…are they just throwing back what they suppose I want to hear? We've both had to handle just this kind of thing many times over the years. I have a professor, very senior guy, leaving on sabbatical next week. Nice home on campus. I'm holding it for you."

"Come on, Wilkie. I'm not a classroom teacher, never wanted to be. When I was a Captain, the Marine Corps wanted me to teach at the Naval Academy, even though I attended West Point. I said 'not interested,' but somehow it got elevated out of the personnel system and up the chain and eventually I, a mere Captain, was forced to see the Big Man himself, the Commandant of the whole doggone Marine Corps. Captains don't get invited into the office of the Commandant, and Captains are as far removed from that four-star as we are from Jupiter. So the Commandant looks hard at me and says, 'Pack, you're going to graduate school, then you'll get your ass to Annapolis to teach. That, I'm telling you, is your duty.' Steam bubbled from his ears when I replied, 'Sir, you can send me to grad school, but you can't force me to go to class, and I won't. Then you'll boot me out of the Corps, and neither of us will have gotten what we wanted. I love the Marines and I hope you'll find a way to let me stay.' You know how that turned out, so we probably shouldn't pursue this line of conversation."

"I'm not finished," Buffer said. "Now, I'm just asking you to go down there and root around, look at the house, decide if you'd prefer a six- or twelve-month gig. You can work up your own title, department, and syllabus. Think of all the good you could do—you've been in combat as a military leader; you've been the Superintendent of the United States Military Academy, which in my book trumps the standard university president in status and responsibility; you've led a Constitutional Convention movement; you've run a state as its elected governor; and you're a gifted public speaker. I have to believe you'd have unparalleled influence as a teacher. As I said, you alone can determine the length of your tenure. We have a doctoral program in Interdisciplinary Studies. Are you kidding me? You're the premier person for that. You're extraordinarily rare, General, having had your foot—and really your brain—in such a variety of sectors of American life. I'd have killed to be in your classroom if I were of the right age."

"Wilkie," Pack replied, "there's no one I admire more than you. I'd do about anything for you, but in this case you're not seeing clearly, in my opinion. Just look at me. I'm not cut out to stand in a classroom and talk. I'm seriously not. But out of respect, I'll go down and have a look around. And maybe I haven't mentioned it, but Keeley has planned for us to visit her mother on their island in Greece for our honeymoon. I don't want to let her down on that. She's an only child, and seeing her mother is really important. Because we haven't set a date for what we intend to be a small private wedding, we haven't arranged the Greece trip yet. Keeley and I will talk once you're gone, set up some dates on the calendar, then we'll get back together to discuss when I take the visit to the university. How's that sound? And keep in mind, Keel's got a say in this too."

"That's an absolutely satisfying answer, Simon. All I ask is you give it your good-faith consideration," Buffer said.

Wilkie and Cissy shared breakfast with Simon and Keeley Saturday morning. They all walked in the woods near Pack's cabin for an hour, then the Buffers got on the road just before noon.

This was the first chance Pack had had to fill Keeley in fully on Buffer's proposal. He had driven her home an hour after dinner last night. They sat on the porch and he filled her in A to Z. Then Pack began to explain why he gave the idea even a moment's thought. "You've known Wilkie since you worked together on the campaign five years ago. You understand he's a good man. But I've known him a lot longer. He's been professionally loyal to me in so many ways I can't recall all of them. There were civilians in DOD who hated me a long time, men and women who wanted me out of the Corps by whatever means necessary, but then-Secretary Buffer, a onetime Marine NCO, cut them down to size faster than you can say go. He even fired several Pack-haters. Then after he resigned, before the President could fire him, he foregoes making millions in favor of helping me in an election. He was at my bedside after the helo crash. He's not just some guy asking a favor. He's a stalwart friend, true blue, who thinks there's something in this proposal for both of us." Pack paused, and Keeley spoke.

"But the truth is you profoundly do not want to do this, do you?"

"No doubt about it. I like teaching, but in my own way, to soldiers and Marines and athletes, just not in a damn classroom. Taking him up on the offer would be torture in many ways, but to please him, I'd willingly do it. I've seen most of the Deans' homes down there, and frankly they're fine for anyone. Old and regal and stately. If we have maintenance issues, they'll be attended to swiftly at no cost. But houses don't attract me. And neither does a salary I'm confident I wouldn't earn." He closed his eyes and pushed his head back.

"OK," Keeley said, "I know where you stand. You *will* go down to assess the situation as a professional courtesy, then you'll give him a reasoned reply. I'll readily go along with any decision you reach. If you say it's not for you, fine. If you think you want to do it for one semester, fine, or one year, fine. But in the meantime, let's work out a timeline."

+++

Keeley had told Pack she had banking to do, financial matters to attend to in town. She had attended to a financial matter all right, in a big way that for the present must remain unknown to Pack. She had had to, because Pack had no interest in a pre-nup agreement.

+++

The next day Keeley came forward with the schedule. She let herself in the cabin and called downstairs to Pack, who was typically in his basement office by five in the morning. "OK if I come down, honey?"

"Come on down. Just working on my stamp collection," Pack called back. Pack had been a serious philatelist for years, and owned quite a respectable collection. To have such a preoccupation with stamps challenged the image most had of Pack. In fact, he spent quite a percentage of his discretionary income on stamps. But for him it was more than collecting; it also entailed close study of stamps and postal history as it ties to American history, a fact established by numerous such specialty books lining his shelves.

Keeley stepped into Pack's office, yellow legal pad in hand. "While I'm talking, look at a calendar, please. Hold your foolish comments til I'm finished. First, I've looked at the university calendar. Wilkie said he'd like you to take part in the summer session. We would need to move in and you would need to prepare yourself for your assignment, so I think 1 June is the no later than time for us to be in place down there. Second, we need some time to decide what we want to take from the cabin, as well as to prepare our places for an extended absence, so let's get that done by 15 May. Wedding, 20 guests max if we can keep it to that, on or about 1 May. You hearing me, mister? A month-and-a-half from today. We have some gear-kicking to do. Finally, I'm going to Seattle and Phoenix next week, if they can take me, to visit your daughters. I want to speak to them face-to-face about this wedding. I want to do it alone. They need to know I won't pretend to be their birth mother, and they need to see my eyes and face as we talk. Therefore, I suggest you arrange your visit to the university during my absence. Tomorrow I have a few financial matters to attend to, so I'll be going into town about mid-morning and might not get back until mid-afternoon. If you think of anything you need from town, I'll pick it up for you. All right, what do you have to say about all this?"

"You mean, do I need anything from town? Nope," Pack answered, understanding that really wasn't the question of moment.

"Try again, Pack," Keeley countered, giving him a determined stare.

"Very well, bride soon to be," Pack said. "I accept your schedule without change. That includes my agreeing to set up my visit while you're away. Your decision to go directly to the girls doesn't surprise me. In fact, I kind of thought you might do something like this. I'm even proud you'd like to do the job alone. Now each of us has to put meat on the bones of the plan in our own areas. I'll start by calling Wilk today. He'll probably want someone down at the university to work up an itinerary for me, although I won't offer that up as an idea." He paused, holding up a palm as a stop sign. "But you didn't mention the honeymoon. What will we do about that?"

"Great to the first part, husband soon to be. I'll start making my travel reservations today. As to the Greece trip, we'll do that later. In the meantime, I'm calling mother and asking her to visit us for a month or two either here or at the university. Now…I'm going back up to the kitchen to begin my list-making."

That evening, Keeley served them a one-course fish stew dinner. Afterward, they retired to the sofa after cleaning up. "Keel," Simon began, "I'd like to talk more about Wilkie's offer. You taught at Yale. You know better than I what goes on in the world of higher education. How 'bout you we talk it over and you educate me a little bit?"

"Sure. What particular aspects you wanna discuss?"

"Well, to begin with, I feel slightly dishonest. I kept it simple, didn't give Wilk a full, complete answer. I wasn't dishonest with him, but I didn't explain in detail all my misgivings about taking him up on the offer. I told him I'm not a classroom teacher and never wanted to be one. Even if I did want to teach, I'm sure I wouldn't be good at it. Like that. The total truth is more complicated. What Wilkie Buffer's asking me to do isn't something he ought to ask. It's *his* job. As one person in one university, I can't genuinely help him, not really, not in the way he expects I would. Anyway, when Jim Dahl was my chief of staff, he and I had several really long, dreary sessions about the state of higher education today, because there is simply no doubt we're not about to grow good citizens if we can't find a way to improve the education system. As an aside, I heard a university president from Florida say the other day that the main purpose of high schools is to graduate students who'll prop up their local economies. That's one purpose, sure, but more important, I'll argue, is to teach students to think critically and to be good citizens. I'm rambling, I know, but as I do you'll hear my opinions and I can't think of anyone more qualified to tell me if they're generally right or wrong.

"It's often said that the chiefs of universities today, whether they're called chancellors or presidents or something else, are expected primarily to be fundraisers. I don't have to tell you, Yale's endowment is staggering, in the billions, along with a handful of others. A number of those heads now get paid in the millions, and I'm not passing judgment, just pointing out they're not at all different from teachers in the biomedical sciences, meaning they're expected to pay their own way."

"Tell me about it," Keeley said. "You know I was in the biomed sciences myself...." She shot Pack a faux-menacing look, adding, "And my expertise came in handy, didn't it?" Keeley had 'broken the code' on a notebook full of chemical and mathematical notations that helped Pack act fast enough to prevent a contamination of an Alabama water supply that would have adversely affected the health, and in some cases, lives of hundreds of thousands of people. "You're exactly right. The truth is that I was expected to pay myself, and if I didn't I was in trouble. Professors do that by writing grant proposals, and the amount of time spent on those can be criminal. They write their proposals, sometimes on topics of highly questionable merit, in painstaking detail to have them reviewed in-house, then out for three anonymous peer-review critiques. Your name is on the proposal, but you of course sometimes don't know the reviewers, so if you've ruffled feathers or been a pain for the academic/scientific establishment, a petty reviewer—and there are lots in this category—might torpedo this proposal you've sweated blood on, just for spite. I'll go further: let's say my salary is $100,000. I had better ram through a grant of at least

$220,000. That's my $100,000, another $60,000 for the university coffer, and another $60,000 to pay my assistants. And the noose is always around your neck, because as quickly as you've reeled in one grant, the administrators are telling you they expect another one soon. With this kind of pressure, how much time do you think the professor gives to students, or carefully thinks through the material he must teach? OK, there are rare profs who can do it all, and do it all well, but as I say they are few and far between. Everyone's heard of the 'publish or perish' dictum, and that remains true in many departments, but I think the groveling for grants is more insidious. At the same time, I must admit there is a connection between publishing and grant writing. You often have to publish in order to be heard by others in your field. And just as often the people you have cited in your publication are the ones you'll ask to do the peer reviews."

Pack said, "And even at West Point I discovered problems in the Admissions Office, problems which, by the way, good old then-Colonel Jim Dahl dealt with expeditiously and severely—that's just one of numerous problems he solved in a New York damn minute. But nationwide, you have Admissions people taking in lots of students with SATs below 800, high schoolers simply not prepared for real college work, because they've probably sensed in meeting after meeting the university's desperation for revenue. They don't much care that professors who give out too many D's and F's will face penalties from that same administration."

"I hear you, Pack," Keeley said, "but I can't say Yale had that problem. Their problem was the inverse, professors handing out A's to everyone just because they came from the top of their high school classes. Grade inflation is a bigger problem in Ivy League schools than anywhere. Heck, if a kid gets a B at Harvard or Yale or Penn he feels personally insulted, and wants the administration to crank up an investigation of the professor. You can find exceptions, but in my view the exceptions prove the rule."

"Keel, I know enough about the education system to say with certainty that those in charge—beginning in our case with Wilkie and extending to university presidents and deans—face a huge daunting assignment, and it takes special people to clean up the mess. It's a big, big job, a tough job," he said, shaking his head and spreading his fingers, virtually in awe of their task. "In most cases, in my considered opinion, you have people ill-equipped to tackle such an assignment. Why? Because they've spent most of their adult lives in the academic environment, where the idea of rough-and-tumble means something different from that in other professions. This doesn't apply to all professors, by any means. There are those who have gained invaluable experience in other ways, such as having been high school teachers and senior administrators, but they're definitely in the minority. On the one hand, nearly all college campuses are lovely, with shaded walkways and carpets of green and ornate structures. The campuses are designed to convey a sense of serenity soothing to the spirit. On the other hand, under the surface, it seems all the parties on campus today are complaining about one thing or another.

"Students complain about professors being too tough. Professors complain about underprepared students. Professors punish students whose politics differ from their own. Then there's the byzantine world of gender politics, where new jargon appears almost weekly. Entire academic establishments live in fear of offending tender young egos or faculty fellows."

Keeley leaned forward eagerly to say, "And you can't neglect to mention the issue of international students. A few minutes ago we were discussing what universities will do when desperate for revenue. One of their biggest cash cows is the international student population, no matter how unqualified it might be taken as a whole. Schools can charge confiscatory rates and get away with it, providing they continue to push those students through the system to graduation. School leaders are as willing to drop their ethical guards with respect to foreign student admission as on any issue facing them. Often, the fault is more the schools' than the students'. For example, a hundred Kuwaiti student applications appear, the university sees dollar signs, and voila, all hundred gain admission. The university knew right away with high certainty that few were actually qualified, but no matter, what's important is it'll be paid more than any group of American students would produce. So a professor at the direct interaction level gets one of these underqualified students, and it's no surprise to him when he discovers the international student has a language barrier and understands little of what the professor is saying. After just a few days, the student is hopelessly behind, but has a project due. He turns to plagiarism, which is what many international students do. The professor complains to his next higher, but the admonition comes back to the professor: 'Doctor Throckmorton, you must take into account the obstacles that young person faces, obstacles over and above what our American contingent faces, and extend some latitude in recognition of his limitations. I'm sure you'll treat this situation with the sympathy it deserves. By the way, you're doing a great job, Mark.'"

Minutes passed without conversation. Then Keeley laughed. Pack turned to look at her full on until he couldn't suppress a little laugh too. "I'm laughing because you are. What's your reason, Keel?"

"Because," she said, "whether it's true or not, sure seems you're doing all you can to talk yourself out of becoming a teacher…pardon me, of becoming a *professor*…if only for a semester. Just relax. Maybe there's a reason for you to do it. You made a pledge to Wilk, so follow through and see where it takes you. Besides, you can learn some essential skills."

"Such as?" Pack asked, knowing she was playing. Pack himself was the master of opposite talk, which by example Pack had taught her meant in a facetious vein, and the tendency had rubbed off on Keeley.

"Well, dear, you could improve your writing skills. All those papers detailing the objectives of the Constitutional Convention were far too clearly composed. You must learn how to impress through muddying, which you will if you're asked—as I'm sure you will be—to review the scintillating prose of a fellow academic who's trying to get published in *The Journal of the Modern Language Association.* Our relationship could be so much stronger if you'd come out of the professorial tenure with full command of the postmodernist understanding of American culture. And think of all the cultural offerings on campus; we could spend four evenings a week attending poetry readings, modern dance performances, *mise en scene* theater— I'm sure you would like Artaud's Theater of Cruelty--, and lectures on the failures of Montana governmental institutions, with special focus on the failures of Governor Simon Pack's administration. See, Simon, without hurting your feelings, I want to tell you kindly that you could use some rounding out. I like you, yeah, but let's face it, you've led a pretty, uh, dull life."

That was the end of depressing talk about the plagues of the university that night. Pack found delightful ways to tease Keeley to conclude the sofa time. Then she said goodnight and drove home.

CHAPTER TWO

Early April

Keeley and Pack would leave the cabin on different schedules, each to be away from the cabin for a week. Pack had a drive of three-and-a-half hours down to the university, and was leaving Monday morning. The night before he left, Sheriff Joe Mollison, one of Pack's closest friends, dropped in for a brief chat. Pack explained he and Keeley would be away for a week, and the good Sheriff stepped up immediately to say he'd make sure both Pack's cabin and Keeley's house got checked daily, and further, that he would pick up Keeley on Tuesday evening to take her to her connection.

Once Mollison drove off, Pack said, "I respect what you've decided to do, Keel. You'll be a hit with the girls, I can promise you that. Enjoy every moment of the journey."

"What I haven't told you is I'm—that would be *me, me, me*— giving each of them money for a plane ticket to the wedding. I know they would come anyway, but I just don't want them spending their own money. No blowback, please," Keeley said.

"If I've told you once, Keel, I've told you a hundred times, your money is yours, and you spend it as you wish. That's OK with me. And thank you, although that would be better coming from them than me. Just gift them within reason, my reason, if you would."

Keeley insisted on making breakfast sandwiches for Pack's journey tomorrow, which she did before driving home. Pack followed her to her house, waited until she was fully indoors with lights on, before pulling away with a short beep.

The next morning, at oh-dark-thirty, Pack went outside, walked in the darkness around the property, reminding himself how much he loved this cabin, these woods, this bucolic setting, this state, this nation. A fox skittered around him. How many life forms are with me, on this property, right now? he wondered. He didn't want to give up this life to become a college teacher (he still wouldn't think of himself as professor), not for a month or a year. He loved the things that occupied his time here. Books in the evenings. Writing real letters by hand to his few close friends. Chopping wood for his stoves. Clearing brush. Making repairs on the cabin itself. Creating furniture in his well-lighted and -outfitted garage. Cleaning his tools, most of which had the feel of jewels in his hands. Going camping and canoeing and hiking. "But a promise is a promise," he told himself, "and I'm going through with my pledge to Buffer."

He loved the pre-dawn darkness, always had, knowing most people were in their cocoons, and he was mostly alone. Because he had the drive in front of him, he wanted to get the blood flowing with a fast walk up and down the dirt road connecting his property to civilization. After thirty minutes, he came back to the cabin, poured coffee into his oversized insulated container, took from the fridge the thick ham and cheese sandwiches Keeley had prepared, picked up his pre-packed bag, threw it into the truck, and drove away.

+++

Wilkie had had everything set up for Pack's arrival. He had instructed the university president to in-brief Pack, then hand him over to a series of escorts.

University president Richard Eaglesky greeted Pack with gusto. "Come in, come in, sir, and we wish you a hearty welcome." He could've become president on looks alone, Pack thought. Nearly as tall as Pack, slender, good teeth, lush silver hair worn State Department-long. Pack had met him before, indeed three or four times in connection with his duties as governor. He pointed Pack to a chair, and laughing, said, "I'm having the same problem with you I had with Chancellor Buffer. I asked immediately what he'd prefer to be called. Would it be Doctor or Secretary or Professor or Director, and he said 'A simple Chancellor' will do, thank you. So with you is it General or Governor or something I'm overlooking, sir?"

"Truth is, it's not something I think about. In my mind I think of my primary identity as Marine, but used in private life that alone sounds pretentious in its own right. My answer to you is that among faculty I guess I'll go with Simon. With students, I'd say any title that's respectful, including Mister Pack, but I would not accept Simon from them."

Eaglesky nodded acceptance, then shifted the subject. "What would you think, Simon, if I say I did not vote for you?"

Grinning, Pack replied, "Bad choice." He quickly added, turning serious, "Richard, all I want is a well-informed citizenry. If people understand the issues and know the positions of the candidates, they can and should vote as they please. But I also believe they ought to have a sure grasp of American history, especially including the Founding."

"And I agree," Eaglesky said. "Please be my priest for a moment and accept my confession in total confidentiality." Pack nodded assent, but knew he didn't need to. Eaglesky continued, "You're correct. I did make a bad choice. I would have voted for you if you had run again, and I did vote for your protégé, Governor Dahl. See, Governor—yeah, you just asked me to call you Simon, but out of respect, I'd ask your forbearance if I address you as Governor—I actually have known few military people, and I figured 'OK, here's this guy who was a big jock and a General, which by definition means he can't be too smart, surely not governor material.' But you proved me awfully wrong. I became a close Pack observer, and it didn't take me long to understand you're a man of both probity and intelligence. Accept an apology you were unaware was either deserved or coming. You were a positive force for Montana, and you've given us the most highly qualified leader of any university system in America."

"It's good to hear you say that. He's been a personal friend a long time, and I respect him to the nth degree," Pack said.

"I also have become professionally and personally close to the Chancellor, and I have learned much about you from him. His eyes are never as bright as when he's talking about you, Governor. And I've found you can stand behind a person he affixes his stamp of approval on."

"Just so we're clear, Richard, what I promised the Chancellor is that I'd give good-faith consideration to his offer of a position here. I did not say I would accept. And I'd like you to know my lady, soon to be wife, and I were discussing the immensity of your job a few days ago. She taught at Yale some years ago, and her insights mirror those I acquired as Governor. I once had a young Captain Aide-de-Camp. I called him Duck, telling him he was to appear as serene as the duck on the pond when in public, but that beneath that exterior I expected him to paddle as furiously as a duck trying to escape a predator. The university appears similarly placid on the surface but I know it's also a place of cutthroat competition. Keeping everything under control and operating in the student interest is a tall order."

Eaglesky said, "And I'm sure you also learned great lessons as Superintendent at West Point, a job not unlike mine at all. So I'd like you to know my door will be open to you at any time, and I'd also welcome constructive criticism. And that offer stands whether you take a position here or not. Governor, you're not looking at a thin-skinned man.

"And one other point that's critically important to me that maybe you don't know. I don't pretend to be the best university president, but I am president of the largest school in the state, and I suppose because of that the Chancellor sees me as first among equals. He often takes me to his discussions with Governor Dahl. And I said discussions, not briefings. Your successor gives us huge portions of his time because, like you, he sees education as a foundation to the health of the state. He normally schedules us in late afternoons so that we can continue into the evening. Governor Dahl takes us home with him for dinner, and sometimes we don't wrap up until midnight. You don't think I tell my people how seriously this governor takes what they do? He listens, he takes notes, and he makes suggestions, as we all do. Participatory democracy at work, sir, and it invigorates each of us. I can see why you relied on Governor Dahl. He has not left education issues in total to the Chancellor. It's my responsibility to stay away from politics in my job, but I'd debate anyone on my faculty who finds fault with his education policies."

"Warms my heart to hear you say that about Jim Dahl. He was a helluva field Marine, that I can tell you. And I would've been nothing at West Point or in Helena without his counsel and executive talents. Mind if I ask a question the answer to which I'll keep in full confidence?" Pack asked.

"Shoot," Eaglesky said.

"First, my preface: I spent a lot of time as Governor trying to understand the impact Chancellor Buffer was having on Montana higher education. At the same time, I understand well he's not a one-man operation, and to achieve the success he was after has required the willing support of university presidents like you. Given that, how has he done?"

Eaglesky paused for nearly a minute, shifting his gaze from floor to ceiling. "You might interpret my pause to indicate either doubt that he's succeeding or that he emphatically has not succeeded. But that's not the case. Nobody could have succeeded fully given the time he's been running the system. But if I were giving grades, he'd get a solid A. He is succeeding. He holds me and my fellow university heads accountable, and he has introduced metrics that no one had thought of, or maybe had the courage to institute, before. If we can't explain our failures, we'll probably be on probation; if we fail with respect to the same metrics a second time, we'll be sending resumes out of state. It doesn't take much thought to figure out that we presidents have passed something similar down to our own subordinates, and they to their subordinates, and so on. I don't have the stats available to the chancellor, but my guess is that a quarter of subpar performers at various levels have been weeded out. Chancellor Buffer doesn't play, Governor. He's a true gentleman, but he is hardhearted when it comes to meeting his expectations. But you're quite correct that there remains much more intradepartmental weeding and general bucking up to do."

Pack said, "I imagine quite a few of those who've been rooted out were happy to go. After all, if you travel just two states westward, what he's doing would never have gotten off the ground. He'd be a pariah."

"That's right, Governor," Eaglesky said, "but we're in the Treasure State, thank God."

When Pack walked out of Eaglesky's office, he thought maybe Buffer's offer wasn't really so bad.

+++

Although he couldn't say he felt at home, he liked the people who escorted him around the campus. They were friendly and bright. Pack believed they were giving him the truth as they saw it. He was sure President Eaglesky himself had carefully selected these men and women.

Some of the spiel was boring, the minutiae of a professor's life: what committees they served on, how much time meetings and student conferences consumed; writing SOPs; grade calibration within the departments; the competition to lower credits for some courses and raise them for others; standard methods of evaluation of student work; how to direct a dissertation; allocation of office space; general reorganization within the university; how to earn bonuses; the drive to capitalize on the Internet as a means of delivering courses; the constant push to lower overhead costs. These people prized industry as much as he.

Three professors guided Pack that day, Monday, the first day of a projected five-day orientation Pack was free to truncate at any time. He made it through Tuesday as well, listening with care to everything said to him. He had trained himself in special techniques for absorbing and cataloguing large dollops of information in areas outside his normal ken. He said goodbye to his last appointment of the day on Tuesday and went to the spacious early 20th-century home of the departed Dean. The university president had invited Pack to dinner, but Pack declined. He wandered through the big house, but tonight it didn't suit his mood. He was looking for a small space in which to sit and think. He found a book-lined study about the size of a large closet. Between the shelves sat a recliner and standing lamp. There he pushed back, and tried to think of the day. With eyes shut, he saw spread out before him a murky map of his life. These people he had been with today were like traffic cops trying to direct him down a street he didn't want to follow. They were good people, professors diligently pursuing their interests, but he sensed an absence of the passion that habitually had animated him and the people around him. Oh, yes, he thought, we need these people in the worst way, they're as necessary as any group in society, but...I'm not programmed to do this job. Or am I excusing myself for my inability to do the job?

For reasons he couldn't explain, his thoughts drifted back to martial matters. He could see Chesty Puller in his mind's eye, old Chesty telling his Marines as they trained to deploy to Korea, "I want you to be able to march twenty miles under full load, the last five at double time, and then be ready to fight." He thought back on his infantrymen, foul weather warriors, with love brimming in his heart. He had led them to disrupt, psychologically dislocate, and disorganize enemy resistance. He told them that their mission was destroy the enemy's hope, and to do that they had to destroy his center of gravity. He raised Marines who could move alone at night, who could function in a decentralized environment, lessons he had tried hard to drill into their big Jarhead skulls. He retained that old passion for the martial life. No experience or set of experiences in his illustrious football career could match that connection he had with his Marines.

He recalled those long years marked by enforced periods of privation, cold, weariness, wilting heat, muddy uniforms. It takes special people to love such conditions. Pack did and his Marines did. His Corps was no place for the metrosexual, the whiner, the handwringer, the sissy boy, the sybarite. And in his Corps the leader, whatever his rank, endured pretty much every difficulty his Marines faced.

Does my preference for a life of discomfort make me superior to these people I would be expected to work with in this university? Nope. Not in the least. I probably can't do what they do, and they probably couldn't survive in a combat unit. Next his mind turned to his erstwhile life riding the rails, hearing the roar and clank of the moving train, and the freedom of traveling anywhere he pleased on America's 142,000 miles of tracks. And of the good and bad men he met during that brief pit stop in his life. At some point such thoughts receded and he drifted to sleep on the recliner.

He dreamt of struggling futilely to open his mucilaged eyes. He was the driver and sole occupant of what looked to be a 1940's style darkly-painted car. His seat reclined at a perilous angle, one so severe he could not have seen through the windshield even if his sight had been clear. But in this dream, seeing through the windshield would have been useless, in that the car hurtled backwards and down a long declivity into oncoming traffic. His feet stamped around, attempting to find the footbrake, but they could find nothing. He found the emergency brake by feel, but ratcheting it upward had no affect on the vehicle's path toward destruction. He could intuit the danger he was in, but he could not regain control. His car missed other vehicles by inches, and only a guardrail stopped it from flying off the mountain into a great black void.

At 0400 a groggy and still-dreaming Pack awoke in the chair, his phone burring and vibrating in his pocket.

+++

Fabled Swiss psychiatrist and psychoanalyst Carl Jung during his life provided examples, drawn from his patients, of a phenomenon he called synchronicity. In one notable case, he listened in his office to a patient describing a recurrent dream in which a little white dog emerged from the woods. The dog beseeches the man to follow him through the woods. The man follows the dog into a vast nothingness. As the office session ended, Jung asked the patient to go with him for a stroll through the woodland outside. As they meandered slowly down the path a little white dog, just like the one the patient had but minutes ago described, appeared from nowhere. It looked at Jung and the patient, as if imploring them to follow them, which they did.

In another case, Jung was listening to a patient describe a dream she had had the night before about someone giving her an expensive piece of jewelry, which happened to be in the form of a golden scarab beetle. At that moment, a beetle flew into the glass of Jung's office window. Jung immediately opened the window, and as the beetle flew in, he grabbed it out of the air. He then placed it on the desk, saying to the stunned lady, "There is your beetle."

There are other examples not from Jung. Over time, there are instances of synchronicity having to do with lecturers on the subject of death. As they reach their climactic point, they drop dead at the lectern.

Or, as has happened to many of us, we're thinking of Aunt Bessie for the first time in years, and just then the phone rings and it's Aunt Bessie on the line.

In the illustrations mentioned here, there is no causal relationship between the events, but one cannot deny they are meaningfully related. Some describe synchronicity as intellectual intuition.

+++

State University Chancellor Wilkie Buffer sat at his office desk early on a Wednesday morning thinking hard about the essay he was presently composing. In addition to his state duties, he had continued to write pieces for syndication, as well as for various academic journals. For a reason he could not explain, his thinking was interrupted, in what he reflected was an almost violent manner, by Simon Pack's connection with trains. He had never had such a thought before. Buffer was not a professional Jungian, but he could hold his own in conversations about Jungian theory. He surmised that deep in Pack's mind was lodged an ancient form of understanding connected to trains. Whatever it was grew out of instinct. Buffer imagined Jung would call Pack's unconscious preoccupation with trains an archetype. He was nearly certain Pack himself had never made the connection between himself and trains.

Pack had ridden the rails after retirement from the Marine Corps and before assuming the Military Academy Superintendency. He had felt the thrum and vibration of many variations of rail cars, and absorbed their smells into his nostrils and clothes. He learned how to mount moving trains and where to sequester himself once on board. He slept in hobo encampments near rail yards. He killed two men whose interests were inimical to America's near the Las Vegas rail yard. Such was his connection to railroads that even West Point cadets gave him the sobriquet Heroic Hobo. He killed the leader of al-Qaeda America just outside the rail tunnel under Washington Hall at West Point. Yes, there was something profound connecting Pack to the idea of trains. Buffer loosened up his mind and let it roam. "*Let's see,*" Buffer thought, "*trains are awesomely powerful, more so even than large planes. They can trample an automobile as if it is nothing. And they are shape-shifters. A 150-car train appears much different from above than from the ground. From above, it is a serpent repeatedly coiling and uncoiling. They are servants of man, moving vital goods to wherever they're needed countrywide. From inside, they're cocoons. Trains fascinate Americans, who incessantly record stories and documentaries about them. Trains opened up the nation. They are carefully woven into the history of our nation. A train is very much, to employ the military term, an LOC, a line of communication. It is a fabricated steel river every bit as vital as the interstate highway system and the river network of our country.*" Wilkie was enjoying this, thinking he was onto something significant about Pack as well as trains. He thought more. "*A train is a string of entities that have decided to go together. We speak of a train of thought. And guess what? A train is an integrator, a totality that binds cars of various shapes, sizes, and purposes toward a single end. A friend told me the other day about one train he personally knew of that was an astounding 194 cars in length. Parenthetically,"* Buffer reflected, *"more and more we see these extravagantly long trains as cost-saving measures by rail companies...but that's another story. What we have with a train is one or more locomotives that pull cars into line. If there were no tracks to guide them, the locomotive(s) would pull the cars into a straight line. That's what Simon Pack was as the Superintendent at West Point, and in other command positions in his Marine life: someone who pulled the cars into a straight line and directed them toward a common purpose. Carry this extended metaphor several degrees further: Simon Pack was the driver, the engineer, and he chose the riders and even the composition of the train, and how the many cars would be sequenced for the journey."* Buffer leaned back in his chair, believing he had just found the links between Pack and trains. Pack was powerful, Pack was a shape-shifter—Marine, polymath, award-winning football star, brilliant athlete in multiple sports, Governor-political leader, locomotive force behind a Constitutional Convention whose effects would be felt decades ahead, a worker with his hands, the liver of a simple life, a man of uncomplicated tastes. Simon Pack was one very large hobo bindle of contradictions.

And, it just occurred to him, Pack informed him only last night that he was excited for Keeley to experience the thrill of the *Empire Builder* journey to Seattle. It was his idea, he said, for Keeley to travel by train to Seattle to break the marriage news to his younger daughter.

At that moment a staff member came in with coffee and asked if he had heard the news about the awful derailment near Sandpoint, Idaho. The staffer added, "That train just passed through Glacier Park and Whitefish a few hours earlier. More than a hundred have perished, they think." Wilkie Buffer had just experienced synchronicity. But he also felt instant sorrow for his friend Pack. He called the Interdisciplinary Studies office at the university, where he knew Pack was scheduled to be today. An administrative person over there answered, then got the person Buffer requested. The female professor said, "Just minutes ago the Governor bolted out, sir, said to tell Dr. Eaglesky it's an emergency and he had to go immediately. I was just about to let Dr. Eaglesky know."

"It's OK," Buffer said, "poor man had no choice. I guess we've lost him as a future Professor, Lisa. Let's pray he hasn't lost anyone." Lisa didn't understand immediately what Chancellor Buffer meant, but within a second or two she had figured it out, and put her hand to her mouth in shock. Buffer simply disconnected the call and phoned his wife.

+++

Pack made his first call before charging up the road to his cabin, and maybe over into Idaho. That call was to Sheriff Mollison, his best friend locally. "Joe," Pack started, but Mollison interrupted immediately.

"I'm on it, Simon," Mollison said. "Have been on it since the news came out." It was Mollison who had dropped Keeley at the train station. "I've got several sheriffs over in Idaho on speed dial, and they're doing their best to find out about Keeley. As soon as I have something solid, I'll get back to you."

"Thanks, Joe. What hospitals are they using? Maybe I can go in that direction," Pack said hopefully.

"Hard to say," Mollison said. "It's a mass casualty situation, as you know, so they'll probably be evacuating casualties to several trauma centers within MEDEVAC range. This happened in a rural area, so helicopter will be the preferred form of transport, as it has been so far. Not confirmed, but I've heard they'll use two hospitals in Coeur d'Alene and several in Spokane. There're just a lot of blanks to be filled in yet, but my sources are working it. Maybe your best course is to come here, join me, and when we have good info, we can go over there together. I believe I can get us a chopper."

"All right, Joe, be there in about three hours. Thanks."

+++

Five Hours Before Pack's Phone Burred

Chesley Mason and his college buddy were sharing jokes in the lounge car. Chesley was on the way to his parents' home near Seattle to celebrate his Spring break from North Dakota State University in Fargo. He was taking his best friend with him for the week. Chesley was the MVP of NDSU's powerhouse FCS (formerly Division I-AA) football team. At his coach's urging, Chesley had signed with an agent, who promised him he would go in the first round of the NFL draft. Even in high school, people had told him, "Son, no matter where you play, scouts will find you if you're good enough." He hadn't put much stock in that, but nonetheless had faith in his own abilities. Now that he was on the cusp of signing for big money, Chesley drank only non-alcoholic beverages, even in the anonymity of this *Empire Builder* lounge. He wasn't going to let anything screw up his big chance. He didn't mind that his buddy was drinking heavily and had for hours; he wasn't going to drive a car, after all. Chesley would remain in the lounge as long as his friend continued having a good time.

Dr. Dave Chastain had spent a week back East with his wife and five-year-old daughter. He reckoned that a huge benefit of both sets of relatives living in proximity to one another lay in not having to take separate visits to their families. An hour before midnight they were in their sleeper compartment. The little girl was tucked in tight next to her mother. Dr. Chastain himself got into bed but couldn't sleep. He got up quietly and sat for a while listening to the soft sounds of their sleep. He took a seat next to the window, aimlessly wondering where they could be along the route. Then he began to reflect on his career. He was too junior to be the chief surgeon, but his reputation as a neurosurgeon was sterling, given his performance ratings and general comments from patients and peers. He was indeed a valued member of the neuro staff at the region's only Level II trauma center, Sacred Heart Medical Center and Children's Hospital in Spokane. A strong good feeling of satisfaction spread over him as he reminded himself how very much he had to be thankful for. Good family, loving wife who supported him through a wicked schedule, a beautiful, intelligent child, a comfortable home, and a vocation that enabled him to save lives. David Chastain stretched, took out a novel, and began to read under his nightlight.

Major Russell Cooper finished Command and Staff College two years ago, then went off to his fourth combat theater tour of duty. One leg was missing below the knee, a relic of his second tour. Once back in America, he flew to Minneapolis just so he could take this train ride. Five years ago he was the Aide-de-Camp to Lieutenant General Simon Pack at the United States Military Academy, and although the General never mentioned anything related to trains to him, Cooper longed for this small connection to the Heroic Hobo. He also liked the idea of passing through the state he was pretty sure General Pack still lived in. He gave a salute, in fact, as the train pulled away from West Glacier. It was a salute to the man who'd pinned the name 'Duck' on him.

This was the best way to de-stress Cooper could imagine. He remained a bachelor at age 32, and had no serious prospects. This was a solo ride, as most of his life had been. The cycle he was in had consisted of one stateside military assignment for a year or two, then a combat tour, rinse and repeat. He was among the most highly decorated Army officers of his year group, and he had earned every medal. He knew well all the tools of his trade, and his soldiers followed him because they observed it. He was a man who could keep them alive. But he was also an audacious fighter who didn't stop until he and his men pursued the enemy to its destruction. On this trip Russell Cooper never left his sleeper compartment. He read, looking out into the darkness every now and then, seeing few lights winking along this desolate stretch until, at eleven, he turned in for the duration.

Keeley Eliopoulous left the lounge car around midnight. In her sleeper, she showered and got into a nightgown. She missed Pack already, and hoped he missed her too. No matter, this was an important and necessary trip, and she was happy Simon had recommended this mode of travel. She'd been on many trains in Europe, but this was particularly comfortable. Now all that remained for her to do was sleep, dream, and wake up for breakfast...and meet one of her future stepdaughters...who she hoped would greet her with a smile.

CHAPTER THREE

Worley Fisher was 71 years old and healthy as a mule. He was up by 4:30 A.M. every day tending to his 5,000 acre spread. He couldn't recall the last time he was bedridden, and he'd never spent a night in a hospital. He knew how to nurse every sick animal back to health. Several of his outbarns housed a fleet of heavy equipment that took up the space of a Kubota dealer. Mr. Fisher had a crew that maintained the fleet in tiptop condition. He even got considerable use from his Excavator, a powerful piece of equipment that only a powerful rancher could afford. He was lead dog of the farmer's co-op, and if some pestilential force struck a ranch anywhere within a 30-mile radius, Worley saw to it the afflicted rancher's operation survived until said rancher got back on his feet. Even his ranch foreman feared and respected him.

The train tracks leading to the Lake Pend Oreille Bridge more or less bisected Fisher's land. Shortly after midnight, Worley bolted upright in bed upon hearing loud noises. One look out his window told the story of what had gone down. He was curt with his wife. "Alert the bunkhouse, then get on the phone tree and tell them a train's down at the bridge and we need trucks, stretchers, lights, and blankets foremost, and maybe more later." Worley himself called 911 and took off for his own pickup with an armful of blankets in his arms.

Worley was first on the scene. What he saw up close when he shined his flashlight through the misty 30-degree air was six Amtrak cars thrown onto their sides in the open field. They lay at varying downward angles looking broken and defeated. He'd seen this train in the daylight thousands of times, and knew the consist normally was between 10 and 15 cars. The absence of even one locomotive told him what had occurred on the bridge. Within minutes Fisher saw headlights of vehicles approaching from numerous directions. The rancher armada was forming. He focused on sizing up the situation in order to issue sensible instructions to the others as they arrived. Worley knew about discipline and organization. He had been through the hell of Khe Sanh as a young Marine. Most of these ranchers had served in the military, and he'd always heard that one in ten farmhouses out here contained a registered nurse. They were dependable people in this type of emergency.

Worley had a rough scheme in mind. The first 'armada' vehicle to appear belonged to Rancy Hill, an Idaho state trooper who lived nearby. Rancy was still young, and had a chance to advance in rank, but facts were facts: the best troopers didn't get assigned to rural outposts like this one in Sandpoint. Worley began talking to Rancy right away. "These cars have emergency exits. The double-decker has two window exits, one on each end. We can boost men up there and get the ambulatory out. Those most likely to contain passengers are priority." He pointed to all except the lounge and dining cars. "We'll put the walking wounded in our trucks, where they'll be covered in blankets, and transport them to the nearest three ranch houses. We'll get them shelter and anything urgent, and we'll tend to them in the fashion of a mobile aid station until professional EMTs, etcetera, can arrive. You let the emergency vehicles know where they can be picked up. Those who've experienced traumatic injuries will remain inside or lifted out on stretchers—they'll be examined individually. If we get those with minor injuries away from here you'll have a cleaner, clearer landing zone for the MEDEVAC choppers. 'Course, it'll take a really top-notch pilot to fly through this soup, if they're even allowed to." Trooper Rancy Hill started to say something, but saw through the beam of headlights that Worley wasn't quite finished. "I guess you recognize, officer, this train's missing some cars, including the locomotives. I'm afraid they're resting a hundred feet down in the lake. You'll have to tell the railroad that. I'm sorry."

Everyone's neck generally feels fine until he sticks it out. Trooper Hill considered Worley's words, and it was clear if he went along with moving people away from this site, he'd be sticking his neck out pretty darned far. "I don't know...." He was halting, feeling he was about to stutter.

"Trooper," Worley interjected, "we don't have time to mess around. Let's go bold and get this situation under control. Roger?"

Rancy Hill stiffened his spine. "Go ahead. Just give me exact locations of where each group is going."

"Good call, trooper. Just stand back, make your calls, and we'll get to work," Worley said.

The good-sized cadre of ranchers circled around Worley Fisher, got their instructions, offered a few suggestions, and set to work.

Worley used the trooper's megaphone to announce as loudly as he could to those inside that could hear that help was on the way.

+++

Inside the Train

None of the passengers possessed a manifest, and none but the most experienced travelers had a good idea of how many were aboard. In fact, the sleeper car carried somewhere between 34 and 44, each coach car carried up to 96, and an unknown number were presently in the lounge and dormitory cars.

Chesley Mason's college buddy had been drinking for hours before Chesley persuaded him to turn in just before midnight. He fell asleep immediately on his bunk still wearing his clothes. Chesley also fell asleep right away, but for a more mundane reason: he was exhausted. Before the train overturned, Chesley felt the car begin to shake violently, and he tensed, waiting for the worst. When his car flipped, he was deliberately leaning the wrong way, supposing it was going to careen in the opposite direction. Like many others, he was flung out of bed swiftly. His face struck a metal bar protruding from the opposing side.

Chesley's virtually lifeless friend, in a state of deep alcoholic inebriation, was similarly cast from his bed, but he made the happy discovery upon waking up on the floor that he was unhurt, outside of a contusion or two. "Get up, Ches," the friend barked, "it's over now." And indeed it was over for Chesley. The friend came to his senses and checked Chesley's wrist and carotid for a pulse, but there was none.

Evil in Disguise

Major Russell Cooper woke instantly when the intense vibrations began. He had removed his prosthesis for sleeping comfort. He set in his mind exactly where he had placed it as he got out of bed and grasped a grab bar as tightly as he could while stooping to lower his center of gravity. As his car finally tilted over he was prepared, although he figured his shoulder joints would be sore for a time. When he felt the car come to rest, he felt around for the prosthesis, and from his new position awkwardly attached it and the shoe it fit into. The lights remained on. He left his cabin to search for people in need of assistance. He opened the door of another single-occupant cabin, where he found a lovely woman down, bleeding from the head and unconscious. He thought about picking her up, then remembered she might have sustained a spinal or neck injury. Before he left her in search of other victims, something caused him to do a double-take. He knew this woman was special. He had seen her before. He had followed General Pack in the news as Governor, and was now certain he had seen her at Pack's side. He noted her cabin number, and scurried further throughout the car in search of others. He ran into Dr. Dave Chastain, who said, "My family and I are OK in 2D...I'm a doctor...have you found anyone who can use me?"

"Yes, in 2F. I'm sure she's the wife, or special friend, of the recent Governor of Montana, Simon Pack. She's bleeding and unresponsive. She needs you."

"Going there now. See what you can do about getting the ambulatory out. I heard the blast saying there's help outside," Chastain said calmly.

Cooper began rounding up all who could walk and instructed them to follow him. He pushed out an emergency exit window and pulled himself up and out. He spread out across the exterior and used two arms to pull up the first person, a man in good shape he designated to be first so that the two of them could pull the others out. Most were injured in one way or another, but none appeared life-threatening. Once he and his associate had hauled out the last one, Russell Cooper went back in to get a tally on those who would require stretchers. He would, however, leave specific extraction details to the man who had identified himself as a medical doctor.

Before Major Cooper went in again after pulling out the less injured, he wrote a note and gave it to the man who clearly was in charge, Worley Fisher. The note said, "I used to work for General Simon Pack, the former Governor of Montana. I encountered a lady inside who is his close friend, or possibly wife. She is alive and already is receiving medical attention. A Doctor Chastain intends to get her transferred to Spokane's Sacred Heart Medical Center, it appears. Please get this information to him. Very Respectfully, Major Russell "Duck" Cooper. 555-467-1238." The major wasn't a hundred percent certain he was right about the true identity of this woman, but if Pack's lady was safe at her home, there'd be no harm.

"I'll do it, Major," Worley Fisher said gruffly. "I been watchin' you, and thanks for your help. You'll be welcome to stay at my house, and I'll even drive you there when the time comes. Meantime, my truck's over there, so have a seat in it and get warm."

"I'll take you up on that, Mister…?"

"Sorry, name's Fisher, and yours?"

"Russell Cooper, US Army, sir. But I hope you're here when I come back. I've got to go back in and help the doctor who's still inside evaluating those we can't pull out."

"Don't worry, Major. I'll be here. I'm told the EMT people from Coeur d'Alene will be here in maybe a half-hour. Choppers from Spokane aren't cleared to fly yet. Don't expect the fog to burn off until mid-morning. And I think I should pass this note to the Trooper, Rancy Hill, who has better comms than me at this point."

Russell didn't know the nature of the work being done in the other five train cars, but Rancher Fisher had rounded up one medical doctor and several veterinarians to accelerate the triage process inside them. He had stretchers at the ready, and was prepared to ferry them inside if and when they were required. Some of the stretchers weren't pretty, being homemade, but they were functional. Trooper Rancy Hill had used follow-on law enforcers to cordon off a broad area around the site in order to prevent interference with Fisher's operation. The first media people had arrived with their bright lights and microphones, but so far none had broken through the cordon. But the lawmen created openings for the land armada to pass through and back again. Both Rancy Hill and Worley were pretty confident some higher-ups were going to pepper them with criticism for hauling off the walking wounded to the three ranches, but Hill was already adopting Fisher's mantra, "when in charge, take charge." Trooper Hill was nervous about his decision at the start, but now he was calm and entirely mission-oriented.

Before going into the exit hole again, Cooper overheard Rancher Fisher issuing what the military call a 'convoy briefing.' Worley stood in the center of the circle of trucks, and began to speak. It went something like this: "Ladies and gentlemen, we're going to get you to a place where you'll be warm and have light and have as many needs tended to as we can handle. We'll treat you with respect and kindness. Hope you have a comfortable but short stay with us until the medical professionals arrive."

Back inside a third time, Cooper went looking for Doctor Chastain. Before he found him, he saw a woman who was awake but in great distress. He saw that Doctor Chastain had been there because next to her head was a page of notes, which Cooper took to be an initial diagnosis. He didn't read the note in full, but at a glance he saw the phrase "Severe dilatation of the stomach." Cooper took the old lady's hand and told her quietly that help would arrive shortly and that faster than she could imagine she would be relieved of her pain. He placed another blanket over her. He stopped to reassure two others who had pages of notes beside their heads as well.

Eventually, he saw a blanket drawn fully across a body. Only the feet showed from under the blanket. They were men's shoes. That was Chesley Mason, the North Dakota State football star. Dr. Chastain's note was brief, signed by himself: "Pronounced dead at 1:15 A.M."

When finally he found the Doctor, Chastain was at the side of Keeley Eliopoulous. Chastain looked up to see the Major. "Did my wife and daughter get out?"

"They sure did, Doctor, and the rancher running things out there, Worley Fisher, will be able to tell you which ranch they were transported to when the time comes. Is there anything I can do to help you?"

"How much longer before EMTs get here?" Chastain asked.

"Fisher thinks under a half hour now."

"To take them where?"

"I heard him say Coeur d'Alene."

"I do neurosurgery in Spokane. Spine and brain work. My hospital there is the only one in this region that contains the equipment some of these patients will need. This lady is definitely in that category. They can be stabilized in Coeur d'Alene, but the hard cases will need to go to Spokane. Can't we get the MEDEVAC birds over here?"

"Looks like it'll be mid-morning before they fly, something like five to seven hours from now," Cooper answered.

"If that's actually the case, go back out and inform whoever's in charge that Sacred Heart Medical Center must prepare to fly every available airframe to Coeur d'Alene. Tell them Doctor Chastain says so. I'm about finished here. Go with me to the other cars, OK? After you speak with the rancher about those aircraft. Maybe we can speed the process up if you write while I dictate my initial findings. This lady right here, I'm sure, will be under my own care." Cooper figured Chastain didn't care right now that he knew this woman and the man attached to her. But he did not stop himself from saying, for a second time, "It's good to hear you'll look after her, doctor. I know her husband, and he thanks you in advance." Doctor Chastain couldn't worry about special cases right now.

Then Major Cooper was gone, saying on his way out, "I'll be back to help you out, Doctor Chastain."

+++

Sheriff Joe Mollison got the weather reports, and the same conditions that prevented the helicopters from lifting off in Spokane prevailed there at Mollison's location. When Pack arrived, Mollison would drive his official vehicle to make better time. The distance was about 190 miles to the crash site, which he thought he could make in about three hours. Easy drive down 93 and west on 2 through Libby and Troy and Bonner's Ferry down toward Sandpoint. It was still early morning, and although he was alert now, he might falter a bit within a few hours, so he filled a gallon Thermos with black coffee for the trip. And he threw in a couple of energy drinks for insurance against fatigue. Now till Pack got here he'd just watch and listen to the news and hope for a call from Bonner County.

Ten minutes later his phone rang. It wasn't from the county sheriff, but from a man who identified himself as Idaho State Trooper Rancy Hill. "In a roundabout way, I was told you're friends with Governor Pack? We can't contact him, so you're next. Is my info correct?"

"Sure is, Trooper. I've been waiting for one of my counterparts over there to bring me up to speed. And I know where Governor Pack is right now and why you can't reach him, so I'll get the message to him…oh, probably inside an hour from now."

"OK, I got a handwritten message here I ought to read directly."

"Send it," Mollison said. "Just go kinda slow."

Mollison thanked the trooper, signed off, and turned his attention to the television screen. The Amtrak spokesperson explained that they were reviewing the manifests, but cautioned that it would take weeks to produce a reliable casualty accounting. Despite warnings to remain on board until they reached their chosen destinations, some passengers always got off before then without telling the train personnel. Someone could therefore be reported as missing, only to show up elsewhere weeks, or even months, later. There were some circumstances over which Amtrak had no control. Further, some who were originally in the cars that plunged into the deep water were most likely still in the lounge car at the time of the derailment. The woman on the screen refused to speculate on the cause of the fatal derailment. She took questions, the first of which was "Is it true this engineer was arrested for DUI two times during the past three years?"

The woman was prepared for the question. AMTRAK was well aware the first conclusion habitually jumped to was engineer error. "False. Maliciously untrue," she added.

+++

Most psychiatrists likely would aver that Pack's lead attitude is intuitive and evaluative. The archetype of this kind of person is the Hero. Not many of us wear the Hero mantle. Pack would surely be unaware of the mysterious ways in which our minds function, because he flatly didn't care. He just knew who he was. The Hero operates on needs, not wants. Moreover, the Hero—unlike most archetypes—is willing to sacrifice, even his own body, to get what's needed. And Pack got cold and remote when things got tough and rough. He didn't permit the typical human reactions of fear and insecurity to take the lead as they did in most people. Rather than feeling overwhelmed and terrified, he unconsciously opted to be courageous and powerful. During the onset of stresses, his mind became possessed of clarity, not cloudiness.

When finally he pulled up in the lot at the Sheriff's office, Pack wore his serious game face. He wouldn't be opposite talking with his friend Joe Mollison today. "What've you got, Joe?" he asked at once.

"Good to see you, Simon," Mollison answered. They'd been friends a long time, and Mollison never hesitated, in the fashion of fellow locals, to call Pack by his first name. "On the positive side, read this first," Mollison said. He looked on as Pack took in the note in a matter of seconds.

"I'll be damned…small world…Duck found her. Hurt but alive. Thank God. Ready to go? Spokane, OK Joe?"

"Grab that Thermos and let's get on the road, then," Mollison said. "Helo's been ruled out for the time being. I think we'll get there faster by road than by waiting until a chopper can get up."

Two hours into the drive, Pack had barely spoken. Mollison quit counting at three cups of coffee, but Pack took none. After the second stop Mollison required in order to offload the coffee, he apologized to Pack for slowing them down.

"Naw, Joe, pardon my manners. I should be making talk to help you stay alert and awake. I can do that, and I will." Presently he started up again. "How long has it been since that helo crash Paul Fardink and Tetu and I were in? Doesn't matter, except that it really hasn't been that long, something along the order of sixteen, eighteen months. They say I was hurt pretty bad, but I was up and back to full activity within a couple of months. I want Keeley to be unhurt, but it seems she is, so now I hope she fares as well as I did. Yep, I'd be satisfied if we could be guaranteed that outcome," he mused.

"We're warhorses, Simon," Mollison offered, "and we both know there are no guarantees coming with injuries. But Keeley's kept herself fit as a fiddle, so the docs have a lot to work with. Has anyone spoken with her mother yet?"

"I think Keeley invited her to spend some time with us after we're married…." Pack paused, realizing there now was a real chance the wedding might not happen. "But I'm not sure she got around to it yet. I'm thinking I'll call her after a day or so."

"Simon, you're my friend, and your judgment's the best, but I think you ought to alert her now, get her on the way over if she can do it. Mothers can help their daughters in special ways the rest of us sometimes can't, you know? Heck, I'll make the call for you while you're dealing with the hospital. OK?"

"You're right, Joe. Let's contact her. I'll copy the number for you," Pack said. "I guess you could say I have an inner circle that ought to know, also. For example…"

His phone rang. It was another illustration of synchronicity, in that Wilkie Buffer was on the line, and he had just about brought out Buffer's name. Mollison imagined it must have been an awkward call, in that outside of a few perfunctory grunts, Pack did not hold up his end of the conversation. Still, Wilkie was smart enough, and understood Pack well enough, to know Pack wouldn't be talkative at this time. Buffer accomplished what he wanted, which was to let Pack know he sent his condolences, and would visit him and Keeley when the time was right. Buffer assured Pack he would go wherever he needed, and whenever, to be of help. Pack thanked his longtime colleague and hung up.

"As I was saying, Joe, you can help me out a lot by informing Jim Dahl and Tetu where Keeley and I stand. I'm sure they'll let a few others know….And that's about all I have to say at the moment. Don't think you have to babysit us. You were great to drive me over, but anytime you need to go, no problem."

"Simon, I'm staying until we have better resolution than we have now, which is zero. I brought paperwork, and I have a phone, so I'll stay in touch with my office. A hospital always has a cafeteria, and in the big ones they're open twenty-four hours, so that'll be my office. If I get a motel for a night or two, I'll leave word for you."

Pack phoned ahead to the Medical Center. Once he was connected with Admissions, the person on the other end must've given

Simon the usual "Well, sir, if you're not next of kin, we can't release that information." Mollison glanced over at Pack. He had witnessed Pack's 'volcanic visage' once or twice before, and recognized it now. He reached over, hand out, for Pack to give him the phone. Pack complied. Mollison spoke calmly, "Howdy, ma'am, this is Sheriff Joe Mollison for Governor Pack. I'll be there shortly to discuss the matter with you. May I have your name, please?"

CHAPTER FOUR

Pack and Mollison had reached Sacred Heart before Keeley. The first serial of MEDEVAC birds wasn't far behind them. Much as Pack wanted to see Keeley, he knew the most critically injured would arrive first, so from that point of view he was willing to wait a while longer. Sheriff Joe Mollison was running point for Pack, and had gotten assurances he'd be paged as quickly as Keeley was under full control of the hospital. 'Full control,' the lady explained, meant not only that the patient was inside the hospital but also had undergone necessary imaging and other tests, and a plan of follow-on action decided.

Several hours passed in the waiting room when a young nurse approached Pack and the Sheriff. Looking at Pack, she said, "I know you, sir. Former Governor Pack. Pleased to meet you." Pack shook the extended hand. "OK, sir, Miss Eliopoulous has been asking for you. Obviously, she is conscious. Dr. David Chastain flew in with her. There aren't neurosurgeons better than him, if I can editorialize. Anyway, I'm going to escort you to another section of the hospital where Dr. Chastain will meet you in about half an hour."

Pack was relieved, as was Mollison, who gripped Pack's forearm. Pack wasn't going to ruin his relief by asking more questions of this nurse. Chastain would tell him what he needed to know. Thankfully, the nurse didn't say more either. All the news was about those who had perished in the derailment, a subject Pack wanted to leave alone for the time being. There would be a time to mourn, just not now.

Dr. Chastain finally entered the small space where they waited. He looked exhausted, with dark spots showing under his still-youthful eyes. He was a neat, trim fellow of medium stature, but clearly he needed rest. After shaking hands with both men, Chastain got down to business. "She was unresponsive until a short while ago. I flew aboard her chopper. I feared the worst, substantial brain damage. But as you've been told, she has regained consciousness. That, of course, is positive, but there are negatives. First, she has lost her vision—for now. She might regain it tomorrow or next week or next month...or possibly never. These things are tricky. She is not panicking. In the short time we spoke, I have to guess she knows as much about the physiology of the brain as I do. She's a very bright woman, and knew immediately what trauma to the occipital lobe means. The type of lesions I observed on imagery were consistent with scotoma, but no, when we presented her with the eye chart, she couldn't read it, not even scotomatously, meaning partially but with blind spots. What she saw was a shadow, as if her eyes are darkly veiled. We have to keep her under observation until we're convinced the likelihood of severe complications attenuates to near zero."

"And the severe complications, what are they?" Pack interjected.

"Well, first let me say she doesn't appear to have lost memory. I would not have anticipated memory loss from the images, but until I asked her some questions, I couldn't rule it out. No damage to the frontal or parietal lobes. But to answer your question, there's still a chance she could experience seizures and what we call complex hallucinations. And she could also experience aphasia, an inability to express thoughts or to understand clearly spoken language. But that's worst case. For now, none of that.

"She has another problem, though, that's more immediate, and that she wants me to bring to your attention. She's had to be heavily sedated for a high level of pain arising from a problem that's clear and familiar to me. I was on that train and can attest to the violent manner in which Miss Eliopoulous and quite a number of others got thrown into unyielding objects. She apparently struck something with her lower back. Her L3, 4, and 5 discs shifted and pinched nerves around her spinal column. This caused sharp pain and numbness in her right leg and hip. If, at this moment, she could bear the pain to walk down the hallway, she would probably fall. I can repair this problem with spinal fusion surgery. With the damage done, no amount of medicine or physical therapy will fix her back. So, here's what I'd like to do: you and she talk over what I've said, and if you give me the go-ahead, I'll schedule it for tomorrow. I'll keep her morphine level up so that the pain is minimized until surgery. I frankly need sleep before I'm fully prepared to do it."

"So you've performed this surgery before?" Pack asked, rather rhetorically.

"Hundreds of times, with an almost 100% success rate," Chastain said.

"Will this surgery adversely affect the brain's recovery?"

"No," Chastain answered flatly.

"And how long will the back surgery recovery be?"

"Well, Keeley will continue to have pain for at least four weeks post-surgery. Pain in her leg will dissipate totally, but there will be pain from the surgery itself. After four weeks, she'll probably be walking normally, and within six months she can resume her normal range of activities. She might feel numbness in some places for up to a year. Of course, I'm speaking only about the back issue. The head injury will follow its own schedule."

"Go and rest," Pack said. "Thank you for taking good care of her and for getting her here. We'll probably need your expertise tomorrow. I'll see that you get our answer soon."

+++

The Sheriff had taken a powder to let Pack visit Keeley alone. Pack took her hand, and her eyes opened. More than anything it was her eyes that attracted him. He had always been attracted to her rare kind of eyes: kind, deep, solemn, knowing, wise. Eyes that could twinkle on the right occasions. The lineaments of the eye were of greater meaning to him than hue. Color was just frosting on the cake, in the end not all that important to him. And now those eyes were essentially sightless, but that didn't matter much either. She tried to smile, but that was an effort given the morphine cloud she floated on. He also was thinking she was a true match for him, filling in the considerable gaps in his own personality and intelligence.

Keeley made an effort to shift, just the least bit, in the direction of Pack, but pain seized her and made her grimace. She breathed deeply and settled herself once more as the pain diminished. "I can think, Simon. You know, 'I think, therefore I am'? I'm going to be fine." She was speaking in a 33 rpm voice, words oozing out like xylem sap from a maple tree. "God has spoken to me. I know that in whatever condition I leave this hospital, that's part of the plan. Know that, Simon. I'm going to be fine however this turns out."

"OK," Simon said soothingly, "I believe you as long as you don't turn maudlin on me. You relax as much as you can and let me say whatever comes into my head. Can you do that?"

"Uh-huh. I'd like that, Simon."

"Well, for starters, I like our Doctor Chastain. Seems highly competent, and to his colleagues he walks on water. He was, incredible as it sounds, on that train with you, and looked after you all the way from there to here. And he treated others on board, too. I think he's a good man. He wants to do spinal fusion surgery tomorrow, says he can make that better. You'll need good care for a while, but who's better than me to give it? Yeah, I know, hundreds of thousands of professionals, but nobody can care more than me. That's what you want in a *care-giver*, right? When we get home, we can hire a nurse to do some things outside my expertise—if there should be any—but sign me up, boss, to be primary caregiver. And I don't want an answer now, just relax like I said, but with your approval, I'd like us to get married right here in the hospital once you're feeling better, and…."

She did smile. Keeley said with eyes closed, "Love you, Simon. I approve all of it. Go on."

"And we can forget about living in two places. You'll finally be home in the cabin. OK, lots of friends want to visit you here, but I'm holding them off till you're better." Pack hadn't heard that from anyone, but knew it was true nonetheless. "I'd like your mother to come soon as she can. Tetu and Swan want to come, and Wilk and Cissy, and Governor Dahl. And instead of your going to Seattle, daughter two will come to you. Just so many have you in their thoughts, Keel."

"How many died in that accident, Simon?"

"I don't know for sure. More than a hundred," he answered.

"Say prayers for their families, Simon. OK?"

"I will, Keel. A lot of people are hurting. Look, I'm sure I've been here too long already. You need rest. You know, the first sign you see entering Station 73, as this area is called, reads *QUIET, PLEASE...HEALING IN PROGRESS.* So I'm going for now, but will be back the next time I'm permitted. There's a lot I'd like to tell you."

Keeley said, "Not yet. Why haven't you asked me about, or mentioned, the head injury? Does it frighten you?"

"No, it doesn't frighten me. It does concern me. I suppose I haven't mentioned it because the doctor said you know as much about occipital injuries as he does, or words to that effect. I understand that you can't see me clearly right now, but in time that might change."

"Yes, it could change, for worse or better. What if I am permanently blind?"

"If you were forever sightless, I'd hurt for you, but not for me. Who you are will not change whether you can see or not. And let's be optimistic. He said they detect no damage to another lobe, which is superb news, don't you agree?"

"Oh, yes, not having my mental faculties impaired seems like a huge victory, for sure. But I want you to know if I'm forever sightless, I'll uncomplainingly learn to live with it. I'd be lying, though, if I claimed the prospect of that condition doesn't frighten me, Simon."

With that, Simon Pack squeezed her hand gently, placed a soft kiss on her lips, and padded soundlessly out of the room.

They knew to contact him of any changes in Keeley's condition. He left Station 73 in search of Joe Mollison.

+++

As expected, he found Mollison in the cafeteria watching TV. The Sheriff was agitated about something, frowning and spitting mad, judging from the slit of his eyes, the crease in his brow, and the jut of his jaw.

"What is it, Joe?" Pack asked.

The Sheriff was about to speak, thought about it, then said, "Nope, let's have your report on Keeley."

"I'll give you the full report, but get whatever it is off your chest first. You won't be able to hear me if you don't."

"All right, then. It didn't take those sorry rotten bastards long. One of the networks is claiming ISIS has taken responsibility for the train wreck. Whaddaya think, Joe ISIS walks up to a correspondent in Afghanistan or Iraq or Bumscrew Egypt and tells him that? Or did it come from social media? Nice if the TV people would mention the source. I'm not doubting the report, though. The whole damn world keeps me in a state of royal pissed-off these days, Simon."

"Maybe it's true, maybe not. Let the NTSB investigators do their thing first. The people working in this field are pretty good, have a record of getting to the very bottom of these things. You gotta admit, Joe, this isn't like 9/11, where we had immediate visual proof. So calm down, buddy."

Mollison put a hand on each side of his head as if drilling inside to purge the angry thoughts, whereupon he threw his hands out and away from him, signaling they were gone, for the time being. "OK, Simon," he said in lowered tones, "I'd like to hear about Keeley."

Pack gave a full accounting of Keeley's condition, stressing that she wasn't out of the woods by any measure, and would be confined to Sacred Heart for some time. Staff here would follow her dual disabilities for however long it took to pronounce her cleared to go home. Pack added, "To summarize, I believe the back problem is eminently treatable, but will be a source of pain for at least a month. No surgery is planned for the head injury, but whether it will heal enough to restore her eyesight is not as clear. In the case of both injuries, Dr. Chastain was adamant in stating his belief in the enormous restorative powers of rest. I'd like to spend most of my time up there with her, but he says that's not in her best interest. I'll have to ration the amount of time I go up there. I guess that in short I'll fall back on the overused expression 'cautiously optimistic.'"

"Thanks, Simon. Tell her I'm thinking of her all the damn time, but that we think it's best for me to pack up and get back home. I'll stay in touch. And brother, if you need anything, any kind of help, yell and I'll be on my way in minutes. How about you let me take you to pick up a rental car on my way out? You'll need one."

On the way to the rental agency, Mollison told Pack that when he had a moment here and there he should call Governor Dahl and Tetu and Buffer and a few others. "Let me tell you, my sense is that if you don't head them off, they'll show up here uninvited. They care about you and that lady, hear me well on that." Pack acknowledged he felt a duty to do as Mollison suggested. He mentally added one other person he intended to call and thank—his former aide, Russell Cooper.

+++

The next morning Pack was at the hospital before the sun came up. He ate a full breakfast in the cafeteria as he waited to get into Keeley's room at seven. He expected no change in her demeanor from the day previous, and he found none. Careful not to disturb her, Pack let her sleep. At seven-thirty Dr. Chastain came in, studying this patient's chart. He looked refreshed and sharp. After giving a smiling nod to Pack, he woke Keeley. He explained each step of the process, including post-op and subsequent return to this room. She understood and asked no questions. It was then three hours until surgery. Keeley was placid, showing no case of nerves.

They moved her to the Main Pre-Op Center, where a retinue of staff members—RNs, NPs, Lab Techs, NAs, Doctors and Chaplains—asked that boring but essential question: "Who are you and why are you here?" The head nurse must have assumed all patients were nervous at this stage, in that she used lines on Pack and Keeley she had doubtlessly used on an untold number of others: "Hey, who is this guy tagging along with you? Your boyfriend, right? He's been making eyes at you ever since you got here. And don't think I haven't seen him poking his hand under that warm air blanket we have on you….I think he's been trying to crawl into that bed with you, but golly darn, I'm not gonna let him! Now, mister, shoo, git on outta here! You can't go into the OR with her."

And yet another Nurse Ratched wannabe who joked: "Surgeons here don't wear scrubs. It's Oshkosh by gosh and DTC Fire Hose workwear and Buck Naked underwear. Our men don't use scalpels either, just the Buck knives they carry everywhere. Last week, we wheeled a man into the OR, and his answer to 'why are you here?' was 'heart transplant, ain't you people 'posed to know that?' Doctor screamed back at him, as he peered leerily at his blade, 'You're shit outta luck, pardner! This here's the castration station.'"

That was about as much humor as ever displayed around an OR.

Five hours later, she returned to Room 715, dazed and confused, eyes still sightless…but with back fixed. The surgery, Dr. Chastain allowed, was successful. Nevertheless, the staff remained vigilant, particularly given the disturbing lesion on her brain. A great deal of pain lay in front of Keeley Eliopoulous.

Between the second and third weeks of Keeley's confinement at Sacred Heart, Simon commissioned a hospital chaplain to perform a wedding ceremony.

CHAPTER FIVE

After a month-and-a-half, Dr. Chastain declared Mrs. Keeley Pack fit to travel home, which now meant Pack's cabin, and his cabin alone. The first month in Spokane had been especially rough on Keeley. The staff monitored her continuously. Every physical therapy session was a risky venture. They took absolutely no chance of a fall, as a phalanx of medical staffers surrounded her. Getting therapy for her back without endangering her brain health entailed walking an extremely fine line. As it turned out, her eyesight was returning as the lesion on the occipital lobe began to show as just a faint shadow on the CT Scanner. She was able to walk unaided, the leg pain having vanished, but still Pack insisted she rely on the walker a little longer. With what she had been through, thorough precautions, Pack reckoned, were called for.

Keeley's spirit upon crossing the threshold of the cabin was buoyant. Her mother, Daphne Eliopoulous, had been with her during most of the hospital stay, and had been the only outsider present at the bedside wedding. Pack liked her a great deal. Daphne was a regally beautiful woman of 62, who even in the hospital dressed in exquisitely tasteful fashions. Her patriarchal, exceedingly rich husband died unexpectedly last year, making her a much sought-after widow, or so Pack suspected. The quality in Daphne that Pack most prized was her reserve, which coupled with her equanimity, made her queenly. And he noticed that even though she was accustomed to life on a luxurious island estate, she blended in seamlessly to life on Pack's place in the woods of northwest Montana.

Pack drove Keeley home in his rental four-wheeler. Daphne had wanted to drive over four days earlier in the company of Sheriff Mollison, who helped the gracious Daphne re-arrange the cabin to accommodate her still-recovering daughter. Daphne selected a part-time nurse after interviewing half a dozen candidates. She shopped at the markets in town to stock the refrigerator and freezer Pack had left mostly barren. She insisted on being the meal-planner and cook. She performed all the chores Pack figured her maids had done in Greece. If Daphne had a bad side, Pack hadn't observed it yet. He was sufficiently realistic, however, to understand she'd undoubtedly bottled up a great deal of stress, and could uncork it at any moment.

There had been another surprise awaiting Keeley when she first got home. Tetu and Swan Palaita were there waiting for her, as was Governor James Dahl. Tetu had brought along Chesty, the prized dog Pack had given him, possibly as a wedding gift. The visitors had taken instructions to be careful about hugging her, in that her back remained tender. Dressings no longer had to be applied, but Pack liked to keep a close eye on the surgical area. They didn't need to worry, though, because Keeley tearfully squeezed each of them for all she was worth. Chesty remembered Pack's scent, as he proved by jumping all over him as he exited his SUV. Pack called to Tetu the unnecessary admonition to "make sure our friend doesn't leap onto Keeley, OK?".

"Thank you all," she said. "I'd like to remember all those souls who fell to their deaths, and to all the others injured, some much more seriously than I. I am thankful beyond words for having had the great fortune to become Mrs. Keeley Pack, and I am grateful, equally beyond words, that Simon has friends like you. You three, plus Joe Mollison and Wilk Buffer, are at the center of Simon's life-support system, and I doubt he can find the words to express in public what he has expressed to me about each of you in private. Can we sit down?" she said laughing, "My back's still not up to speed."

Pack's spirit was buoyant as well, as evidenced by his return to opposite-talking. "Don't believe anything Keel said about speaking for me. You people never done nothin' for me. I'm the one took care of you for too long—wastin' my time's how I'll put it. We're gonna have a nice dinner here in a few minutes, but just be on guard not to eat overmuch, OK? That's my money with each damn bite you take, got it?"

Daphne had been forewarned that Chesty was coming, so from the kitchen she distracted him with a hambone she'd selected at the market. He followed her to the basement, where he would be out of Keeley's way. When she came back up, Pack went down for a few minutes with his old dog. He spoke to the dog as if the animal were a human. "I miss you, pal. You understand why I handed you off to Tetu, don't you? Sure you do. Remember that cross-country trip we made, the one where you saved mine and Tetu's lives a couple of times? Hope you see little Tommy pretty regularly. That boy loves you also. Don't allow any harm to come to him, all right?"

Back upstairs, Pack heard Tetu chime in, "Matai is back to normal, Mrs. Pack. Tetu is happy to see." He put his arm around Swan, his own wife of a short while. With a grin, Tetu added, "And, Matai, if

Tetu can make up for all the things you say he has not done, tell him, and he will fix it."

It was Governor Dahl's turn to speak. "How many perfect couples are there in this world, do you think? Not very many, probably, but I'm looking at two right now, I'm sure of it. Swan, I don't need to tell you Tetu is as good a man as I've ever seen, and if he's never explained how he came to be at the General's side, have him do it sometime. It's a great story. And Keeley, I can only say your husband is maybe the foremost American patriot, as well as Marine, I could ever dream of meeting. And, oh yeah, the greatest Governor of any state in the Union. And Mrs. Eliopoulous, everyone thanks you too," he said, turning in the direction of the kitchen. "Keeley, we've had some time with your mother before you arrived, and wow, she is a gem of a lady. I'm sure you're as proud of her as she is of you." Keeley gravely signaled that she agreed. More solemnly and quietly, Dahl said, "Finally, we want you to understand we've prayed for your safe return every day, and now we give thanks that has happened." The lay minister Swan uttered an "Amen," which seemed to be the final punctuation to the formalities of the homecoming.

They ate, they clinked glasses, they smiled, they touched hands, and they laughed, until at last the visitors declared that Keeley, the object of their gathering, had received enough adulation and experienced enough excitement, and done enough activity for this juncture of her recovery. Swan said, "We're almost done, but not quite. I checked with Mrs. Eliopoulous and she confirmed the new Mrs. Pack never got her wedding cake. Tetu will tell you I'm not the best cook, but I am a fair baker, so I did my best to create this cake." She went outside for a moment, returning with six tiers of a stunning cake. Students at the Culinary Institute of America could not have done better. Atop it rested two painted figures, reasonable likenesses of Pack and his wife lovingly captured, carved by one of their friends from the Upper Yaak. Pack sliced a portion for Keeley, who fought back tears. Everyone ate, and it was as delicious as it was beautiful.

Pack said, "Thank you, Swan. Very much thank you. We have options here on what to do with this masterpiece. We have our memory and we have our photo. With Keel's consent, I'd like to recommend you take the remainder to Georgeann's General Store and let her dole it out to anyone who would like it. Our way of giving our respects to all of our great friends up there."

Keeley said, "We do absolutely love it and we admire your skill. This is so far beyond my own ability to make...I can't tell you, Swan. But I agree with Simon. Let your friends up there enjoy it as much as we have. And I'd also like to send a small contribution to Georgeann to let her know we're thinking of her and Tommy."

They took their leave after doing the full cleanup and putting away of tableware. They had felt the strength of deep friendships.

+++

Keeley was asleep, Chesty and visitors cleared out. Pack reclined in his favorite chair, under his favorite reading lamp, and resolved to read a book of essays that was next up on his reading list. Before opening it, he decided to pour himself three fingers of Blanton's over ice; it had been a while since he had been able to relax so fully. As he filled his heavy whiskey glass, Major Cooper, 'Duck' as he had ordained him, leapt to the front of his consciousness. If a small fraction of the men in this world were in the mold of Duck, it'd be a fine place. Yeah, problems would remain, but good men would be there to keep them under control. He thought of the sacrifices the young man had already made: lost much of his leg in combat; the Army personnel people in Washington tried to force him into a non-combat arms branch, but, angry, he resolutely told them he would not hear of it—he entered the Army to be an Infantry Officer, and he would stay in the Infantry until, in the normal course of events, he had to leave the Army altogether. There followed three more tours in Southwest Asia that consumed his prime years, years in which he might've been stabilized enough in America to establish a lasting relationship with a woman. Back in America on leave after his last tour overseas, he treated himself to the 'luxury' of a solo trip aboard a train across the breadth of the country….and look how that turned out for him. Pack was a hard man, but somewhere deep he hurt for Duck, hoping he could find true joy with someone.

Pack had phoned Duck in those first days of Keeley's hospital confinement. By that time the Major had found his way to Kansas City, for what reason he did not explain. Too bad, because Pack had intended to let him into his cabin for some R&R. He had also wanted Tetu to come down to meet Duck.

He thanked Duck for his heroic efforts at the crash site, but that wasn't enough. What could he do to brighten Duck's life?

He found the first two essays unoriginal and uninspiring, until he turned to the Table of Contents to find two by one of the country's great men of letters, Victor Davis Hanson. And there were also two by some fellow named Wilkie Buffer. It was a profitable evening, after all. After two hours in his chair, Pack got up to check on Keeley, who still was sleeping soundly and, he hoped, healing.

He returned to his chair, where he would sleep tonight. He didn't trust himself to sleep with his wife, yet. He wanted to, badly, but he was fearful of accidentally hurting her back. Some days in the hospital, following their marriage, she invited him to lie quietly beside her, and he had, but that was during the day, and he knew he could be still. Sometime soon....

+++

During last year's Army-Navy football game, the network four times interspersed a feature on Pack, college star and future leader. He was shown destroying opposing linemen, a couple of whom went on to big careers in the NFL. When the postmaster in town asked him about the feature, Pack replied truthfully he hadn't seen it.

Rarely did he think about the past. His life was about the present and future. When he relaxed with the Blanton's, he was never prone to revel in a past achievement or to re-live a moment in combat that at the time was worthy of national notice. He did not dwell on the energy and intelligence that had been required to convene and prevail in a Constitutional Convention. He was anything but an advertisement for himself.

At the same time, he had followed an old-fashioned code of conduct that wasn't much in vogue in the present century. He spoke bluntly and candidly, and made enemies, most of all in Washington, DC. Pack was fearless, unflinching in his devotion to his personal code, and couldn't have cared less how the public viewed him. He could sleep well, which he did this night.

+++

Two more weeks elapsed and now, in June, Keeley felt strongly she had no further need of the part-time nurse. Swan and Tetu had come down three times to offer support to both Simon and his wife. Keeley was thankful for their support, but now wanted everyone to stop treating her as an invalid. She said to Pack, "Simon, I need a few days of pure escape. Much as I love it here, I want to get away for a little bit. Spend time with you, no telephones, no interruptions, nothing but forgetting my back, my head, the hospital, and the doctor visits. I want to throw stodginess out the window. Whadda you think?"

"I'm up for it, Keel. I spent a fortune on that truck, but it hasn't gotten much exercise. Let's give it some. Where you thinking of?"

"How about someplace Simon Pack would never hang out? Someplace that's pretty much anti-Pack country?"

"OK. I can do that. And where is this Shangri-La?" Pack asked.

"Glitzy Las Vegas," Keeley offered.

Pack hadn't expected that. He had reservations. Maybe she was testing him. He thought fast to come up with a reply, which was, "OK, but you need to know the last time I was in that town, the Mayor and Sheriff of Clark County sent me out of town hoping never to see me in their town again." That was true. In fact, Pack had spent a while in jail before the authorities discovered his identity. They simultaneously discovered that he had, in self-defense, killed two men who were at the right hand of the leader of al-Qaeda America. All charges were dropped, and he was portrayed as a hero, but they also felt he was a menace to the peace in their city.

"Nope, General Simon Pack is, as I can hear him say, a freeborn citizen of these United States, and a couple of tin horn lawmen aren't going to stop him from entering the city limits. What do you think of that answer, cowboy?"

"I think I lost that discussion, cowgirl, and I think we're headed to the Strip."

"Done deal. I'll work on finding some good shows, including Cirque du Soleil, which I've always wanted to see," Keel said. "And I'd like to drive through small towns and go inside little stores on the way there, and I want us to follow a different route back. Let's *amble* our way there, Simon. No rush. And let's make love everyplace we spend the night, whether it's in a $25 motor inn or an expensive place like the Bellagio. And let's not contain ourselves. Let's have it be a joyous affair we'll remember because we laughed so much."

+++

Pack was going with his gut on making the call to indulge Keeley. She was a smart, intellectually responsible and disciplined woman. In the time he'd known her, she'd reached uniformly sound decisions. She had been educated well in the human anatomy in general and the wiring of the brain in particular. She'd spent nearly every day of their marriage confined to bed. She had been a party to a traumatic event, and carried the guilt of living while others on that train had perished. Pack could read her, and what he read was she was growing increasingly ashamed to be a bedridden bride. She needed to show her husband that he had married a strong, vibrant, youthful woman, one who couldn't be held down for long. She had always had an alluring sassy streak, and wanted to put that on display again. "Well," Pack thought, "I'm not going to stand in her way. It's time I let Keeley be Keeley again. After what she's been through, she deserves some hegemony in our relationship. Oh, she had it before the accident, but since then other people have been calling the shots." Pack wouldn't have chosen to go to Las Vegas, but his preferences carried no weight right now, as he saw it. He was happy to subordinate his every desire to this woman he loved.

Their route to Vegas registered about 1,400 miles, much of it over secondary roads. As Keeley wished, they strolled slowly through interesting little towns, getting a kick out of the kitschy merchandise in many little shops. They packed light, in order to give themselves freedom to buy wacky clothing. On a Shoshone Tribal reservation they purchased Native American garb they donned with glee. They drank homemade milkshakes and licked large ice cream cones and ate at trucker stops and hole-in-the-wall cafes and bars. They made eyes at one another and kissed over beers. Inside the truck they talked with strange voices and peppered one another with silly jokes. Like: Pack— "Wait for me, wudja?" Keeley—"Nope, you're not a cook and I'm not a waiter." Or, when Keeley jokingly said, "You're too ugly for me, know that, Pack?" To which Pack replied, "If I had a dollar for every woman who found me unattractive, they'd soon find me attractive." Keeley frequently poked him in the arm, and every time he pretended it really hurt.

One evening, as Keeley showered, Simon took out a pen and wrote a note he would hand to her in the truck the following day. Pack couldn't stop himself from laughing at the words as he composed them. He would be Mr. Sobersides when he informed her she had received an urgent message left at Reception (in this fleabag establishment 'Reception' amounted to a greasy stoner who seldom looked up from his video game). The message read:

"Please, i am Sldr Joneee Kuala Lump, and will be pleased you to hear my story as it will be of sincere benefit to all your kind life. Please, in my Sldr Events i am most disconsolated to state uncovered, whilst in a nation of sincere bad repute, a most generous cache of funds which of no person does know on the side of me. In that year i was a Sldr of tiny morals and, so made away with said funds. Now i am Sldr of Faith, so to state, and wish to bestow the most full sum on the poverty victims so to atone. Ask yourself sincere are you also to join me as Sldr of Faith. Please sincere to send your monetary assistance

to JoneeeKualump@bahkeestan.ae. You will learn of progress, kind
friend, as we unite hearts to display our love with billions of rupees and
large dinars to the sad. Sldr JKL will be in delight of your sharingness
in these noble effort."

Keeley read it with as much delight as Pack had drawn from
the composing of the nonsensical draft. Life need not be lived without a
measure of mirth.

They did agree to have dinner at The Uptown Café in Butte,
which was a place of fine dining for the Wild West. In fact, they went
to Butte only because of its reputation as just about the most maverick
town in America, and the locals took great pains to protect its status.
The people of Butte wanted to be left alone as much as the people of
the Upper Yaak River Valley. Just about every soul walking the streets
of Butte recognized Pack by sight, but they left him alone because
that's how life got lived there. There were no photo requests, no
autographs sought, and Pack knew that's how it would be.

They ambled their way down two-thirds the length of Idaho
and the full length of Utah, avoiding the population centers. They
bypassed smaller towns such as Idaho Falls and Pocatello and Ogden
because they judged them too 'big' for this trip. The highborn, well-
educated beauty Keeley told Pack to pull over so she could pee in the
wide open space of the desert, and as she squatted she grinned, laughed,
shook out her hair, and waved at him as if it were the most delicious
experience ever.

Not very often, they turned serious. Pack said, "Keel, maybe
you're thinking of this as our honeymoon, and if you are, that's fine,

because it's as good a one as I could dream of. But just know we're going through with that trip we've planned for Greece too. We promised your mother, and I want to keep it. I want to see where you grew up, the places you played, the schools you attended, the desks you sat at, your toys, your dolls, every bit of it. And while we're at it, we can go to other places in Europe if you feel like it."

She was looking out her window, stroking her long dark tresses, sounding wistful. "I know. I know, Simon, and I want that just like you. There will be time for that. And thank you for treating my mother so well. She likes you, you know?"

"I did nothing. Your mother takes care of herself. She's the one who helped me, not the other way around. I'm sure you drew greatly on the example of your father, but I know for sure you took so much of who you are from your mother."

That evening, their fifth on the road, they stayed at a rustic lodge in Gardnerville, Nevada. They dove a thousand kisses deep. They made love, long and slow and tender. When they finished, Simon rested on his side and stroked her hair. He told her how profoundly he loved her. He reminisced about that day they met on an old battlefield, and how different things would have been if she had not been so forward in insisting he take her full panoply of contact information. "It's true that I loved you then, at that moment. I saw those intelligent eyes and knew you were special. I couldn't get you out of my mind. A few days later Tetu caught me gazing longingly at your telephone number and he called me right out. He knew the love bug had bitten me hard, and he urged me to do something about it. I called you, and felt I was in fifth grade again, like I had never asked a girl for a date, and it was awfully awkward for me. That call didn't last three minutes, I'd guess. And then, without warning, you showed up at my cabin, which we grandly called a campaign headquarters, and you took my breath away. And now, we've just made love in Gardnerville, Nevada, and you're my wife. I'm the luckiest man alive, Keel. I love you with all my heart. I think we're a good team, dearest Keel."

Pack turned over onto his back, and lay with eyes open, looking at the ceiling in the dim lighting that came from around the margins of the drapes. Keeley was silent for what seemed a long while. Finally, she said, "Just now, during our lovemaking, I felt like I had died." She could tell that startled Simon, as the bed shook a little. "Don't get concerned, pal, I didn't mean that in the literal sense. I mean I felt so thoroughly complete as a person I would have been happy to pass into the next world. I was all goodness, see. It was as if I had never directed an ill action toward any other person, ever. I was created in the image of God, and almost wanted Him to settle my earthly accounts and send me on to Heaven. I was pure love…because you brought that out in me. And dear friend, you must let me tell you no other man on earth could make me feel that way. Let me go further, and humor you. For argument's sake, I'll agree…not truthfully…but just for argument's sake, that you are not the handsomest man." She poked him on his arm for emphasis, with a wide full-mouthed smile that caused her magnificent eyes to crinkle at the edges. "I'll concede you have a thousand deficiencies, which you absolutely do not, but let's say I go along with you. Let's say I acknowledge you're not the brightest. But

95

even if I concede on all those points, you're still the best and only man for me. Can General Governor Matai Pack get that through his head? The former, very former, Keeley Eliopoulous loves Simon Pack for all she's worth...buster."

+++

They were inside their imposing hotel room more than out of it while in Vegas. They had no problem making love two times a day every day. They showered together, they helped one another dress, they joked and they said nice things. They ordered most meals through room service. They watched movies, alternating preferences. Simon ordered flowers for his wife even though the hotel provided fresh flowers daily. He stroked her still-wounded back often and applied fragrant oils to it.

They amazed themselves by never exhausting topics to discuss. They couldn't help themselves from repeating the refrain, "Can you believe us? We never ever run out of things to talk about. Isn't that beautiful?"

They discussed books; she was quick to make recommendations to him. "Keel, I'll read it, but I already have an on-deck list of at least a dozen," he'd whine. But she was Keeley, and immune to those whines, and she'd tell him no, this one needs to be next. Pack learned she was always teaching him something more than what lay in the pages of the particular book. It was as if she was sending him coded messages that sometimes he could decode immediately, but normally it took time. She would never offer a clue, just wait for him to find it. Sometime after the reading, he would be floored by her shrewdness—she had coaxed him into a book because she knew he would eventually recall the single passage she knew would be important to both of them. Usually her coded message was time-sensitive. He caught on to her game, and she recognized he did, but they left it there. It was cement for their relationship, the most durable kind, because they knew they were holding a secret that neither had even expressed.

She told him without embarrassment about her every flaw, such as she felt she possessed. Her cool open way of saying anything on her mind was something he wasn't used to, and he found it invigoratingly startling. She said breathily, for instance, "Pack, when you're an old man do you know how privileged I would feel to wipe your butt?" No woman in Pack's life had ever spoken so crudely but lovingly. He loved her more for this quality. Pack ran out of words to describe his limitless love for her. He found himself merely shaking his head slowly with eyes wide, and she understood him to be saying, "How is it possible to love you with more force than I did a half hour ago?"

Keeley got her Cirque du Soleil. No, she got three. At the Bellagio, she saw "O" and loved it so much she asked to go to another. So they got tickets to New York, New York to see "Zumanity." That didn't sate her appetite, so they took in a third Cirque show at The Mirage, "The Beatles, Love."

On their fifth day in America's City of Lights, Keeley said, "I'm ready to go home now, Simon." She had said it in such a low tone it struck Pack as ominous, but, doubting this interpretation as poor snap judgment, he stayed silent to allow her to say more. "I am ready to go home," she said again. She eyed him with a quiet passion of ultimate focus. "Can you understand how much this journey has meant to me? I say journey rather than trip because it was as allegorical as real. It meant everything. We journeyed more in ten days than I daresay most people will in a lifetime. You didn't question me. You let me have my way, and didn't caution that we should go to the doctors one more time to get professional clearance for it. You showed me how clever you are, how well you understand the wife who would give her life for you, and you just…acceded to my wishes in an important moment. I felt more freedom on this trip than at any point of my life. In a manner of speaking, all my sins are washed away, and I am a better person than I ever aspired to be. I haven't exactly expressed myself clearly, but do you at least vaguely understand me?" She faced him, saying in the same subdued tones, "Simon, it will mean everything to have you say you understand me."

He walked over to her and held her close. "I think this embrace answers your question, Keel. Yes, my dear, I do understand you. I can say you have given me the fullest experience of my life. We will leave tomorrow."

They undressed each other and settled into bed again. When they thought their lovemaking couldn't be sweeter, it was. They were one. They said more words of love, said aloud a prayer of gratitude for the plushness of their relationship, and fell into a deep slumber.

The next morning, the day of their going back home, Simon Pack awoke but Keeley did not. Keeley was going to a different home, and she had known it. Man is incapable of explaining and understanding the great eternal mysteries.

CHAPTER SIX

During the course of his life General Pack had drawn deep draughts from the sweet stream of joy and the poison puddle of sorrow. He had watched Marines die in excruciating circumstances, young men cut off before leaving their imprint. He had consoled too many young widows and fatherless children. He had witnessed breathtaking bravery and human heroism. He loved his Marines, many of whom, despite the ignobility of their births, had distinguished themselves by the nobility of their deaths. He had been celebrated at fetes and he had mourned at funerals. He was like most of humanity, truly that was so, but it cannot be gainsaid that as a matter of objective fact, he had experienced higher highs and lower lows than most of the rest of us.

Keeley's passing was the lowest of the lows.

+++

Montana Governor James Dahl, Pack's protégé and longtime confidant, turned his duties in Helena over to the Lieutenant Governor and headed to Pack's cabin. He would conduct himself as he had when working for Pack in other positions in and out of the military: foremost, he would be there. He would not proffer opinions or offer advice. Pack would communicate through body language what he needed from Dahl. If his time in the cabin entailed sitting in the same room with Pack without speaking for ten hours, he would do so.

He resolved also to serve as Pack's civilian chief of staff. This meant he would screen those trying to get to the famous man, make minor decisions on his behalf, and let him know when momentous decisions were required.

He turned the volume down on the home phone, listened to all the messages, and summarized them in writing for presentation to Pack at the appropriate moment. Dahl had never seen Pack like this. His mind was far away, pulling him away from the concerns of the hour. But Dahl knew decisions related to his wife's death had to be reached, and soon.

Keeley's human form was back in northwest Montana, and the funeral director was seeking disposition instructions. Dahl was acutely aware a decision needed to come from Pack, but before he could work out when to broach the sensitive subject, there came a knock at Pack's front door. Dahl led the man in and directed him to Pack's basement office. "Governor Dahl, I hadn't expected to be speaking with you, but here we are. I'm Mark Ballon from the First National Bank of Kalispell. Is this a good time to speak with General Pack?"

"I'm afraid it isn't," Dahl answered. "He's not feeling well. That includes not wanting to talk much, so I'm trying to help out by acting as his agent until he feels better. Can I help?"

"Well, Governor, you understand this is irregular." He rubbed his forehead, thinking. Then he said, "I'll talk around the matter, then let's decide how to deal with it, OK?"

"Fine," Dahl said. "What've you got?"

"So, about three or four months ago, before the train accident, Mrs. Pack—then Miss Eliopoulous, of course—walked into my office. Oh, she had made an appointment, so it wasn't like she arrived unexpectedly, but I didn't have a reason to think this would be a big deal. I didn't know her by sight at the time, had never met her…she didn't have an account with us. She said the General wouldn't discuss a pre-nuptial agreement. So instead she instructed me to prepare a will for her. I'll tell you it took a lot of time to research the details of her request. Bottom line is she left her husband the totality of her extensive finances. *Very serious money*, sir. I've never associated with anyone who possessed such money. She signed the document. My business now is to determine where he wants to situate these considerable funds."

"Can you give me Power of Attorney limited to this decision?" Dahl asked.

"We can do that, sir," Ballon answered. "We can draw it up today, and have it ready for the General's signature by this evening. Then it's a done deal. Can we get a head start on the disposition of the money?"

"You call when you want me to come by the bank," Dahl said.

"I can do better, sir. I can have the Community Banker here within a couple of hours, if you agree."

"Good, I'll get it signed. In the meantime, deposit the funds in his name in your bank, if it isn't already there. If he wants to move it later, he's free to," Dahl said.

"Will do, sir. There's one other matter Mrs. Pack addressed in the will, and as it pertains to funeral arrangements, I think I should call your attention to it directly. I have it in writing right here." He passed the document to Dahl, who read it.

Keeley asked to be interred outside the cabin next to Pack's first wife. Dahl was moved, admiring Keeley's uncanny foresight yet again.

"Thanks, Mr. Ballon. You've been a big help. I'll be certain to let the General know of his wife's expressed desires."

+++

June is historically the month of greatest precipitation in northwest Montana. The temperature sat in the mid-70s at 1 P.M. as a steady drizzle fell under gray skies.

The service occurred right there on the property around Pack's cabin. As far as Pack knew, Keeley's death had not been formally broadcast. Word spread quickly, though, because he was beloved in this state, and those people he had represented as Governor didn't want him grieving alone. People who did not know where he lived found their way there, and most found it hard to believe that a man of Pack's stature resided in such a modest dwelling. Most never knew Keeley, and few knew anything about her. But they knew if Simon Pack had wed her, she had to be a special lady. And so it was a state's way of showing respect.

Most Marines from the area came, as did some military connections from as far away as Washington, DC. Pack's daughters were there by his side. They had taken part in another funeral less than a decade ago on this same plot of land. Daphne Eliopoulous, Keeley's grief-stricken mother, had returned mere weeks after going back to her island home. In a year's time, she had lost both husband and only child.

Georgeann, owner of the only General Store in Yaak, had helped set up tables in Pack's garage as a place to stow the food so many people brought. There had been no viewing at a funeral home, so all the condolences would occur here, outside the garage once the service was over.

They had streamed down from the mountains of the Upper Yaak, from the statehouse, indeed from all over the state. Some people parked their vehicles on dirt roads a mile away. From the high ground the cabin sat upon, Mollison marveled at all these people, from the commoners to the dignitaries, snaking their way up the road. Several fellow Governors showed up. Nobody counted the number who attended, but once on site Sheriff Mollison saw the need to call for support to help with traffic control for the exodus. Flanking Pack were Tetu Palaita and Governor Jim Dahl. The person Pack chose to conduct this funeral service was not a denominationally ordained minister, but one ordained by the Higher Power, in Pack's estimation. Pack had no need to provide talking points to some minister who did not really know Keeley. Swan knew her well. There was no chance the large crowd would unbalance or overwhelm Swan Palaita.

As the lovely Swan commenced the service, the sun broke through the branches of the stately larch trees. Her seven foot, 365-pound husband Tetu began to shake and tears rolled down his face unabashedly. Tears, we are told, result from a surfeit of emotion, from the broad scale of human emotions, all the way from unbounded joy to utter grief. It's not always easy to know why people shed tears. Tetu wasn't the only person to weep. Mollison observed Judith Buck, mountain woman extraordinaire, tough as the leather she tanned, weeping quietly as she recalled Keeley's calming presence during a crisis in the Yaak not long ago. Georgeann wept too, as in her mind's eye she watched Keeley sitting with her son Tommy, his life hanging in the balance, after being poisoned. Mollison looked around to see other faces familiar to Keeley: Ranger Ranklin Shiningfish of the Kootenai tribe, and a couple of FBI agents from the Kalispell Field Office. The hills were still, but for the occasional sound of a bird, and Swan's voice carried strong to the farthest reaches of the assembly. She spoke from the heart.

"Brothers and sisters gathered here, please take a moment to send up your own silent prayers for our dearly departed Keeley Eliopoulous Pack." Swan waited. Then, "General Simon Pack could not have been loved more profoundly by any woman. She spoke with me about his integrity, his strength, his compassion for all people. She admired him. And he felt the same about her. And, while we mourn her passing, let us also give thanks that we were able to know her. She had degrees, and was a learned scholar, but she never flaunted her intelligence. She walked with us all as equals. The life she lived showed who she was, a genuine rare lady who cared for everyone, regardless of station. She was at home everywhere. She was a Great Spirit. She has helped me establish programs to help tribal communities work through some of their special problems. She offered me encouragement as well as good ideas.

"God bestowed generous gifts upon her. But she also in turn bestowed gifts generously upon others. I hope I may follow the example of this woman's grace, humility, and Christian charity. Now, Almighty God, accept this person into your embrace of Eternal Peace. Amen."

Pack had requested brevity, and he got it. He figured God already knew who Keeley was, and didn't need the public affirmations of her goodness. She needed no panegyrics. And she didn't need humorous little anecdotes to allow the crowd a moment of nervous laughter for relief from the gravity of the occasion. He just wanted the service to be done, and the people who had come to go home. Simon Pack wanted to be alone. He wanted no more consolation, just seclusion.

+++

General Pack wasn't the only one at the cabin who had decisions to make. Governor Dahl had been there three days and had to get back to his duties at the capitol. He went downstairs to Pack's office, and confronted him. "Boss, we have to talk." It had been a long time since he had called Pack 'Boss' and even at that point he'd used the word only two or three times.

Pack turned toward him and nodded, indicating 'go ahead.'

"I've never seen you like this, General. Maybe you should see a doctor. Seems to me you may be clinically depressed. If you are, I don't want to leave you in this state."

Pack swiveled his chair toward Dahl, taking a moment to collect his thoughts before speaking. "Look, Jim, I'm not clinically depressed. Time will help heal me, I know that. But this was an awful blow. I am fighting melancholia like I've never felt. We had a delirious love. My beautiful Keeley's death ruptured my psyche. Our journey together was the best thing I've ever experienced. I felt like…when we got back here I was ready to burst into some tremendous state of productivity for the general good…I didn't know what it could be, but I believed it would happen. She gave me new life. And now instead of blooming, I'm wilting. I'm consumed with thoughts I don't want to think about. How, in hindsight, was it so clear she knew she was about to die? On the taped recording in my head, I have replayed every word she said during the journey. I mean it, Jim. I think I can recall every word that lady said to me, from beginning to end. How, on our very final night together, did she appear to know she wasn't going to wake up the next morning? What caused the clot that was as powerful as a gunshot? How would she want me to live now, without her? I usually have answers, but I have none. For the present, I've lost my will to live, but I have faith I can recapture it.

"That was quite a throng of humanity that came for the service, and I suppose I couldn't have prevented them from coming if I'd tried, but you know what? I didn't want to see any of them. I probably seemed ungrateful, not taking time with anyone afterward, but I simply couldn't do it. To me, they represented enemies of Keeley, people trying to detract from her memory, and…."

Dahl interrupted his mentor. "Now wait a minute, General. I believe you're being selfish. Why is so hard for you to imagine all those folks came all the way out here in the woods bearing respect for both you and Keeley? They damn sure did. I spoke with most of them afterward when you walked away and went to the basement without a word. They came with love." In a more mellow voice, Dahl said, "Believe me, boss, they came with love. And I covered for you. They didn't think you were ungrateful. They understood you were hurting bad inside, and they also understood you needed to be alone. Remember when you were the Supe and the President was about to fire you? You went to a desolate area of Camp Buckner to be alone with your thoughts, and you left General Bass and me in charge? Same as now, and I saw that right away."

Pack looked past Dahl and shook his head slowly. "You're a good man, Jim. Always have been. You're a better man than me, truth be told. I've felt your presence here since the funeral, and I've appreciated it. Now let's do whatever business you have for me, and you go on back to where you're needed. And don't leave thinking I'm going to take my life or anything like that. I'll be OK, but it's not gonna happen in the snap of a finger."

Dahl stood up, slapped Pack on the shoulder several times, then kept his hand on Pack's shoulder for a time. He sat back down, pulled out his sheaf of papers, and briefed Pack on all the phone messages. A call from 'Duck' caused Pack to blink hard and swipe at his eyes. Duck had inquired as to Mrs. Pack's health. "Sorry to report that one to you, boss, but I figured you'd want to know."

Dahl continued, reiterating that Keeley's fortune was now Pack's; Pack had signed the Power of Attorney, and Dahl had subsequently gone to the bank to sort out details, but at the time Pack showed no interest in what he was signing. Indeed, he showed so little interest he might not have remembered it. So now Dahl pointed out again that a lot of money sat in the First National Bank of Kalispell until Pack decided otherwise. Pack said to Dahl, "Jim, do you realize she did that *before* I asked her to marry me? She was quite a phenomenon, wasn't she?"

Once he finished going through his notes, Dahl said, "General, I know you want to be left alone for a while, but with your consent, I'd like to stop by for a chat with Sheriff Joe to ask if he'd drop in a couple times a week. Can you let me do that?"

"Yeah, Jim, go ahead. Joe Mollison has more good sense than you'd find in most ten men. He knows how to handle me in my present state."

They both stood, and exchanged a strong manhug. "If you need anything…."

"I know, Jim. I'll remember what you've done. Now get out of here."

PART II

FINDING HIS WAY

CHAPTER SEVEN

August

The world around him had proceeded apace. His daughters visited. Mollison made his routine checks. Tetu and Swan came around a few times. Jim Dahl was dealing with the remnants of the mollusk infestation, but now he faced a statewide health crisis. There had been 35 fires categorized as major during the past summer; most had been extinguished but a few still burned. Kids had been unable to go outside for recess, houses and businesses had had to keep their windows closed, lots of people wore masks everywhere, and whole towns had been evacuated from both smoke and fire. Months of smoke inhalation had resulted in hospitals overrun with bronchial inflammations and associated maladies. The fires alone had already cost the state $1.5 million a day to fight. Dahl had a full plate of serious issues facing him, and a money crisis was now one of them.

Pack had tuned everything out. He was unaware of anything outside the confines of his cabin. He had no taste for the things friends and family were involved with. He trimmed his mail pickups from six days a week to one. Scores, maybe hundreds, of unopened envelopes lay on his kitchen table. Many bore postmarks of small Montana towns. Many bore postmarks from all over the country. Some bore APO addresses. He took them to be condolence notes. He was not up for reading them.

He woke up on an August morning and looked at himself. He hadn't bothered to shave in months. That wasn't bad, he decided. He'd keep the beard. He resolved to clean himself up, though, and do something with himself. He had to make use of his talents again. He was shortchanging himself and everyone who had ever known him. He had to reinstate an acceptable level of psychic and physical fitness. He'd lost weight and didn't like the shape he was in. Time had come to start eating right, thinking right, doing right. Time to clean the cabin, fill the refrigerator, organize his office, clean and sharpen his tools.

Pack showered for the first time in weeks, and found his favorite work clothes in the closet. He put on his L.L. Bean boots and went to his place of making, the garage, checking the status of the tools he'd need for the first job he had in mind. The bench he saw in his mind's eye would require a careful craftsman's touch. He wanted to situate it in a place where he could view the burial sites of his two wives. He might even want to manufacture some sort of cover for the bench.

For Pack, every construction project, like every military operation, got created at least three times. The first was in the mind, a mental picture. The second was in the form of a rough sketch, on paper. Then perhaps a more refined sketch that included precise dimensions. The third act of creation involved the real thing, the gathering of materials, and the cutting and sanding and staining. So, today he commenced by going from garage to basement office to put his mental image onto paper.

Within a week, he'd made his bench. It worked as a way of unchaining whatever dark forces had bound him. He resumed his daily postal calls, and promised himself he would open up to the world again. He began to read all those notes and long letters. Maybe he'd invite Mollison to meet him at the Sundance for breakfast. Maybe he'd make that phone call to inquire about the lives of his daughters. Maybe he could drive to Helena to pay his respects to Governor Dahl. Maybe he would drive up to Yaak for a night in Tetu's Lodge, and stop in to visit Georgann and Tommy in their General Store, and maybe even go for a drink across the road at Montana's Armpit and tip one to the proprietor, Nick Surgeon. And he would use his long evenings to fertilize his mind with good books, as he always had.

By the end of August he had turned his resolutions into actions. Pack had re-engaged the world.

+++

August, the Pentagon

General Harris Green had been responsible for installing Simon Pack as Superintendent at West Point, the United States Military Academy, in one of the darkest hours since its establishment in 1802. At the time, General Green was Vice Chief of Staff of the Army, and getting Pack—a recently retired Marine three-star--into the post had been a masterful feat of political maneuvering. Now Harris Green was still a four-star, but had ascended to the highest uniformed military position, Chairman of the Joint Chiefs of Staff, or CJCS.

The full Joint Chiefs were present, in addition to a squad of others with particular interest in the subject of the briefing. The Colonel began his presentation: "Sir, this is an Information Briefing. The subject is a 35-year-old male who goes by the name Blaise Paschal. As you will notice, his surname appears to be a knockoff of Pascal, the French mathematician-philosopher. We doubt this is his actual name, but in fact we don't know for sure. We think he has served in the Marine Corps and the CIA, but we cannot confirm either…"

Green cut the briefer off. "You're shitting me! You can't tell me whether he's worked for the Marines or the CIA? Records for both are a mile long. What the hell happened?"

"We don't know, sir. Somehow, somewhere, he got sheep-dipped, which as you know means his past got meticulously expunged, including credit cards and phone numbers and birth records and fingerprints. His last two jobs were working with government-contracted mercenaries, and both those outfits claim he had former military colleagues attest to his prior military service."

"Go on," Green said.

"There seems no doubt he was, and still is, a very, very good Marine. One of the retired Generals running the mercs—and I'm sure I don't have to name that General for you—called him a supersoldier. The profile we've assembled paints him as a tactical genius. If he's the Marine we think he was, he could mold a platoon into an elite force. He wasn't interested in units above platoon level, which may be why we

114

think he voluntarily terminated as a platoon sergeant. He is qualified in about every individual skill. SCUBA, numerous hand-to-hand fighting techniques, parachuting—including HALO—rappelling, skiing, mountain climbing, expert medical badge, all the basic infantry skills. He takes to martial skills like a duck to water. If this isn't enough, he's fluent in Arabic. I do mean fluent, sir. The aforementioned retired General told me he witnessed this fellow in the middle of a group of Iraqi officers, speaking about fairly technical subjects. After the event one of the interpreter-translators said 'He speaks as if it's his native tongue.' The interpreter added that astonishingly he heard Paschal flipping to various dialects depending on the dialect of the Iraqi speaking to him."

Green said, "Very interesting, but what's your point? I don't have all day."

The briefer said, "Sir, the White House arranged this briefing. What we suspect this man of doing is having the effect of literally upsetting the international political system, probably without understanding or caring he's doing so. The National Security Advisor informs us the President has personally given the green light to take this man Blaise Paschal out.

"You will remember an American vehicle was ambushed in Fallujah in '04. In fact, enemy vehicles boxed them in and rained withering fire into the vehicle from the driver side. Paschal was in the right rear seat. We believe now that he escaped by leaping out of the vehicle, off the bridge, and into the river below. It was dark. Somehow he eluded them. Whether they knew he escaped is open to question, but probably they did. The enemy hanged the bullet-riddled bodies of the remainder from the American vehicle and lighted them on fire as they dangled from the highest beams of the bridge.

"Paschal disappeared entirely for years, until recently. Since he reappeared, he's been a killing machine. We are pretty sure he has murdered American military contractors, key Iraqi government figures, and ISIS leaders—anyone, in short, he holds responsible for the murder of those Americans that day in Fallujah. He has taken a stick to a hornet's nest."

General Green rubbed his hand through his burr cut, holding up a hand. "OK, a few comments and questions. One, I know the legal issues involved in killing an American, but still, why haven't we gotten to him? For starters, answer that."

"He has repelled every attempt to capture him. As you know, we have small teams at various places in the Middle East who go by different names...like Purple Haze and Alpha Element...whose specialized mission is to find, fix, and destroy, or capture, individual HVTs, High Value Targets, like Mr. Blaise Paschal. These are formidably trained men, but four times they've gone after him but haven't returned. He has preyed upon the predators."

Green again: "Who do we think he served with in the Marines?"

"He was in only one unit, General, the 1st MARDIV," the briefer answered. "Or so we think."

An idea popped into Green's head, but he kept it to himself. "And what years do we believe he was in 1st MARDIV?" Green asked.

As quickly as the briefer replied, Green knew Simon Pack had been Commanding General of that Division during that period. He had hoped for that answer. Maybe Pack was a resource he could use. Yes, a Division was large, thousands of Marines, but Pack had a recall for individual troops like no other man at his level of command. He might remember something about this man Paschal....

"And where is he now?" Green asked, not hopeful of a direct answer.

"Three months ago we lost him. A man meeting his description has killed HVTs in Pakistan, Iraq, and Afghanistan. This story hasn't made the news yet, but our government certainly has heard about from our allies. Could be someone got to him first. But if ISIS got him, they would assuredly be parading him or his body before the cameras. For other reasons, we would know if friendly forces or contractors had killed or captured him."

"Who's funding him?" Green asked.

"Short answer is he's probably a millionaire, and can stay on the lam for a long time with no external funding. He made excellent money in his contract jobs, and he spent almost nothing. Probably been that way all his life. Squirreled away a very nice nest egg. Of course, it's also possible he steals what he needs.

"In sum, sir, this man is not a soldier gone mad from the stresses of war. Instead, he is a quite sane individual out to avenge the deaths of those men alongside him in Fallujah. Unfortunately, his definition of who ought to be held accountable is vague at best, and criminally extensive at worst. Yet he seems to have an chart-busting IQ. He is proceeding methodically and intelligently, by his lights."

+++

Two days before the Pentagon briefing, northwest Montana

Sheriff Joe Mollison was eating breakfast with Pack at the Sundance, their eatery of choice since he and Pack first met. "You're my friend, Simon, and I tell you it does my weary eyes a world of good to see you're getting back to normal. Don't take that as implying something was wrong with you. If any man was entitled to grieve, it's you. In fact, you wouldn't have been normal if you hadn't grieved. Now you're returning to the man Keeley married, is all I'm sayin'."

"Yeah, I understand, Joe. And damn right you're a friend, a great one for a long time. As I reflect quickly, Simon's gotten more from this relationship than Joe has. Usually it's been me asking for your help, and every time you've come through. Another way to look at it is that you weren't helping me as much as you were helping the people of the State. In any case, you earn every cent this county pays you, and a lot more."

"You like my advice so much, Simon, listen to me on this piece. Some person, or maybe more than one, at First National Bank in Kalispell hasn't kept your information confidential. The particulars of your bank account down there have spewed out to the point half this valley knows your net worth. That ain't good, Simon. Not good at all.

Think of the target you've become. Oh, for sure, every charitable organization in the country will have you on their contact lists, but that's small beer. There'll be a lot of potential hostiles out there trying to rip off a slice of what you have. The unscrupulous will be looking for chances to sue you. Just a minor touching of fenders will be cause to sue for fake injuries. And think about your residence. Somebody will want to break and enter to find what they expect will be riches inside. If I were you, I'd find a top-flight security consultant to do a site survey and set up a comprehensive alert and prevention system. Where am I going wrong?"

"I'm pretty upset with the bank. I'll have a talk with them. The horse is out of the barn now, though. Maybe I'll tell them they'll have to up my interest rate, or I'm leaving—I guess I'm not serious about that…quite yet. But what you're missing, Joe, is that I have a veritable armory of weapons and ammo, and anyone attempting to break in would have to face me firing those weapons. Let me tell you, I'm not a rookie with those handguns and long guns. Put another way, Joe, I have the tools, but I'm the weapon. Besides, what they also don't know is that I have very little of actual value in the cabin…the weapons themselves and my stamp collection would be the top dollar items," Simon said. "I could fend off an infantry platoon by myself. If Tetu were with me," Pack added wistfully, "we could handle a company."

+++

One day before the Pentagon briefing

119

Pack was back at work in his garage, building a replica of his big
kitchen table. Last visit to the local Soldiers' Home he saw a use they
could put it to. The guy who managed the place always accepted Pack's
donations, which came about once a month. Pack figured the manager
wouldn't object to the table. But he had to get it done first, and he
wasn't halfway there. It was Friday, which meant it was cigar day. He
permitted himself to enjoy a cigar once a week, only on that one day a
week. He put down his tools, drew his favorite out of the humidor, an
oscuro 6x60 El Rey del Mundo Ronco, and sat on another of his
creations, a backed bench with redwood stain that sat outside the
garage. He wasn't facing in the downhill direction from the bench, so
he could hear, but not see, the approach of a vehicle.

A Ford Transit, of the type many tradesmen favor, inched
down his gravel drive off the dirt road. Pack immediately recognized
the face and frame of a Marine from his days as CG of 1st MARDIV.
Big fellow, nearly as big as Pack. Black hair cut short, thick brows,
dark-complected, clean shaven. Maybe six-three or -four, 230-240.
White patches of skin and hair gleaming sharply on his hands, arms,
and face contrasted with his darker pigmentation. What Pack saw of the
patches on one side of his body were mirror-imaged on the opposite
side. Vitiligo, Pack surmised, most typically the result of an unusually
high level of stress. The hair and the trim physique said Paschal could
still be in the Corps. The name of the unforgettable Marine wasn't
coming to mind right away. He did remember it had been a somewhat
uncommon name. The big fellow got out of the high-profiled vehicle

and had a hand out for shaking. He was smiling, showing straight rows of white teeth. "General Pack, sir, I'm sure you don't remember me, but I was in your 1/7 at Pendleton. Blaise Paschal. I was just passing through, and wanted to offer my congratulations on all the success you've had since I last saw you. It's an honor. Allow me to say you're my model of a true leader."

"I'll be damned. Come on over and have a seat, Blaise. It's always a special pleasure to see an old comrade. How in hell'd you find me?"

"I saw the Sundance and figured someone inside would know where you live, and bingo, I found someone on the first try," Blaise said.

Pack found that reply confounding. Most people around here could not locate his cabin. Then he remembered word had clearly gotten out before the funeral service here on the property, so there was no cause to question Paschal. Pack liked it better when the locals were ignorant of his place. Truth was, Paschal had stopped to eat at the Sundance, but he hadn't had to ask anyone. He had scoped out Pack's bio in some detail before coming here.

"Still in the Corps?" Pack asked.

"No, sir, left as a First Sergeant," Paschal lied. Pack knew that was a lie. When the covert ops guys from the government came to Pack in his 1st MARDIV days asking if he had a Marine that fit the profile they were searching for, Pack mentioned Paschal. He knew they had stolen a good Marine away from the Corps when Paschal decided not to re-up. Paschal hadn't come to thank Pack for steering him into another line of work. Had he failed to make it through their program? No, he would've succeeded with flying colors.

"Good, what then, what have you done afterward?" Pack inquired.

"Never married, took care of my money, decided to see the country, so I've hired on to work lots of jobs with my hands. Dug ditches in Miami, day-labored in Houston, lots of things. Working outdoors, mostly, and it's been fun, kept me in decent shape."

"Sounds a little like me," Pack said. "When I returned here after West Point, I worked for a contractor buddy for fifteen bucks an hour, doing about every sort of work that goes into homebuilding. So, yep, I know where you're coming from. That can be satisfying to body and soul. Also, I hooked up with some hobos and rode the rails for a while to get a different glimpse of this country," Pack said. Paschal already knew the details of everything Pack had told him, but wasn't giving anything away.

"All right, then, how about some iced tea or a soft drink?" Pack asked. "I've worked up a pretty good sweat this morning doing some woodworking, and could do with a cold beverage myself."

"Well, General, if you keep a cold beer around, I could handle one," Paschal said.

"Done deal," Pack said, "one Moose Drool coming up."

As Pack was rising to fetch their drinks, Paschal said, "Beautiful property you've got here, sir. This is exactly the lifestyle and the type of cabin I aspire to."

"It really suits me, but I guess to a lot of folks it's not much. Wanna come in and have a look around? Couple minutes and tour's over," Pack grunted.

Once inside the kitchen the ground floor could be taken in in a single protracted look. Still, Paschal surveyed every wall at a deliberate slow pace, commenting with admiration as he gazed at each object. "You can have a look at the basement if you're genuinely interested," Pack said. "Not much down there, though."

"You bet I'd like to see it," Blaise Paschal said. "I'm in awe of this cabin, General, I really am. It's my dream, that's exactly what it is."

Pack led the way down the basement staircase. Both sides of the staircase were festooned with testaments to Pack's athletic career. College Football Hall of Fame. First team All-American recognition in both football and lacrosse. Photos from various locker rooms and on the playing fields. Winner of various events at the Penn Relays. Pack told Paschal these walls were a concession to his first wife, who had insisted on displaying them prominently. Pack let her display them, if not exactly prominently.

Paschal said, "Holy hell, General, this is impressive! I never knew of any of this. Pretty sure none—or not many—of your Marines knew about this part of your life. I'm sure you're proud of this. 'Course, you know who you're talking with—me, who hasn't set the world on fire, not even a little bit, and whose knowledge of politics is zero. Why wouldn't I be impressed by a man who's been a General and a Governor?"

Pack ignored his visitor's questions and bootlicking, and opened a small refrigerator from which he pulled two bottles of Moose Drool. He handed one to Paschal and invited him to sit in one of four recliners. "I spend more time down here than upstairs," Pack said. "It's cool, as you can feel, even now in the heat of summer."

"You said I wouldn't remember you," Pack said. "You're right, in the sense that I don't always remember either faces or names, but you're wrong in this case. I do remember you. Your platoon seemed to win every platoon competition in the Division, Blaise. You were a great trainer, had a way with your men. Your commanders mentioned you frequently. That said, more than once I heard them describe you as an eccentric. Said you didn't fit into any of the typical categories. Said you weren't close to your Marines, that you were virtually emotionless, yet they admired you and worked beyond exhaustion to fulfill the objectives you set for them. A big part of that came from your being expert at every skill you led them to master." Pack never mentioned he was the one who fingered Paschal for another job.

"I don't take offense at a word of that, General," Blaise said. "I was a little weird, and still am, but yeah, I was damn near expert in the tools of the military trade. Everybody told me that, but they didn't need to, cause I knew it. You know, I never faced any Marine willing to go toe to toe with me in a fight. Maybe they really respected me, maybe not. I didn't care. But I did care that they feared me, which for damn sure they did, every manjack one of them." Paschal sat back, squinting those heavy-lidded eyes, like some mutant serpent about to strike.

Outside, thunder rumbled in the heavens and lightning began to flash in a late summer light show.

Paschal took his time finishing his Moose Drool. "Great beer, boss. One of the best domestics I've ever had. I oughta be moving along now."

Pack walked him back up through the garage. "Thanks for coming by, Blaise," Pack said, proffering his hand. Blaise gripped it solemnly and said farewell. Rain began to throw down hard. Pack watched as the large vehicle pulled away and down the dirt road.

+++

Paschal drove downhill out of sight of the cabin, pulled into the drive of a small ranch, and waited for half an hour. He took out his phone and called Pack. "Hey, General, sorry to bother you, but somewhere up there I think I misplaced something important to me. I'm on my way back up if you don't mind. I'm sure it'll take me just a few minutes to find it."

"Of course," Pack said, "garage door'll be open." As he hit the end call button, Pack wondered how Paschal had gotten his number. Only a couple of people in town had it. But he let it go, thinking Paschal had likely come upon it innocently enough, and in any case he'd be gone soon. Marines were special people to Pack, and got a pass in situations others might not. Maybe it was a weakness, but no Marine had let him down yet.

The blinding rain gave Paschal the opportunity to wear his deep-pocketed North Face rain jacket into the cabin. Pack met him in the garage. "You know what, General? I'm thinking through my movements, and think I dropped my driver's license in the basement. Can we go back down?" Paschal asked.

"Yeah, basement's a dungeon without lights, and the light switches aren't in the obvious places, so let me lead you down," Pack said.

When Pack descended to within a step from the bottom, Paschal pulled a taser from his rain jacket pocket and zapped Pack in the back of the neck, 50,000 volts for ten seconds. Pack dropped in a heap, the 15' wire never growing taut in Paschal's firing hand. Within seconds Paschal had secured Pack's hands behind his back and slapped a set of Smith & Wesson stainless steel cuffs on them.

Paschal gave him a minute to regain his senses before announcing, "Sorry about that, General. Had to be done. Here are the rules: don't make any stupid moves and you'll probably live. Know that anything you try, like a head butt or a kick, I've seen before and will counter in a most violent manner. Now I'm going to give you a slight tug, but you'll do most of the work in hauling your oversized ass up to your feet."

Pack thought, *Instinct is totally useless without action to support it. This man set off every alarm, but I ignored them. He was a Marine, and 99% + of Marines never stop being Marines in thought and deed. For most Marines the credo is 'no bullet, no shell, no demon in hell shall break this bond called brothers'. But this is one of the bad*

apples making up that fraction of one percent. Whatever this was—
heist, kidnapping, ego trip—Pack already was thinking of Paschal as
the Devil, and when Pack awoke after a long nap, the Devil would be
saying, "Shit, he's awake!"

"Where's your mobile phone? You'll tell me or I'll turn this
cabin upside down until I do find it. Or maybe I'll just torch the place."

"Upstairs, on the table beside the landline," Pack said.

"Very good. Nice start to our relationship," Paschal said. He
found plastic trash bags, in which he tossed toilet paper, a bucket, and
duct tape, as well as all the food he could salvage from the refrigerator.
"Gonna make myself a sandwich before we *didi mau*. You want
something? Could be a while before you eat or drink again. Like I said,
Governor, you follow the Golden Rule and you'll live. If you cross me,
don't do exactly as I say, you die. I don't care which option you
choose, but I think you ought to care."

Pack sat on the sofa while Paschal sat in a kitchen chair across
from him. Once he ate his sandwich, he'd feed Pack and let him sip
water through a straw. As Pack ate, Paschal smashed Pack's mobile
phone with the hard heel of his heavy boot.

"What's this about, Paschal? Why?" Pack asked evenly.

"See, Governor, I have reason to be pissed, angry as hell in
fact, at the whole lot of you damn Generals. The two guys in charge of
my last company--civilian company I'm referring to, understand--were
retired four-stars, buddies of yours most likely. When they were still in,
their reps were spotless. They were walking gods to most people. Then
they sent me and my comrades out on an impossible mission. We were

under-resourced, but they didn't give a damn. If they'd invested more in that mission, they'd have had to give themselves a smaller bonus. They were traitors. Who knows, maybe you'd have been no different from them in that situation."

"But maybe I would have," Pack said.

"Doesn't matter if you would have or not. You have two things they don't have and will never have," Paschal said.

"Fame and…money," Paschal said. "And incidentally, I pretty much think this cabin is a shithole. I sure as hell wouldn't live like some modern-day Thoreau, all Walden Pondish. Or some transcendental holier-than-thou turd like R.W. Emerson. Reverse snobbery, is how I see it. And I damn sure wouldn't if I had your money. Anyway, you're the most famous General in the 21st century; have to be a groundhog not to recognize the name and face of the famous Pack. You being you will get the attention I want. And, man, did you ever screw up by letting everyone know how many dollars you're Packin', pun intended. Packman's gobbled up a lotta money, and some of it will have the honor of becoming mine.

"I've read a lot about you. Ironic many people say in interviews you're a recluse, yet anything I wanna know is right there on the Internet. Doesn't do much good to live like a hermit if no one respects your hermitage. You could ask me how much you paid for this land and the shitheap cabin that sits on it and I can tell you. You can ask me about your wives and I can give you loads of details. Who your friends are. Who your enemies are. Your dog's name. On and on. Social media is a wonderful invention for people like me, not so much for people like you. Amazing the inside info people share on Facebook, feeling like they're speaking with a couple others, but it's actually going out to the world. And even when they aren't telling the truth about you, they think they achieve something…respect, fame of their own?...by association."

The landline phone began to ring. After the fourth chime, it went to voicemail. The phone was far enough away from Pack and Paschal, and the volume setting low enough, for the message not to be distinct. "Harris Green…my direct number…urgent, I would say."

Paschal went on eating his huge ham and cheese sandwich and talking through the chewing: "I lied about being unaware of politics. I keep up. Could say I detest the current crop of flag officers, but there used to be great ones. Character people like Chesty Puller, Stonewall Jackson, Robert E. Lee, George Washington, Jefferson even if he wasn't a General. Now you've got losers running around the country, faux-angry, ripping down all their statues. Madness. Politicians crumbling in unison with the statues, trembling as they agree with the madhatters. The statutes of limitations may have expired on these criminal politicians, but in my book this country can and should tear down, crush, detonate every statue of imitations, including those of both the pols and madhatters.

"You've described me, from memory, as a detached Marine, one less interested in his men than himself. Thanks a lot, Pack. But maybe you're right. In fact, you are right. So then you ask why I care about avenging the deaths of the men with me in Fallujah. Truth is, it's not so much that I cared for them as that I hate seeing anyone taken advantage of. In the eyes of the people behind that operation, we were small potatoes, so small the loss didn't really matter much. That, sir, I do not like and will not abide.

"And what are we doing in the Middle East? Not enough killing of bad guys, I'm sure of that. Your modern Generals are pussyfooters. You need conscience-dead people like me, at least a few, who say F___ this S___ every other sentence, and go after the murderous bastards with Old Testament vengeful hearts. Think I've waterboarded some of those assholes? Yep, and when I do I tell them, 'Waterboarding is me baptizing you shitheads with Freedom.'"

Paschal kept spewing until finally he'd had enough of hearing his own words, Pack supposed. Staying to his word, he fed Pack the sandwich and let him sip the water. Pack had an idea that was at least worth a try. He spoke deliberately and softly: "Look, Blaise, you were a troop leader once, and you counseled Marines when you judged they needed it. You observed them, then you gave feedback intended to improve their performance or help them solve a problem. Now, I haven't had long to observe you, but I didn't need to to see you have a problem. I'll help with it if I can."

Paschal pretended to rub tears from his face. He affected a downcast expression. "Oh, yeah," he said, choking out his words, "I'm a snowflake, and I need help. Send money. Don't criticize me. Don't be mean to me. Don't tell me I'm not you're friend. Yes, I'm dependent, and I can't help it." Then he returned to a serious demeanor, saying, "I'm glad you asked, Governor. Because yes indeed you can help me, and we'll talk about how you'll do that when we're on the road. I have more rules you'll need to follow in the van, so listen up." He went on to tell Pack he had the duct tape for multiple purposes, but one was to ensure he didn't speak except when told to. He described the limits of Pack's movement within the cargo area of the vehicle. He told him he'd get one comfort break every hour and a half, and that he'd use the bucket provided. Most important, he said, was in relaying messages exactly as Paschal worded them. Deviate and die, Paschal said. And Pack believed he meant it.

+++

Pack's home phone rang more times that day. General Green told his people to keep trying. Mobile was out of service, the recording said. By the end of the day, Green took talking with Pack as a personal challenge. He had gone through this before, half a dozen years ago, when Pack hadn't answered because he'd become a hobo. At home that night, Green remembered the names of Pack associates he had dealt with those years before. He wrote the names on a torn-off slip of newspaper before he forgot them. He'd have them contacted tomorrow. He would run down Pack, no question in his mind.

Green's aides called Sheriff Mollison the following day. Mollison told the lady he'd been with Pack just a couple of days ago, and the Governor hadn't mentioned a trip. So Mollison said he'd call back after he went to the cabin and looked around.

What Mollison saw got his attention right away. He had tried both Pack's numbers without success. Now he found the garage door up and the front door unlocked. He checked upstairs and downstairs but got no reply. He called for two deputies to join him. Told them to enter through the front door and remove their footgear first. "Wear the rubber gloves and keep hands off until you have photos." They were to search for anything that looked out of place, indoors and around the five acres. Priority was inside. With Sheriff Mollison in the basement, Deputy Janice Tare called down from upstairs. "Over near the landline, Sheriff, I'm snapping a photo of a mobile phone that's been obliterated. Could be the Governor's." Mollison himself had already detected that two people had used drinking glasses just off the kitchen. Shouldn't be a problem lifting prints, unless, of course, the intruder—if that's what he or she was—had wiped them clean. Further, he saw muddy feet tracks brought in from the rain. Two different sets. No attempt to clean them up. Had to be a man. Big feet, looked like prints from boots. Mollison's boots were size 12. These prints were bigger.

Only Mollison knew where to find Pack's weapons and stamp collection, the two categories of things he identified as valuable. He told his deputies to look for things obviously missing as well. Mollison moved swiftly to Pack's basement office and found the weapons case intact. The stamp collection was stored in two places, Mollison knew, and when he covered both areas he found the collection intact also.

Mollison never thought he'd be talking directly to the Chairman of the Joint Chiefs, but there he was doing just that. He told Green what he'd found, not adding, not subtracting. Just the facts. The facts were enough for Green to draw ominous conclusions. He asked

Mollison to call him again as his investigation matured. Green didn't mention Blaise Paschal. Not yet.

CHAPTER EIGHT

Blaise Paschal's lead Drill Instructor quickly became his hero, although in the boot camp environment he couldn't let that be known, by look or by word. During those 12 weeks of fighting the omnipresent forces of friction, he heard that DI wax eloquent in his woodsy way on a thousand topics. *I'm a GRUNT, maggots! You can only hope you have what it takes to become a GRUNT. I'm about to tell you what a GRUNT is, maggots, and you better listen up, cause I'm describin' the noblest damn creation on earth, and this is my religious education for you: the GRUNT is that filthy, sweaty, dirt-encrusted, foot-sore, camo-painted, ripped-trouser'd, tired, sleepy, sonuvabitch who's kept the wolf at bay for over 200 years.* Other times he'd announce another bit of religious education, like: *No bullet, no shell, no demon in hell shall break this bond called 'brothers'. If you don't believe this bond exists or can exist, raise your scrawny hand now so I can kick your ass out before you have a chance to join my Corps. I'm in the ass-kickin' bidness, maggots, and bidness is good.*

One day out on a training range, the Drill asked one of his quiz questions. *How long does it take the average person to become a US Marine?* Blaise Pascal knew it wasn't smart to speak at any time it wasn't absolutely necessary, but he raised his hand, unable to stop himself from answering. Standing, he said, *Sir, an average person will NEVER become a US Marine!* He sat back down. The DI stood there, looking from man to man throughout the platoon. Then he said, *Stand up, maggot, you're damn right, 'cruit, take a bow.* Blaise wasn't sure the DI meant for him to bow, literally, so he sat there. *Get up here front and center, maggot. Give me 50 squat thrusts, then you get up and bow, you understand me?*

Life was rough during those 12 weeks, but Blaise never thought about quitting. He had developed grit, knew what it meant to persevere in the face of nagging, constant tribulation. He was a good recruit, very good, but that brought no special favors. In fact, he observed that everyone truly received equal treatment. The Drill Instructors would hammer the high performers about as much as the poor performers. If they sensed a recruit believing he was good, they'd single him out for treatment every bit as harsh, if not harsher, than the screwup. Everyone got dipped in the cauldron of white-hot molten iron.

The Drills had a little training room off the open bay where the platoon slept. One night, after they'd put the platoon to bed, they talked among themselves about their recruits, something they did every night. They spoke about the strengths and weaknesses of every man, and especially about what they needed to do to raise the level of performance of each one. During week nine one of the Drills said to the other, "Whadda you think about Paschal?" The way the Drill presented the question led the other to reply, "I think maybe we have a star, Drill." Hardass DIs simply didn't issue broad commendations like that. It was rare they complimented a recruit, even in private. But they agreed about Blaise Paschal. "We'll know for sure after we try our best to run him out the last three weeks, won't we?"

During his five years in the Corps, Paschal achieved a noncom rank equivalent to most others who'd served twice that. He was never close to either his men or the platoon commander. The company First Sergeant and Paschal had an unspoken understanding—as long as he kept his platoon squared away, the First Sergeant would leave him alone. The Marines under him wanted to be like him, to possess his swagger and confidence, with the ability to back it up.

He probably wouldn't have stayed in for 20 or more anyway. Maybe he'd become a professional MMA fighter. All he knew was he'd look for a more solitary pursuit. Then two men sidetracked him, and made his decision for him. This happened a few weeks before he had to declare his intention to Re-Up.

+++

It started with a phone call. The man calling said he represented an outfit called Global Communications. Paschal sensed straightaway it was a front organization. "If you call back to this number, you won't get anyone. We'd like to meet."

"And your name is…?" Paschal answered.

"Just call me Joe Doe for now. Here's what I need you to do. Take three days leave." He gave the dates. "We've greased the skids. The leave will be approved. We'll mail you a round-trip ticket to Omaha to meet us. Along with the ticket you'll receive instructions on the hotel you'll be staying at. Simple. Give your name and the clerk will give you the card key to the room we've arranged. You will never contact us. We'll call your room and tell you where and when to report for our meeting. Now listen closely: *you are not to discuss anything I've said with anyone. We will know if you do so, and the meeting will be terminated. Do you understand this part of our instructions?"*

"Understood," Paschal answered.

"Submit your leave request immediately. My partner or I will call you back precisely twenty-four hours from now. Answer on the second ring. We'll expect your answer to the meeting at that time. Questions?"

"What's your partner's name?"

"Not important," Joe Doe replied. The phone call clicked off.

Blaise Paschal would not find out who had fingered him. Had to have been someone connected to the black ops world. Someone with clout. He didn't know anyone personally with those qualifications. He didn't socialize much, though, and had never heard the war stories that might have given him a clue.

+++

Paschal was accomplished at keeping his mouth shut. He went to Omaha and thence by rental car to the fresh-looking ochre stucco motel set off the Interstate by itself. After checking in, he sat in his room reading a book as he awaited the call. Less than an hour later, the phone rang and someone, not Joe Doe, but presumably his partner, issued the same clipped instructions as before. Because it was only mid-afternoon, Paschal had anticipated the meeting would come off later that day.

Instead, the voice told him the meeting would be at 10 the next morning. They would call shortly before the rendezvous to let him know where to go.

Blaise reasoned that if he, or they, were in the same hotel he might be able to identify them in advance. A small area used for breakfast in the morning and as a bar in the evening sat near the reception area. The bar was already open. From the seat he chose he could see anyone coming in or going out of the motel. He ordered a soft drink. By five he'd ordered another soda. The small bar had begun to fill in. By six it was bustling. A bit after six he saw a well-built man walk through the door. Paschal thought he observed the man do a double-take when he spied Paschal, but he couldn't be sure. The man had been about six feet tall. He wore a black shirt that looked to be silk, with the sleeves rolled to halfway between wrist and elbow. Muscular forearms were visible. His trousers were the same shade of black. His full head of salt-and-pepper hair was swept straight back, and longish. Paschal believed he had identified one of his interviewers. He sat there another hour. He had learned that locals liked this place, and most of them tried to engage him in small talk. One of the TV sets overhead was carrying an old Cornhuskers football game the locals desperately wanted to brag about to this stranger. Paschal finally decided the man in black wasn't coming down to the bar. He gave up and went to his room.

Paschal had a cell phone and he had the landline phone beside the bed. He touched neither. He believed the guy would know if he spoke to anyone about his location and reason for being there. Besides, he had no one to call. He was also pretty confident the room was bugged with both audio and video monitors. He decided searching for them wouldn't be a good idea.

At 9:30 the next morning his room phone rang. The man, Joe Doe this time, told him the meeting would take place right there in Paschal's room. Have the door slightly ajar, Doe said. We're coming in without knocking. Paschal knew then his supposition about the bugs was correct; either they or their techs had been in the room before Paschal's arrival and installed listening and/or video devices. He felt a little creepy knowing they were watching him even as he answered their call, and might have been watching him since the moment he arrived. They were sizing him up already.

During his half-hour wait, Paschal had a feeling he was ignoring something he should've considered. What it was came to him, but he dismissed it as unimportant, which he had to, because it was too late to fix it, if indeed it was important. It was how he was attired. Should he have put on a well thought out ensemble to demonstrate his respect? Or, should he be telling them, what you see is what you get, not wear anything other than his habitual knockaround clothes? Paschal wore a polo shirt with cargo pants and black walking shoes.

They walked directly in at a minute before 10. The first guy was the one Paschal had spotted coming through the door last night, dressed in identical black clothing that may have been the same outfit. The other was a couple inches shorter than his partner. He was even more powerfully built than the first guy. He wore a short-sleeved dark shirt that showed muscle, a lot of snaking veins, and scars from some kind of wounds. Pronounced keloid scars.

Before either spoke, the man in black went to the wall-mounted television and turned it on, tuning the volume up high. Black was unsmiling, holding a scowl, and he didn't sit. Scar Man pointed to a position in the center of the sofa where he wanted Paschal to sit, and then took a chair to Paschal's right. The latter smiled and offered his hand and a friendly greeting to Paschal. The *Thanks for seeing us* kind of thing. *We've heard good things about you.* Like that.

Blackie fiddled with a nightstick in front of the TV as Scar explained this was an interview, and it would be unlike any other. Both men quickly shifted and assumed positions on either side of Paschal. Blackie poked him in the ribs, not too hard, with the nightstick. Paschal wouldn't have tolerated pokes any harder than he was getting. The room would've turned ugly. But both men leaned into him, asking one question after another rapidly, trying to throw him off balance. He kept his cool and waited for the questions to stop. Then he answered each one in the exact order it was asked. They had not thrown Paschal. Then they created scenarios and asked what he would do. He answered calmly. They didn't exactly emit any tells, but Paschal sensed he was doing well. Finally, they put a pencil and paper on the credenza in front of him and gave him a geopolitical question to answer. Thirty minutes max, they said. As Paschal took up the pencil, they got back in each of his ears and did their best to distract him. He stayed on task. At the end of thirty minutes, he handed over his completed essay.

They asked if he knew whom they actually represented. "Hint: it's not Global Communications," they said.

"I know," Paschal said.

Blackie pulled out a cred pack and opened it without a word. Paschal, of course, knew who they were.

Scar said, "We have to tell you what's next. In fact, there might not be a next. My partner and I will go over this interview in detail. We'll make a recommendation to our highers on whether they should pursue you. I don't know what we might conclude about you, Paschal. But for the moment, let's say you go to the next step. You'll receive instructions in much the fashion you got them from us. You won't know where they came from. You'll go through psych testing. If you're still given a green light, you'll be invited to take a practical exam. You'll be given few instructions. That means you'll be given a mission in one of the shittiest, meanest sections of this country. If you pass that test, you'll go for 12 weeks of intensive training in tradecraft. Stuff like tailing a target in a vehicle or as part of a team. How to fight. How to employ lots of high-tech gadgetry. How to leap from a moving vehicle. How to handle a hundred different weapons and use them effectively. How to blend in with locals. Above all, how to gather intel on targets and how never to lose your target. If you pass that—and let me tell you, few get that far—you'll be assigned deep cover jobs all around the world. Nasty jobs. Sometimes to collect intel, sometimes to go face-to-face with an adversary. Find him and take him down, is a nice way to explain it. Wherever there are bad guys acting in ways inimical to national interests. I've done jobs from Capetown to Cairo to Paris to

Oslo. All the rules still pertain, but the big one is: *we have an eye on you, and if you speak about any of this to anyone, your prospect of employment with us will be terminated. Clear?"*

"Clear," Paschal answered.

"We'll call in twenty-four hours for your decision concerning continuation of the process." Before walking out of Paschal's room, Blackie turned off the television.

+++

Paschal didn't re-up, despite strong pressure from his chain of command. He thought of himself as a lone wolf. He eschewed team sports, never played football or basketball or baseball or any other. Martial arts was the type of individual endeavor he preferred. You got the hell beaten out of you if you hadn't developed your skills or if you lacked courage. There was no teammate to turn to. He hadn't even liked working in a 30-40 man USMC platoon all that much. He certainly was at the point in his USMC service where he emphatically did not wish to be promoted above the platoon level. What the two guys in Omaha had described was a perfect fit for him, he believed.

He succeeded in all their training programs. He operated at first on two to five man teams. Directions normally left room for initiative, even demanded it. His instincts were rated superior, as was his overall performance. Within 18 months he became a team leader. They assigned him to increasingly more dangerous and important missions. Before some of the jobs they sent him to three-month long language immersion courses at the Defense Language Institute. The program required rapid absorption. The excellent students, of which Paschal was one, entered three-day programs of iso-immersion, meaning isolation from English was total. It concentrated on handling real-life situations in the course language. He took to new languages with a facility few classmates demonstrated. People from prestigious universities occasionally asked him which universities he'd attended, to which he gave many different answers. Neither his fellow students nor his professors were privy to his background, including the organization that employed him. While there to learn Arabic, he pretended to be a German expat in America, so he affected the accent of a German speaking English. "I am from the Max Planck Institute," he told one questioner, "but beyond that I am not free to comment." Another time he passed himself off as an Oxford man there at the behest of the British army.

CHAPTER NINE

Sheriff Mollison got in touch with General Green. "I'll get right to the point, General. His cabin's been smashed up. Doors were open when I got there. Found his cell phone crushed to bits. We can both draw the obvious conclusions. Bottom line: I don't know where he is or when he'll be back."

"To tell you the truth, Sheriff," Green said, "I guess I just expected my call to him to be brief. I wanted to ask a question about a man who was in one of his old units. Maybe he wouldn't remember the man at all. Chances of his being able to help were slim, but the subject is important to people in very high places, so I had to try."

"What else can I do to help, General?" Mollison asked.

"I know you're good, Joe, Simon's told me so. But I need you to call Governor Dahl and get his resources on the case too. My instinct is barking at me, and when it does, something bad is usually about to happen unless I act. What else can you tell me about the scene you found at the cabin?"

"Once again, General, the Governor was missing, place was thrown open, destroyed phone, two drinking glasses, two beer bottles, boot tracks that weren't Simon's..."

"Men's boot tracks, what size?" Green asked.

"Checking the prints now, but about a size 14," Mollison said. "And we're canvasing the area to see if anyone saw a strange vehicle in the area about the time we think this occurred."

"OK, Joe, to be honest, I might seem to be involved in a local matter, criminal or civil, that I have no business in. But at the same time, the subject of my call to Pack is very important. Maybe I'm jumping to an unwarranted conclusion, but before this call, I had more than a little fear his disappearance and my call were connected. After hearing your report, I'm nearly certain they're connected. If you therefore would mind leaving brief updates for me—for at least a few days—you'll be doing work beyond the jurisdiction of Glacier County."

"Happy to help, General. WILCO," the Sheriff said.

"WILCO, huh?" Green said. "I'm guessing you wore a military uniform too, right?"

"United States Marine Corps, General, just like Governor Pack," Mollison said.

"All right, Joe, many thanks. Semper Fi, partner."

"Semper Fi, General. Out, here."

+++

Paschal had stolen the Transit van in North Dakota. Thanks to the exploitation of the Bakken Formation, North Dakota was producing 30 million barrels of oil a month. Now, because OPEC had driven prices down in the short term, Bakken production was off its high, but the area around Mountrail County remained a congeries of makeshift motels, mobile homes, and strip clubs for the roughnecks. Drug dealers and pimps prowled without serious threat of being caught. Paschal knew stealing a vehicle in such a disorganized environment would be easy. Most of those guys who performed hard labor for a full shift on the oil rigs hit the clubs after work and drank themselves into a stupor. Easy pickings. He hotwired the Transit after removing its license plate in favor of one he'd stolen several states away. Paschal smiled, seeing in his mind's eye some sap staggering out at 3 in the morning looking for his truck; he'd wander around for an hour amid the sea of vehicles thinking he didn't remember where he parked it. In his state of deep inebriation he'd have trouble getting sympathetic attention from an already-overworked lawman.

Either the truck's owner or the company he worked for had spent considerable money on the tools in the cargo bay. Lots of big heavy spanners and wrenches. Paschal had dumped all of them in a lake enroute to Montana. The bay was clear, but remained greasy from the oil- and mud-encrusted tools. Pack lay on the hard floor coated in muck.

If he got his head in a certain position, he could view the digital clock on the dash. They'd been on the road about two hours. Paschal didn't speak to Pack. Pack did not speak to Paschal. Pack couldn't speak. His mouth was duct-taped. Paschal pulled into a rest area and pulled Pack's pants down, signaling him to go in the bucket. "Sit up, stand up, do whatever you need to to use the bucket. Be quick," Paschal ordered. Pack finished. Paschal said, "How's the mouth?" He laughed as he said, "Don't answer that." Then, "Roll over, big fellow. Sorry I gotta do this, but see, I can't trust you not to start banging around in here trying to attract attention while I'm gone. Just bear with me and

146

I'll unhitch you when I get back from taking care of my own business. Be good and maybe I'll bring you back a snack or two." He used the hooks bolted into the wall of the cargo area to cinch Pack down tight. There was no give in the ropes. Paschal knew his knots.

Paschal returned. Before stripping away the duct tape, he admonished Pack. "If you say anything, anything in any tone, I'll cut your throat. You're doing well so far. Let's keep it that way." He fed Pack a chocolate bar and a package of peanut butter crackers, intermittently giving him water to wash it down. He undid the ropes and reapplied the duct tape and drove away. Pack couldn't tell from the windowless cargo area where they were, but he could hear the outside traffic. He could feel the sway of the van as it negotiated a winding road. Judging from the volume of traffic and the time they'd been driving, he estimated they were on US 93, probably heading south in the direction of Missoula. Paschal would be taking care to observe the posted speed limit, not too fast or too slow. Pack's shoulders were aching, but he kept his concentration.

A torrent of rain like the one earlier in the day at the cabin came billowing down and the sky grew dark. Pack felt the vehicle come to a prolonged pause then climb a ramp, then turn right, which had to mean they had been near Missoula and now were traveling west on I-90. The increased speed and fewer buckles in the road confirmed Pack's supposition. He took note of the time they entered the interstate traffic flow.

At around midnight Pack felt them exit. Bright lights flooded from above. When Paschal stepped out to fill the fuel tank, Pack heard the low rumble of big trucks idling. Pack connected all the data he'd collected during the day. He concluded they were in Idaho, and this clearly was a major truck stop. Paschal drove the van somewhere around the lot and parked. He sat still for a couple of minutes. Then he riffled through a tote bag on the passenger seat from which he withdrew something so small he concealed it in his closed fist.

Blaise Paschal reverted to a playacting mode, dialing his personality into that of an imaginary figure, as he was wont to do. Every now and then he called to mind a Bernard Lewis assertion— concerning a key reason many Arabs found bin Laden appealing--that comported with the reality he'd observed: "Eloquence, a skill much admired and appreciated in the Arab world since ancient times." Then he began his version of eloquence: "My good man, the most esteemed General Governor Simon Pack, I am concerned you might have experienced a touch of discomfort on our little sojourn. I shall therefore come to your aid by administering a sedative, a mild one, mind you, quite gentle, to let you enjoy your overnight rest. So, get up now, and prepare for slumber by evacuating in your nice bucket. I shall tug down your undergarments and give you a moment in privacy to complete your lavatory operation. You must be in fine fettle tomorrow morning, sir, in order to perform up to the star billing I'm according you."

When Pack had finished, Paschal set the bucket outside the van while he sat Pack back up straight to receive his "mickey." It wasn't the Aleve PM he told Pack it was. Within moments Pack was out cold. Paschal smacked him on the face a few times to be sure the drug had

worked to its potential. Had to be sure he'd administered a dose
sufficient to fell a man Pack's size.

Paschal exited the truck, dumped the contents of the bucket and
set it back inside the truck. Before going into the men's washroom, he
looked around the mammoth parking area filled with truckers sleeping
in their cabins, and was happy that amid this sea of large vehicles, his
would not be noticed.

+++

During the trip down from his cabin, Pack had kept in his mind a ledger
of time-distance-turn information. At the same time, he'd thought about
the circumstance he'd fallen into.

Pack was a practical man. He knew that we often encounter
unexpected circumstances. We assess them. We look at options open to
us. We decide which options we'll take, in which sequence. We have to
determine a means of mastering the circumstances besetting us; if we
don't, the circumstances will master us.

Keeley had told him things he didn't much appreciate at the
time. Like, "Simon, you must consider the possibility you cannot
accomplish physical tasks, in some cases stupendous feats, you
accomplished just 10 years ago. Maybe, Governor, you need to install a
governor on your urges and impulses to be the combat Marine you once
were. I get it. You're still a better man physically than most men half
your age, but you've nonetheless had a bit of the edge taken off your
reactions. Just remember that before you charge into an attack on a

group of well-armed men as you did less than a year ago. I've seen the incredible penchant you possess for finding trouble. Get away from being Simon Pack, the man who follows the path of greatest resistance. Follow the example of water, which chooses the path of least resistance. Don't let your pride morph into hubris, OK? It's time, maybe, that you work your brain harder than your body."

Pack feared no man. He'd always carried in his head the words of Joshua, chapter 1, verse 9: "Be strong and courageous, for the Lord will be with you wherever you go." He certainly did not fear Blaise Paschal. In fact, he dreamed of the moment he would say to a defeated Paschal, "I have a moral base, and you do not. That's the difference between us, but it is a big one, my friend." He entertained no doubts about losing to Paschal in any fashion. Pack just knew he would come out on top in the end.

Paschal had not presented Pack a chance to exercise direct physical opposition, and in Pack's assessment, Paschal was too smart to afford him one. And, he had to admit, Paschal might be—because he was younger, was quite strong, and quite adept at using some of the best fighting instruction in the world—able to take him in a fight. Pack intended to heed Keeley's counsel and follow the course of water down a mountain streambed.

+++

When morning arrived, each man went through his ablutions and tended to his toilet needs in the same manner as the previous evening, and Paschal watered and fed Pack. "OK, Pack, it's time for your starring role. Don't botch it. I'm going to hand the phone to you once I have Mollison. You will read the contents of the paper I give you precisely as written. Don't think about adding or omitting even a word. When you're finished you click off. Understood?"

Pack nodded his understanding.

Paschal got connected to the Sheriff. Paschal spoke in a passable Hispanic accent. "This is Ricky Sanchez. You are an officer of the law and also a friend of Senor Pack, so you can and will make this happen or he will die, that is certain. Record these instructions exactly. Here is Pack."

Pack read the sheet of paper containing Paschal's orders. In pertinent part, they told Mollison to secure $2 million from Pack's account in Kalispell. In $100 bills, unmarked. Pack himself authorized the withdrawal of the money. Carry the money to Governor Dahl in Helena. Have Dahl, and Dahl alone, deposit the cash into the bottom of the trash receptacle that lay 100 meters due east of the capitol building. Do this at 1 AM the following morning. Sanchez's people would be watching from multiple locations with night vision devices. Sanchez's agent would secure the sack of money sometime after the drop. If anyone interfered with the pickup, or at any point thereafter, Pack would die instantly. Call the number Sanchez/Paschal gave once the drop was complete. The clock is ticking, Pack said. Do as he says.

The call disconnected as Mollison said, in futility, "Simon, where are you?" Paschal destroyed the burner in the same manner he had destroyed Pack's. He'd toss it into a dumpster on the way out of the truck stop.

Joe Mollison couldn't tout lofty titles, but he was a damn fine country lawman. He had captured the conversation on tape. Such a call had not been unexpected.

+++

The phone lines out of the county sheriff's office were humming. Mollison had never faced a situation similar to this, but he was proficient at figuring out solutions to unique problems on the fly. He called the Kalispell bank president first to get the ball rolling. Told him that however he had to do it, get $2 million packed up. "But, but…" the president began, but Mollison said, "Mister Banker, that's your problem. Figure it out. Get your hands on the cash. It's the General's money, and he needs it yesterday. I'll be by to pick it up in three hours. End of discussion."

He called Governor Dahl, cutting through the governor's staff immediately. "No excuses," he said to the governor's chief of staff, "I need him now. Emergency." Dahl came on, and Mollison whipped through Sanchez's instructions. Dahl asked Joe to calm down, just a bit. "Joe, Joe," Dahl said, "the General's my friend too. Let's discuss this a minute, truly get both our heads on it, OK?"

"OK, Governor," Mollison said. "What's on your mind?"

"First thing is the advisability of alerting the FBI. Second is whether you report back to General Green. What's your view, Joe?"

"Governor, let's talk through what we think would happen if we notify them. The FBI would likely jump in with both feet if we go in from the top. They do that, they maybe get Sanchez, but get Pack killed. Maybe the best approach would be for me to visit the Agent in charge of the Field Office in Kalispell. You met him around five months ago. In fact, you met him up close and personal when you and your State Troopers broke into his office and got the General released from his custody. He knows and respects General Pack. I absolutely believe we can ask him to keep this under his hat until Sanchez picks up the money. That way, before he notifies his boss in Salt Lake, he can have already sketched out a line of investigation. When he offers it to his boss, it'll have the effect of making himself look good."

"I agree, Joe. Our first objective has to be making sure our good friend is released unharmed. There'll be time to go after the bad guys later. You're pretty tied up with this whole deal right now, so why don't you let me deal with…what was his name?"

"Agent Juan Martino," the Sheriff said.

"Yeah, Juan Martino. So, agreed I call him?" Dahl asked.

"Yes, sir," Mollison said. "So now, what about General Green?"

"I know this," Governor Dahl said, "He's a very, very bright man, a quick study, and another in the line of important people who hold General Pack in ultimate regard. But don't you think if we tell him the General's been kidnapped we'd be tying his hands in some way? He's in the federal stratosphere, and would have little choice but to inform the FBI and probably some other agencies as well. If and when he discovers we've held this story back from him, he'll be mad as hell, and probably will want our asses, but again, we have to keep our eyes on the prime objective, which from our standpoint is protecting General Pack."

"So you're saying we don't tell him anything…yet?" Mollison said.

"That's right," Dahl said.

"Then that's settled," Mollison said.

"Not settled exactly to my satisfaction, Joe," Dahl said. "I haven't heard you say Sanchez pledged to release the General once he has the money. Did he tell you that?"

"No, he didn't," Mollison said quietly, "and he cut off before I could pursue the point."

"All right," Dahl said, "what if I call him back on the number he left before the money's in place?"

"I don't think you want to do that, sir," Mollison said. "The guy sounded edgy, as if violating a single instruction could get Pack killed."

"Then I won't call him. But it should be obvious to both of us that our decision to ignore Green and only share this conditionally with the local FBI man, Agent Martino, could backfire on us more than we can imagine. It's a huge risk we're about to take, Joe."

"Then so be it, Governor," Mollison said. "I don't see we have a choice right about now. We must live with our decision. Now I have to be prepared to put a boot up the ass of our banker friend. Once I get the money, I'll find a chopper for the flight to Helena."

"Don't worry about it, Joe. I'm dispatching mine immediately. It'll be at your disposal." With that, both signed off.

+++

Paschal lowered his window and cast the shattered burner into the industrial-sized dumpster at the boundary of the truck stop property. "I removed your mouth tape so we can talk today, General," Paschal said politely. "I have a lot of driving, and it'll be your job to keep me alert by conversing in a civilized fashion. Where shall we begin, Simon?"

"You can begin by stopping your lying to me," Pack said. "See, Blaise, it was I who arranged the meeting that propelled you to the next act in your personal play."

Pack couldn't see Paschal's face, but if he could have, he would've seen dismay registered thereon. After a time, Paschal said, "Why? Didn't you think you were betraying your own service?"

"To the contrary, you would've betrayed yourself if you'd stayed in the Corps. While almost everyone in your chain was saying you were our top target for reenlistment, I had a different view. You needed to go, not because of the Peter Principle, but because you were born to operate in relative isolation. I could see that and, to be candid, I held your immediate chain in lower esteem because they couldn't see that. I knew you'd lied when you said you became a First Sergeant, not only because I knew you'd been lured out of the Corps, but also because I knew you wouldn't have been worth a crap as a First

Sergeant. In the end, you cared more about yourself than about your men," Pack said.

"Hurray, General Simon Pack! You get an A for perception. Patting yourself on the back. Thinking, 'Aren't I special, there I was a two-star with more than 10,000 Marines in my command, yet I could read this lowly junior NCO like a book.' But you failed to consider maybe you actually were signing my death warrant." Paschal paused, giving no sign he would continue this thought.

So Pack stepped in. "And how did I sign your death warrant? Getting you in over your head in the Agency? Explain, if you can."

"I grew up in a pile of shit. I had plenty to hate. And hate a lot of things and people I sure did. But you know where I give myself credit? It's in not being a crybaby. Take a look at most daily papers. You'll see a cover picture of some punk over whom the so-called journalist will draw an eloquent prose picture of a young man we're expected to sympathize with. Father murdered when the boy was seven. Mother on crack throughout son's life. Somehow the poor lad persevered and made sweet lemonade outta sour lemons. Something like that could be written about me. But me, I hate everyone complicit in producing that dreck. Victims make me sick.

"See, I had this philosophy since I had the ability to think. I just didn't know it. One day on the mixed martial arts circuit I fought a guy who'd played football at Yale. In his daily life he was a lawyer, how good or what kind I don't know, but he drove a nice car, I remember that. But he was one of the best fighters I got in the octagon with. Skilled and brutal, great combination. After our match, after the

156

showering and whatnot, I was sitting in the audience watching follow-on matches when this Yale lawyer sits down beside me. He tells me I'm the best fighter my age—I was almost ten years younger—he's fought, I have a bright future, blahblahblah. Then he hands me a piece of paper, maybe four inches square, that he says is his philosophy of life. He'd written in pen in the margin that it came from a playbook of an old-time Yale football coach name of Carmen Cozza. Best advice I ever got. Reinforced what I'd already kind of figured out on my own. It said—and I shall recite it from memory:

If you are poor, WORK. If you are rich, WORK. If you are burdened with seemingly unfair responsibilities, WORK.

If you are happy, continue to work. Idleness gives room for doubts and fears. If sorrow overwhelms you and loved ones seem not true, WORK. If disappointments come, WORK.

If faith falters and reason fails, just WORK. When dreams are shattered and hope seems dead – WORK. WORK as if your life were in peril; it really is.

No matter what ails you, WORK. WORK faithfully, and WORK with faith. WORK IS THE GREATEST MATERIAL REMEDY AVAILABLE. WORK will cure both mental and physical afflictions.

I didn't know a thing about Carmen Cozza, but the man had his shit packed real tight. Don't know if he intended it to be a poem, but doesn't matter, it's advice the self-proclaimed victims ought to pay attention to.

"The animals I grew up around in The Rathole forever talked of their 'lot' in life. What is a man's 'lot,' I ask you? It's not some thing or some place we're destined to be, but a defeatist, excuse-making state of mind. If you don't like your 'lot' you throw it out with the garbage and make yourself a new one. 'Victims' bemoan their 'lot' and do nothing to improve. Winners make their own, and I'm a winner.

"In the movies the military hero usually has great posture, what they refer to as ramrod straight. That's because the hero is supposed to be a winner, and good posture helps reinforce the idea. I give you credit. Marines looked at you they saw a winner, because you always strode around with purpose and confidence, ramrod straight. I learned that from you, tried to think about maintaining good posture, and not just for health reasons.

"Now, General, if I were you, I wouldn't have told me you were the one responsible for sending me on to the next act of my life. I was too good at what I did. Some said the best. I killed whoever needed killing. Anywhere. I believed I could dissolve into the air. I became a master of disguises. I've had more passports under more names and under the flags of more countries than you can count. So good I never fretted going through an airport or any other public place. I thought maybe the Agency had never had a deep cover man as deft as I at killing people and exiting scenes without a trace, or even witnesses. I got recognition from the Director himself.

"But I saw myself developing a bloodlust. I was a vampire constantly in search of new blood. So I quit. Just left, kind of ashamed of myself, being a hired gun, so to say, going from one shootout to the next. Kind of like Gene Hackman in that movie with Sharon Stone, *Unforgiven?* No, I get that one mixed up with *The Quick and the Dead.* But unlike Hackman in that movie, I kind of hoped to fall at the hands of the next one to claim the title, fastest draw and best sharpshooter. I figured that in the eyes of God, I was already screwed. Maybe, even though in my mind up to that point I'd only killed those who needed killing. Still, I was worried about my eternal soul."

"So you don't think redemption's possible?" Pack said after Paschal seemed to have shut down.

"Not time to talk about my redemption," Paschal said bitterly.

"So," he went on, apparently wanting to send a message to Pack, "I did the hard labor I mentioned to you for a year. Here, in the US. Then I got the itch again…I didn't need the money, cause I'd put away damn near every dollar I made, followed my motto, 'live beneath your means'…and I got word these retired Generals had formed a company. Some of the company was involved in training foreign forces, but that was a cover for the guys really paying the freight, the mercenaries. You can guess which one I was. They paid well. But they paid themselves a lot better, of course. Many times better. And you know who was funding it? The American taxpayer. The State Department approves the licensing, but says the host government is paying the mercs. But the Iraqi government was paying us from American foreign aid money.

"I was back in the climate I was meant to exist in. People all around who'd slit your throat if you turned your back. You never knew for sure the difference between friendly and enemy. Another test of my will and reflexes. Then the assholes in charge, your old buddies, sent us on a mission designed to fail from lack of resources. And I've thought for a long while that it wasn't just lack of resources; it was also because they compromised our location. Someone, somewhere in our organization gave us away. I threw the door open and leaped twenty feet into the Euphrates, swam underwater quite a distance, and E and E'd, escaped and evaded capture as I'd been trained to do. I was consumed with hatred for anyone and everyone who allowed my comrades to die, and who I imagine didn't give a tinker's damn. And you know where I hid while hatching my plan to wreak vengeance on my enemies? First, it was right there in Fallujah. You tell me any American with the mad self-confidence, the unmitigated balls to do that? I found an Iraqi civilian about my size, put a bullet in his head, and stole his clothes. I walked around the city as American military units stormed the place. In those forces most likely were some Marines I'd served with. AKs and SKSs are everywhere in Iraq. I had a couple, with ammo, and pretended to fight with the forces called ISIS now. Wouldn't you say I was well-trained, General?"

Before Pack could answer, Paschal had veered into a rest area, and in a far parking space, was reapplying the duct tape to Pack's mouth.

+++

Mollison was at the First National Bank in Kalispell having just completed a fiery harangue directed at the bank's president. Once Sheriff Mollison heard the first "Sir, this is highly irregular" type of expression from the banker, he'd lost his cool and unloaded on the man. Mollison wouldn't be denied. Finally, the Sheriff had refined the issue to, "We'll have the product you desire in no more than forty-five additional minutes, sir." Just because he was still spitting fire, the Sheriff bombarded the banker with threats of legal action for failing to maintain the confidentiality of his depositor, General Pack. "My strong advice to the General," the Sheriff ranted on, "is to put his assets in a facility that'll be more respectful of his privacy." At that point, Mollison walked around the banker's desk, and leaned down to within inches of his face, saying calmly, "Now I'm going to the lobby to wait, the better to allow you to ramrod this job through. And I can tell you, mister, you're in big damn trouble if it takes a minute longer than you promised. Tick tock." The ole Sheriff bit his tongue and held in reserve threats related to Governor Dahl's involvement in this matter, as well as what a couple of well-placed leaks about the bank's untrustworthiness would do to its business. Montanans didn't appreciate loose lips.

So, as the Sheriff bided his time in the bank lobby, he whipped out his phone to call Tetu Palaita up in Yaak. He condensed the kidnapping story to under a minute in length. The man mountain, all seven feet and 365 pounds of him, practically dove through the phone circuit toward Mollison. "Leave key for me at station, Sheriff Joe. I am going into cabin, keep it secure until Matai has returned."

"Happy to, Tetu," Mollison said, "but if the General were here, he'd tell you you must take care of your Lodge business first, this business you've poured your heart, soul, and money into."

"Swan has done wonderful things for us, Sheriff. She has sent three Kootenai men to work for me as a way of working through their problems. They help me, and Swan says I am helping them. I trust them, and they are doing great work. I have been teaching them to do everything. They will appreciate if I leave the Lodge in their hands for a while. And there is Swan herself, who they know they better please. She will keep close eye on them. I am leaving today. Swan will insist Tetu do this. Meantime, think of ways for Tetu to help."

No one could intuit the degree of Tetu's support for his Matai, Pack. He would rush to offer his life in exchange for Pack's. He told Tetu to keep quiet his reason for leaving the Lodge, but there was no need for that; Tetu could be depended upon. The huge American Samoan was fully engaged now.

+++

The Governor's helicopter was standing by for the Sheriff, who now had taken possession of the heavy-duty trash bag that contained 44 pounds of hundred dollar bills.

State Troopers met him at the helipad near the Statehouse and whisked him into the Governor's office. Dahl had brought no one in the building into his confidence. It was a classic Need-to-Know matter and, in his opinion, no one else needed to know.

Mollison had made clear to the banker that this was his chance at a modicum of redemption. In other words, he'd told the banker, you and your staff will remain mum on this withdrawal. Why the General is withdrawing cash in this amount is none of your concern.

Sheriff Mollison handed the sack to the sitting Governor, who was surprised at its heft and weight. "OK, Joe, here's how I intend to do this: at about five this afternoon, I'll leave the office to go home. That'll signal everyone in the building it's safe for them to leave then too. I'll have dinner—and I'm inviting you to dine with me—after which I'll return here around nine. I'll do my best to focus on other matters until around midnight, then I'll time my arrival at the trash bin just before one A.M. The trooper will take me back home, where you'll remain overnight. I'll have you flown back tomorrow morning. Between now and tomorrow morning, I suggest we pray earnestly for the General's safe release."

Mollison said, "Do you believe the kidnapper is Ricky Sanchez?"

"No way, Joe. This is the man that General Green inquired about. He sounds like a murderous bastard, sorry to say. If it were anyone else, he wouldn't have been able to capture General Pack. It was someone Pack knew from a previous life, I think. I think the General is far too shrewd to let some rookie named Ricky Sanchez get the drop on him. And nothing seems to be missing from the cabin, right?"

"Right, sir. I've been there a hundred times, and I saw nothing out of place. Looks like he is after the two mil."

After Dahl made the drop, he called the number Sanchez/Paschal had provided. The first thing Dahl said was, "Let me speak with Pack." Sanchez handed the phone to Pack, saying, "Make it quick. Under thirty seconds. In and out." Pack said, "I'm OK, Jim."

Dahl said, "We've followed his instructions, General. If you aren't released unharmed, the universe of law enforcement will be on him."

"Thanks," Pack said, and returned the phone to Paschal.

Paschal said, "Listen, Dahl, your pal will be freed after I have the cash and am gone. You've done well so far. Be sure to stick with the details until this deal is fully consummated. He dies if you fail at the final hour. Comprende?"

"I understand. I want to tell you, though, what I told the General in case you didn't hear it. If he has a mark from your brutality anywhere on him you will have the full weight of old-fashioned unfriendly American law enforcement on your tail, and we will not be kind when we nail you."

"Have a good day, Dahl," Paschal said as he hung up. He destroyed this burner as he had the others.

+++

Pack had calculated they were in southern Idaho. Could be wrong. But he didn't think he was wrong. He was highly confident they were far away from Helena. Not nearly enough time to get there to make the pickup of $2 million.

They were driving again, and again Paschal removed the duct tape. He wanted Pack to be free to converse. "OK, Simple Simon, let's talk some more. I'll start, but you, kind sir, feel free to hold up your end of the conversation. So. Since I've been back on US soil, I notice 'so' is a new thing. If you're asked a question on TV or radio, you begin your answer with 'so.' Like the government has made a new law. Can't make a sentence unless you open with 'so'. They do it because they think it's coolspeak and because it gives them a second more to form a reply. Weakness is on parade everywhere you look in this country." He paused, then added, "Or the other favorite is 'Look,' a word they think establishes dominance before they make their statement.

"Which brings me to my next comment, namely, that I find myself wondering which country I belong to at this point. I don't know anyone in America any longer. If I have a friend here, please give me his name. But the fact is, I don't think I have a friend anywhere in the world. You think I'm bellyaching? I'm not. I pretty much don't give a shit about anyone these days. Is the bitch who birthed me still alive? I don't give a shit, and it's all OK with me.

"Now about you. See, I don't want to be an unkind host and make this all about me. Let's speak about you a little. I'm frankly of multiple minds about you. Part of me hates you for giving me a nudge toward a life that's been mean to me. You had a small role in helping transform me into the vampire I am. Maybe I ought to kill you for that alone. On the other hand, maybe that's a subject God will take up with you one day, and he'll end up doing that piece of dirty work for me. At least you confessed. You're thinking a man ought to be responsible for himself. Can't argue with you about that. So I suppose I ought to let you live.

"I also see you've taken this like a man. You're not a panty-wearin' squealer. Haven't begged me for anything. Haven't seen any

165

fear in your eyes, and I appreciate that in a man, sir. Don't seem to be many men left in this country. All right, Mister Pack, your turn to talk."

"I can only speak truth to you," Pack began. "I don't like any man who literally invades another's house and upturns it without cause. I certainly haven't enjoyed this experience. You've perpetrated a criminal act on me. If I believe what you've told me, you've perpetrated many criminal acts. You're filled with hatred for people you have no proof harmed either you or your reputation. You could've followed more peaceable avenues for redress of grievances. But we are where we are. You can give yourself up and find an attorney who can make an eloquent, fact-based defense, and then…you live with the results."

"Or die with the results," Paschal sneered. "I am not about to give myself up, Pack. I have places and people who've not yet felt my hammer of justice, and I most assuredly will mete it out. The best way to harvest tender meat from a rabbit or chicken is to stroke its head softly a couple times to hypnotize it before cutting its throat. That's kind of my chosen method of killing men. I insinuate myself into their environments, then when they don't expect it, when they're lulled to sleep, I bring the hammer down. I could've handled you that way, but I wasn't ready to kill you. Who knows, maybe I'll even demonstrate my artistry to you a second time…with a different result.

"I could tell you stories that even you might not believe. And, maybe deep down, one of the reasons I haven't turned you into a corpse is because you were known as a real Marine, a man who'd actually seen the underbelly of the world and thrashed around in the ugly world of death and maiming. To most men, you're the living embodiment of the word Marine. But let me offer for your consideration a couple of vignettes. I was so good at feigning an Arab upbringing that in Afghanistan I worked my way into ISIS. I knew how to do it. Sometimes the way to gain control is to give it up…there in a nutshell is the key tactic instrumental to my success.

"Anyway, Generalissimo, I hung around a shithole village in Afghanistan…and let me tell you, even it wasn't as bad The Rathole I grew up in…pretending I was from another distant part of the country. I went to mosque with them, I sold fruit from carts, I eked out a living knowing they were watching me through slitted eyes. They genuinely believed I was one of them. I could recite the hadith as well as if I'd attended madrassas throughout my formative years, certainly as well as any of them. A couple of the men even had sisters they wanted me to meet. But the important point is that I was fully aware that at some point ISIS would try to recruit me. That time came, and I pretended not to be eager to join them. That, of course, made me more attractive to them. They discovered I had skills they could use. I told them I was weary of war, that I had fought in Iraq. The places I described I had of course actually been to. So at last I joined them and went to the mountains to fight against the Americans. When I got set apart with a group the size of an American squad, ten to twelve men, I plotted each day about how I could kill them all before we actually fought Americans. Insinuation. Think about it. Insinuation, to be effective, requires time and patience. I insinuated myself into their nasty lives. Then my moment came and I killed them all. I knifed to death the man pulling night security with me, then I gunned down the rest as they slept. This happened in a southern province, from which I E and E'd to Pakistan and in time joined another group after getting lost in a big city for a year. I would submit America could have used more men like me. Oh, and I took from them every item of value I could carry. The raptors had a feast with all the carrion of human flesh I supplied them."

CHAPTER TEN

The American Samoan was mad as hell as he barreled down the highway toward Sheriff Mollison's office. He couldn't block out ideas of hurting the person who'd taken Matai Pack. He wanted to be near the action if Mollison got a clue about the captor. Oh, yeah, he wanted to be on that posse. In fact, he intended to ask Mollison to deputize him immediately. Let Tetu be legally cleared to fight on the side of right as quick as the chance arose.

Mollison wasn't in, but Jonelle, the Sheriff's civilian admin assistant, gave him the key to Pack's cabin. Forensics had already cleaned Pack's place, so Tetu was cleared to enter. Tetu removed his footgear before going in, as was his custom. Once inside, Tetu noticed the muddy bootprints still littering the floor. He followed them through the garage, kitchen, dining area, and down the stairs to the basement. He saw the slurry of mud on one of the lower basement steps. Looked as if the wearer of the boots had deliberately smeared the mud at that point. The treads were obliterated from view. He stopped there and thought through what he was seeing. Something happened here, he believed. He began to writhe, unconsciously, as if he were performing some native Samoan dance. What he was actually doing was imagining himself as the attacker, trying to move in some manner, some reasonable sequence of moves that would fell the man in front of him, Simon Pack. This epiphany was telling him the bad guy attacked Matai from behind, right here. Made sense. By attacking here, Matai's fall wouldn't carry him down the full flight of stairs, thereby risking severe injury or even death. The kidnapper didn't want to have the unreasonable load of the large Pack body.

A pile carpet that looked by Tetu's eye to be roughly 7' square lay on the floor at the base of the stairs. Before stepping down upon it, Tetu went back to his vehicle to retrieve his high-mag Taclite. Back inside, Tetu returned down the steps until he reached the last from the bottom. From there, he leapt across the rug. Then he lay prone across the floor, beaming his bright light across the fibers of the carpet. The piling was still indented sufficiently for him to perceive the unmistakable markings of an elbow and forearm. He looked at the length of his own forearm and mentally measured it against Matai's. Tetu was sure this is where Matai had broken his fall. He had fallen forward off the step, that was obvious.

Tetu Palaita's knowledge of forensics was rudimentary at best, but he thought before the piling straightened itself out further, he should snap a photo of it with his phone. He did so from multiple angles, near and at a distance, hoping perhaps someone had the tools to blow it up and confirm his finding. Then, before he called the Sheriff's office with his supposition—and he would regardless—he wondered what difference this would make. Maybe someone had already noticed and noted it. Still, what was done was done, wasn't it? This knowledge wouldn't bring Matai back. But it was important for Tetu himself to know, because he had formed the impression this man was a coward for attacking General Pack from behind. Tetu was tucking that information away, he hoped, for when he would come face to face with Matai's assailant.

+++

Tetu's familiarity with Matai's cabin and surrounding property was surpassed only by Pack's. Tetu had resided here for a time after Pack left the Governor's office. Pack offered to allow Tetu to remain here as long as he wanted, or until he found the employment he desired. In recompense, Tetu did the household chores, chopping and cooking and cleaning and shopping. It was a symbiotic relationship, a natural extension of their earlier times together, both had treasured.

He found Pack's gun cabinet closed but unlocked. He found a rifle he liked and locked and loaded it. He carried it with him while he strode around the property, almost hoping the man who'd taken Pack would return. But Tetu was smart enough to know the odds of that were miniscule. He spotted a fat-trunked tree that had fallen. He set to work on it with an axe from the General's garage tool shop. You learned a lot about Pack, Tetu found early on, by looking at his tools. They were spotless, cleaned and sharpened after each use, each in its appointed place. Tetu swung murderously at the tree all day, chopping it into segments from which he would use the wedges to acquire wood of a size and shape to fit nicely into the General's stoves. It was a way of relieving part of his frustration. He felt impotent. As night drew near, he looked at his blistered hands and went inside for the night.

He made something to eat, and thought about what he would say when he called to check on Swan. He reflected that she was doing so much good up in the Yaak. Gaining the trust of the Kootenai tribe so rapidly it wouldn't be long until all would willingly listen to her. Much of the tribe had been contaminated by poisonous ideas, Swan had said, but now Tetu knew she was helping it purge the poison. When he bought the Lodge, he had no idea that men crippled emotionally would be working for him—and doing a splendid job—at that Lodge. And now Tetu himself was helping them heal by offering them a chance at redemption.

At the same time Tetu was giving thanks for Swan, he hurt just as much thinking about his Matai's loss. Keeley was not here to give him succor, to bring him joy. But Tetu also knew Mrs. Keeley Eliopoulous Pack remained a present source of strength for him. She was with him in this crisis. Tetu knew that to a certainty.

He slept in Pack's bed, rifle as his partner tonight.

+++

Back in Helena, the sun rose the morning after the Governor planted the money as the kidnapper directed. He'd stopped anyone from going near that trash receptacle. At nine that morning he personally went out to check it. Mollison went along. "Sunavabitch, Joe, look at this! It appears the trash bag is the one we left here. I discreetly marked just a couple of bills nobody but me would notice. Let's go inside and I'll give you instructions to see if this is the same *money* in the same bag."

A good many staffers noticed Governor Dahl trudging down the hallway with a large garbage sack, but none said anything. Inside his office, he told Mollison to lock the door. "OK, Joe, you'll see twenty bundles of $100,000 each, just in case you didn't personally count. The bundles surely got tumbled around, and that's no problem. What I need you to do is thumb ten bills down in each stack, and stick a 3x5 card there to mark your place. I wrote lightly in pencil on three of them, six digits on each. Tell me if you see something like that."

As he got to stack 13, Mollison had found the three sets of numbers and read them back to Dahl for confirmation. "Yeah, Joe, same money. Hmmm….why didn't Sanchez, or whatever the hell his name is, pick it up? Did he get cold feet? He said he had an agent who'd grab and go, but nobody."

The Sheriff said, "Or maybe he thought it was picked up but the agent didn't do it?"

"Or," Governor Dahl said, drawing the two-letter word way out, "what do you think of the theory that he never intended to come for the money? Maybe he was smart enough to have thought through what our reaction would be—the part, I mean about deciding not to call the FBI or anyone else—and he got it right? Could be this was a ploy to paralyze us into inaction while he used the time to get so far away we can't tell where he might be by now? And he's probably ditched whatever vehicle he had when he kidnapped the General. Guess what, Joe? I am taking full responsibility for those decisions, and your name will not be mentioned. I'm gonna take flak, but I don't care. Remember what we set as our prime objective? It's time now for me to call Martino and Green. You're welcome to stay awhile or you can take the chopper and go. Your call."

"I'm staying for a little more at least. But before you call those two principals, may I suggest you call that number you used eight hours ago? Try Sanchez one more time? I'm sure he's destroyed that phone, certainly a burner, but you ought to clear that as a possibility," Mollison said.

The Governor gave it a shot, but got back the notice that the phone was no longer in service. He'd been played.

+++

Governor Dahl called General Green first. Green told him to go secure and call back. Once on a secure line, Dahl explained in detail what had occurred in the past two days, and told him the next call would be to the FBI. The line was dead for some fifteen seconds, maybe more. Dahl supposed that Green was upset, and was collecting himself. What Green actually said surprised Dahl. "Look, Governor, I understand your first concern was the General's safety, and I am familiar with your close relationship. I can't find fault with what you decided to do. Besides, you weren't aware of the full story. Maybe I should have made a wiser decision, and given you the full story from the beginning." Green then spelled out everything reported to him about the man called Blaise Paschal. His appearance, his savagery, his wiles, his animal smarts, and his absence of a record.

"Thanks, General. My level of concern has just elevated. Let's hope it isn't too late to get him back," the Governor said. "Do what you have to do now, and I'll get the FBI moving."

He got through to Agent Martino, this time on a secure line from the start. "Look, Agent Martino," Dahl was saying, "General Green is damn high up the chain. He didn't say so directly, because he's not in a position to cast aspersions on a brother agency, but I'm perfectly capable of reading between the lines. What I heard is that the Agency will never admit they sheep-dipped Paschal or even that he ever worked for them. See, they loved him, decorated him, and now they aren't going to admit one of theirs has essentially turned traitor. The one-time Director personally decorated him. No, they made him the slippery eel he is today, giving him fake records and IDs, but they'll never say so. I'm afraid your people have a big challenge." Dahl then related to Martino the day and time of day they believed Blaise Paschal had kidnapped the General. Martino had indeed put the time since his first call to Dahl to good use. He intended to go to Salt Lake to brief his chief—and he already had worked up a solid plan of investigation, or so he thought.

Before Martino returned to Montana he'd gotten a read on how his boss wanted to proceed. Most emphatically, his boss had declared, "this probe will be kept under wraps. For the time being, anyway. Simon Pack had been in the news as much as any individual in America over the past decade. Keep Pack out of the news this time," he had said. "If the full background of this bastard we're about to pursue gets out there, the public will begin to yammer and clamor, wanting us to have taken him yesterday. Unnecessary pressure, people, and we don't need it. We might discover he's left the country again anyway, in which case he's not our problem. The FBI's already rocking with scandals, as we're all too aware, and we don't want to create another reason for the public to hate us.

"Agent Martino, I want you to make sure anyone up in your state who knows about this understands they're not to speak with anyone without the Bureau's express approval. Comprende, amigo?" Juan wanted to tell his prickly boss he was 100% American, and he understood English just fine, but he took the patronizing question in silence. "What if I answered, 'Si, Senor Jefe?'" Juan thought.

CHAPTER ELEVEN

Paschal had paused for fuel around midday, then plunged onward. The vehicle had made so many turns that at this juncture Pack was in the dark as to their whereabouts. Paschal didn't stop talking for more than five or ten minutes at a time. "Listen, Pack, I'm pretty damn sure I told you to keep me alert. If you don't wanna do your job, I'll pull over and slap that duct tape around your head again." Paschal himself drew in a long breath, then said, "OK, I'll give you your last chance…see, I said I'd throw the duct tape on you again…but I can do much better than that. I can just kill you and dispose of your body along this route. So I'll offer the first afternoon discussion topic, and you'll play or you'll be dead. Simple rule I think you can understand. OK…"

Before Paschal could produce a subject for conversation, Pack interrupted with a comment. "So, Mr. Blaise Paschal, I suppose your threat to kill me should be taken to indicate you won't be picking up that money. Don't get me wrong, I have no clue where we are right now, but some primal instinct tells me we aren't near Helena."

"Golly gee, Generalissimo," Paschal said in mock astonishment, "you are the smartest person I ever saw. How in the world did you figure out that stumper?"

"Like I said, Paschal, just an instinctive feel," Pack said.

"Well, genius, there you go, wrong again. We're very near Helena."

"OK, then, so you *do* need me for a while longer," Pack said.

"GOTCHA!" Paschal screamed. "Wrong again, Packoid. I don't need you, and we are most definitely not going to Helena. Didn't I tell Dahl I had an agent to make the grab? And didn't I tell him we'd be watching from afar every step of the op? Yes, I did."

"But you've never had anyone, because you always operate in isolation," Pack said. "Besides, you show no sign that—if you actually did have an agent doing your bidding—you're concerned about a double-cross."

"OK, Pack, so what's your next brilliant deduction?"

"It is," Pack said, "that you never intended to take the money. You wanted to create a furor to show that you could do it. But still I'm curious as why you gave your name as Sanchez? If you wanted them to know it's Blaise Paschal, why even hide it?"

"Good observation, man," Paschal said. "But it wasn't a bad call by me. The US government has sent hunter-killer teams after me several times, and I've left them with bloody bodies. I've taken out high-level politicians of our government's allies, and I've murdered greedy men who once wore the uniform of the US military. Know what that means? It means I'm most wanted, right up there with bin-Laden, although the American public hasn't heard of me yet. So there are people high up who know me, and the public will, but in due time. Even if they won't believe I'm somebody called Ricky Sanchez, it'll take them time to prove it was Blaise Paschal. I couldn't be in disguise with you. Had to be someone you recognized. I should take the credit I'm due, you're right about that. But see, I'm a patient man, and in a short while I'll make it impossible for them not to know it's me. Step right out there, say 'catch me if you can.' Only they'll find they're too boneheaded to tag me after they know it's Blaise Paschal they're after.

"Deep inside I'm a modest man, Pack, and as you've noted, not greedy, because you saw me turn down two million dollars, and don't think I couldn't have pulled it off, brother. So, since we have quite a drive remaining, let's shift topics." Paschal seemed to mulling over a suitable topic, then he said, "What makes a man, Pack, a real man? That's a tough one, am I right?"

Pack said, "You don't mind, I'd like to hear you take a crack at the answer first."

"You got balls, Pack. Ninety-nine of a hundred men in your circumstance would be afraid to raise my ire by not following instructions, but I admire that in you, so I will go first.

"First, a man has got to be unafraid. If a man has a molecule of timidity in his body, he ain't a man. He must be immune to the perils of violent physical confrontation, no matter whether he's a man of the cloth or a professor or a man who studies mountain formations for a living or a member of a dance troupe. He's got to be willing to enter the lion's den with his head up and his blood pressure under control, his only thought being how he's gonna slay that lion. He can't give a second's thought to the likelihood, or even possibility, that lion might devour him. By this standard, being a man is harder than you being able to pass your big-assed self through the eye of a needle.

"Second, a man has to prepare himself. Prepare for what? you ask. Whatever he has elected to do with his life. I don't even know what word describes my line of work, so let's just say, here on the spur of the moment, professional killer. You bet, mister, I've prepared not just all my adult life, but all my life. I look back, I see…let's put it in terms of high school English…'write me a topic sentence, Blaise.' So I do, and the teacher says, 'very good, Blaise, every sentence in your paragraph supports your topic sentence.' That's my life, every part of it supporting the professional killer mission. Got used to crappy conditions and brutality as a kid. Saw my brother gunned down by a drug gang, of which I suspect he was a member. Took advantage of knowledge between the covers of books. Learned tools of the trade in the USMC. Refined those tools in a major way in the Agency. Separated myself from the Agency, found out for sure the life I'd been leading was in fact the deliverer of the oxygen I needed in order to feel alive. Made myself financially independent. Have no family ties, never did have. Went back into the life, became a merc, saw people like me die…without good cause. Dedicated myself to righting wrongs by employing the skills I'd honed to a razor sharpness. There it is." He ran out of steam, got quiet. "Go ahead, Pack."

"Why the need to kill, Paschal?"

"That's off topic, man, but I'll give you the short answer I thought I gave you before: I only killed people who needed killing," Paschal said.

"You seem to define that pretty loosely, but if I accept that, let me ask you, do I need killing?"

"Haven't decided yet," Paschal said.

"See, Paschal, I ask merely from intellectual curiosity. Hear me well, mister: I am unafraid," Pack said.

"Bully for you, Pack. But I don't give a rat's ass whether you are or aren't. I'm in charge. Period, exclamation mark," Paschal said with a lilt. "Now get back on topic."

Pack said, "I agree there's a distinction between killing and murder. That view's been accepted since biblical times. And sometimes things go badly wrong in the military, and a killing actually was a murder. Painful for any commander who's had that happen in his command. But we train our people well to avoid murder. We work at that hard, but, as I said, it happens. We're an instrument of the politicians who use us, and I often have disagreed with the ways they've committed us to action. A brigade or division is too often a chess piece to those lug nuts. But we must do as our citizens' elected leaders direct us. Being the sheepdog to shield the sheep from the wolf is a noble aim. The key word is service. Whatever I've done, in uniform or as Governor, I kept the ideal of service to the citizens of the land always in mind. I am a servant, not a master. I look at some of our cities and states, and I see some in charge who *govern* and others who *rule*. In my humble opinion we have no place for rulers in our system of government. I tried hard to be a *governor.* I'm comfortable with the life I've lived, knowing it hasn't been about me. There have been times I wanted out of the slop and muck and mire I was in, but I never seriously considered any option but the one I chose—subordinating personal wants to the benefit of the people I was blessed to represent. Paschal, it's not my job to judge you. I don't even desire to judge you, but I will say you ought to evaluate my point of view."

Paschal didn't reply. The talk petered out. Perhaps Paschal really was pondering Pack's words.

They drove all night.

+++

The false dawn was visible in the eastern sky when Blaise Paschal hit an exit ramp toward Fort Collins, Colorado. Pack squirmed, his arms and shoulders by this time feeling wrecked from days chained behind his back. Pack couldn't see where they were either generally or specifically. Specifically, they were in the parking area of—judging from the full lot—a totally occupied Holiday Inn Express in Fort Collins.

"Mr. Pack, you've behaved like a man. But I don't trust you. On your knees, big fella. I'll step out while you use the bucket. Keep your mouth shut." Paschal didn't espy anyone in or around the Inn, but if he had, he would've taped Pack's mouth right away. When Pack was done with the bucket, Paschal took it and dumped it a ways away. He got back in the truck. Told Pack he had business that'd require him to be away from the truck for hours, not just a simple latrine break. He climbed in the back and taped Pack's mouth shut again. But before the taping, he gave Pack a long drink of water, into which he slipped another incapacitating drug. Paschal then grabbed his bag and left, locking the doors behind him. He hadn't tied Pack to the frame.

Paschal walked around the rear of the Holiday Inn, found a back entrance open, and walked through a hallway, through the lobby, and outside. He took a taxi loitering there, and was gone.

+++

Pack was out for most of the day. The pressure from his bladder let him know he'd been out a long time. He heard voices in the distance. He began to bang his back and head against the side of the truck. No one responded, and the voices attenuated to nothing. He waited, straining to hear someone closer. He thought about thirty minutes had passed before he heard a vehicle park close to the truck. He picked up the banging again, making "Mmmmm" sounds as loud as he could. Presently he heard a female voice say, "Robert, I think someone's in distress inside that van. Call 911."

'Robert' made the call. Within minutes, an EMT vehicle arrived. One of the crew said, "Can you hear me?" Pack slammed into the sidewall of the cargo compartment. "Do you require assistance?" More slamming.

The EMT lady broke open the driver side window, unlocked the door, and spotted Pack sitting up on the floor. She removed the duct tape as gently as she could, then opened the rear door. Her partner jumped in to help Pack out. "Get the bolt cutters and call the cops," the lady in charge told her partner.

They checked Pack's vitals and asked if he could stand. "I can," he replied, then felt his legs quiver just a little. He leaned back against the lip of the tailgate, and began to flex his arms and shoulders. "Pretty astonishing what a couple of days of being tied up can do to weaken a body, isn't it?" He smiled as he said it. "Glad to see you guys." The lady and gentleman who'd made the call had left the area. Simple Good Samaritans, Pack figured.

"Oh boy," the first cop to arrive said. "If this is who I think it is, we've become part of a big story." His partner was nonplussed. "Are you General Pack?" cop number one said.

They impounded the van and moved Pack to the station for questioning.

+++

Pack's presence at the station was a big deal. "Wow," Debra, one of the admin people in the hallway said, as she tried to catch a glimpse of Pack. "I'm a news junkie. Remember, he was held hostage at that compound up in Montana about six months ago? Geez Louise, Paul, how'd you like to be him? Leads quite the exciting life, that man does. Pretty cool, dontcha think?" A detective was inside a room questioning Pack. As Debra watched, she scooted when she observed the Fort Collins chief of police moving swiftly in her direction.

"Get back to work, Deb," the chief said, smiling weakly. "Stop your hero worship, woman."

"Yes, sir," Debra said. "Consider me gone."

The chief shook hands with Pack, introduced himself, and asked what they could do to make him more comfortable. "As you know, General, you've been the object of a federal crime, and this one is going to fall outside our jurisdiction. The FBI people are hopping to speak with you. The Denver Field Office is relatively close by, and they're on the way to transport you there. If I were you, I'd probably want to be cut loose now, but I'm afraid you'll have to tolerate this questioning for a while longer. The Feds are being close-mouthed about this. Whatever this kidnapping was about is not a blip on their screen, that I can tell you. They appear to know a lot about this character who ambushed you. Buckle your seatbelt, because they'll want every detail they can scrounge out of you. In the meantime, let's send out for something to eat and make you comfortable. If you'd like to chat about anything other than this case, there are people in this building who'd enjoy speaking with you."

"Appreciate it, chief. I'll take you up on the food, but think I'd better have a quiet room to think and make notes on the details of this experience. Don't want to leave anything out. A room in which I can pace around, get my legs and arms back in working order."

"You got it, General. We'll get you paper and pen. What can we order for you?"

+++

The Fort Collins chief had been fine. Pack wasn't happy with this FBI crew, though. They acted as if he were the criminal. He answered their questions, they gave him a break, they asked the same questions again, they gave him another break, and they asked the same questions a third time. Pack reached the limits of his collaborative and cooperative spirit. "Now it's time for you people to listen up. I've undergone a lot of crap in my life, but none to match this from what purports to be a friendly force. If this were a year ago, I as Governor would've called the Director himself and told him what a pack of asses he has in Denver. You people, you dudes, are conducting yourselves as if you're acting in a low-budget, achingly bad movie. So get on with it…no, wait, get me a lawyer. I won't be subjected to this a minute longer. And I defy any of you to call me a prima donna to my face. I don't get pissed very often, but I am at this moment. Seems to me you're an arm of the Department of Injustice. I'd bet an actual felon doesn't summon up the arrogant, superior tone you've laid on me."

The lead interrogator stepped back, and said softly, "Let's all try to lower the temperature, all right? We're going for a break ourselves, and will return after we think about how this is going."

"Do that," Pack said. "And I want that lawyer."

Forty-seven minutes later, as shown by the clock on the wall, one person came through the door. It was the Special Agent in Charge of the Denver Field Office. Pack sat in stony silence, not caring if the man was J. Edgar Hoover or Robert Mueller. The man in charge said, "Governor, I apologize for the tone my agents took with you. I sincerely do, and I hope you will accept the apology. We are releasing you in a few minutes. Would you like us to make a plane reservation for a return to Montana?"

"No, I want to go to a hotel and sleep. Then I'll decide where I'll go and when I'll leave. Don't want to put the FBI out."

"Very well. You've been through an ordeal, and from the sound of it my agents haven't fully respected that. I'd like to wrap up your visit with us by explaining a few things that ought to come only from me. First, this case has a heap of attention in Washington. I mean from the top of the top. Second, Paschal has systematically killed an unknown number of people in high places in Iraq, Afghanistan, Pakistan, Syria, and maybe in the United States. He is a pro, and as such extremely elusive. He is the top target for the Bureau as we speak. Third, records on the man do not exist. We think the CIA removed all traces of his existence from any public record, but they'll never admit that because he was a star for them. Fourth, we will ask you to keep us apprised of your whereabouts for the obvious reason, namely, that after we have reviewed your testimony, we will surely find gaps that will need to be filled in, and perhaps you can help us do that. Fifth—and I know also that you're a pro as well, with a history in black ops—please take care to watch your back and flanks. For some reason, he did not take your money and he did not kill you. Maybe he likes you, in some eccentric way. Or maybe he came to like you during the time he held you against your will. Or maybe—and the odds are against this, but still it remains a possibility—he just went away from the van for the day and expected to find you there when he returned. Point is, he's dangerous, and you might not yet be out of his gun sight."

Pack would let the Bureau do its own work. He was about to develop his own psychological profile of Blaise Paschal…with Keeley's help. Pack imagined he could be the only person ever to have gotten that close to Paschal, the only person to whom Paschal had exposed so much of his inner workings. He had witnessed the man's manic personality, his raw intelligence, the fury in his soul, his brutishness, and the kernel of good character. No one, Pack reckoned, had had the first-hand look he'd gotten. Now he had to make the most of it.

+++

Pack slumbered hard and long in the Denver hotel. He descended to the lobby area just as the complimentary breakfast was preparing to close. He was famished in a way he wasn't the night before. The great hunger was just now awakening. He ate everything they offered, one plate, then another, with multiple cups of black coffee sloshing it down to his stomach. His next order of business was to have a taxi drive him to the Apple store. He bought the latest iPhone. Somehow from the Cloud they retrieved information from his destroyed phone. He asked for his former number, and got it.

His next move was to call Mollison. Turned out—as Pack would have surmised—Mollison already knew Paschal had released Pack. Beyond that, however, Juan Martino would not go. The Sheriff was therefore elated to hear his friend on the line. "Where are you, Governor? I know somebody—and it ain't me—who wants to pick you up, if you'll let him drive the Lariat."

"I'm fine, Joe, thanks for askin'," Pack said facetiously. "Really high degree of concern you're showin' there, buddy. But, I know you will eventually ask, so let me get it out of the way: I've been checked over medically, and except for soreness at being chained for a few days, I am indeed healthy. All right, who wants to pick me up? Think I know, but go ahead."

"Mr. Tetu Palaita, who's been housesitting, more like a defender of your cabin. Big man was locked and loaded, Simon. Since he married, he feels he hasn't tended to his Matai closely enough. Man's been torn up about this. But if you want to get a flight from Denver, we'll all understand."

"Joe, you and I both know there are only two flights a week Denver to Kalispell, and the next one's two days away, so unless I take a bus, I'm stuck here for two more days anyway. It's just short of 1,100 miles from the cabin to here, so tell the big man I'll be waiting for him." He gave the address of the hotel.

"Think he'll be back to see you?" Mollison asked.

"I take it you mean the kidnapper," Pack said.

"Yep."

"Joe, I have a lot to think through about the entire episode. I believe as I stand here at this moment that the honest answer is 'with this man it'd been unwise to rule out any possibility.' You know, Joe, I think I see Tetu's coming for me as an opportunity. I'll sequester myself from now until he arrives to start trying to clarify what has just happened to me. And you also know how I've used Tetu as a sounding board since I met him? Well, tell our friend it might be like old times. Our truck ride might prove useful."

Pack went back to the hotel, got a room for two more nights—two double beds, one for Tetu—and began scribbling with the paper and pen provided.

CHAPTER TWELVE

"Tetu took care of Matai's truck, but he did drive long hours on day one," Tetu informed Pack as he embraced him. "How are you, Matai? Really, how are you?"

"I'm well, Tetu, I really am. My shoulders still hurt, and my arms felt like they were asleep for hours afterward, but it's nothing I'm concerned about. It's good to see you. Hope Swan understands, because if I were in her shoes I'm not sure I would."

"Matai, please understand, Swan loves you too. She wanted me to do this, coming for you. Remember, she knew me when I worked for you in Helena. Besides, this is chance for both of us to let some Kootenai young men show they deserve our trust. That is news Tetu has not shared with Matai. Seeing them succeed at something makes Tetu feel he also is succeeding. Tetu's Lodge will do well with them running things a while."

"OK, Tetu, I'm proud of you, as I always have been. You'll always succeed, my friend. Now let me bring you up to date on what happened. And I have to begin by saying I made a crucial error in letting my guard down around this man while my instincts were telling me the opposite."

It was early afternoon. Pack didn't want to begin the drive back until both of them got a good night's rest. Tetu would occupy the second bed. Pack left his notes in the room. They went to the hotel restaurant to talk over several cups of coffee. Pack filled him in on the facts from the moment Paschal showed his face at the cabin. Tetu listened attentively, in the same fashion he had when he worked directly for Pack as Governor. Before concluding, Pack told Tetu he had a question for him.

Tetu nodded expectantly.

"Can you hold your questions until we're inside the truck? And can we talk only about pleasant subjects this evening? For example, you can talk with me about how your Lodge is doing, about Swan's several important pursuits around the Yaak, and maybe about how our mutual friends up there are getting along? Can you do that?"

"Tetu will be happy to honor that request, Matai."

+++

The folks eating their complimentary breakfasts at the motel looked up when they observed Pack and Tetu enter. For some of them Tetu was the largest human being they'd ever seen in person. Probably thinking they'd better top off their plates while they could, before these two hulksters began clearing the trays. Both the big fellows were toting shoulder holsters under their loose windbreakers. Pack agreed with Tetu that until Paschal was either dead or in custody they ought take no chances.

They'd made many road trips together. When Pack was Governor, Tetu typically drove while Pack either made notes or read. Pack said, "At some point I'll take the wheel. Right now I think it's best for me to have hands free." He jacked the passenger seat back and leaned forward to flip on the Leonard Cohen channel on Pandora; he'd listened to the channel so many times he knew he'd hear--in addition to Leonard--Dylan, Neil Young, Mazzy Star, Pink Floyd, Cash and a little Springsteen. But he put the volume at low, made the music a pleasant background presence.

"OK, we're ready now. Let's talk. Sometimes I do my best thinking when trying to answer your questions, so ask away," Pack said.

"Tetu likes to ask the simple questions first. The five Ws and the H questions. So, where does Matai believe this man Paschal is now?"

Pack gazed out his window, pondering an answer. "Everything I reply to probably any question you ask has to be taken with a grain of dust. He is mercurial. He could go anywhere. But you understand that. The two of us need to engage in deductive reasoning, Mr. Palaita. Take what we think we know in general, then reach some specific conclusions that *seem* to make sense.

"At the risk of not answering directly, let me start with something we both understand, attacking and defending. Each has inherent advantages. If the defending force has excellent intelligence about attacking enemy dispositions and locations, he can tailor his defense to offset attacker advantages. Instead of requiring the attacker to have a three to one numerical advantage, he can force him to have at least a six to one advantage. The defender has the advantage of choosing *where* he will fight. He can position his key weapons to fire with maximum effect. He can clear fields of fire. He can use terrain to funnel enemy into designated kill zones.

"If the defender has no or poor intelligence, the attacker has the advantage, doesn't he?" Pack asked rhetorically.

"Yes, he does," Tetu replied, unnecessarily.

"And why does the attacker possess the advantage if his opponent's knowledge of his movements and formations and dispositions is poor? For one reason chiefly. It is because he chooses when, where, and by what means to attack. We know the defender can't be in heightened alert posture for long stretches without fatiguing himself."

"Right, Matai, but how would you characterize our intelligence? How much do we know about when and where he might attack? Seems we know nothing."

"I must disagree, my friend. We don't know much, granted, but our knowledge is not zero either. Let's think about what we do know," Pack said.

"He has been operating overseas on his personal mission of vengeance for years. Does he feel he's exhausted his target list over there? Probably not exhausted it, but I'm pretty confident he thinks he has done enough killing to say to himself, 'Mission Accomplished.' If that's true, he believes the remainder of those on his hit list reside in the United States. Now that we're whittling down the possibilities, let me ask you if you have a thought about where I'm going with this line of thought," Pack said.

"Tetu does have a thought, Matai, but only because he has learned from you. The thought is that we have to look at where his probable targets live in the United States," Tetu said.

"Exactly correct, Tetu. And both of us know the general location of that place. Both the government people and their military contractors happen to live in and around Washington, DC. Even the big defense aerospace outfits like Boeing, Northrop Grumman, Raytheon, and Lockheed Martin—none of which interest Paschal, I'm sure--all have headquarters around DC. Fairfax, Alexandria, Reston, McLean, Falls Church, Vienna, and so on. It's the power people in those places who need to have their guards up. They have to be near the centers of power, as well as near their lobbyists on K Street. Interesting, most of them are on the Virginia side, probably because of a tax provision, but also because the Maryland side has claimed to become the Silicon Valley of the East. Now, who else might he be interested in outside of those places?"

"Could be someone who angered him. We would not know that person's name, Matai. If he has left the company Paschal worked with, or the CIA, he could live anywhere in the country," Tetu said.

"That's right, Tetu, but the odds are the people he's tracking would be living around DC."

"So most likely if he stays in America his targets will be in Washington, DC," Tetu said.

"That's the way I see it," Pack said.

"If that's true, Matai, why did he come after you?"

Pack paused, because Tetu had struck a good point. "Right. Well, he himself answered that by claiming it's because I'm famous and have money…now."

"But he didn't take your money," Tetu said.

195

"True, he just wanted to show he could," Pack said.

Tetu followed up with, "But if the FBI and everyone involved don't speak of what he's been doing, he hasn't succeeded, has he?"

"Right, Tetu, and I've been thinking about that. Maybe they should make the public aware of his misdeeds, his criminal conduct. You're correct again, Tetu. The man seeks publicity, wants to be known, yet our government is hiding his light under a basket. Maybe I ought to discuss this with the FBI. Get his photo out there. And if they won't do it, maybe I should."

"What kind of man is he really, Matai? Self-absorbed, would you say?" Tetu said.

"I'm not sure I can go that far. He thinks of himself more as an emperor, and an emperor by definition must have an empire he is master of. I see him as having been an intensely private person all his life because he thinks of himself as both emperor and empire. His empire exists in his head. He is never alone because he always walks in this empire. Where he lives—the Middle East, Paris, Copenhagen— matters little to him, because the elements of the empire live with him, in his mind. And the empire exists wherever he is. I think people, some real, some imaginary constitute his empire. From time to time he has to re-assert control, and sometimes that involves weeding out enemies, which is what he's doing now."

"Does he have tattoos?" Tetu asked, apropos of nothing.

"None that I could see," Pack answered. "Also, no jewelry or rings or piercings. But he did have very noticeable white patches streaking his arms and face. Why?"

"I'm not sure I know," Tetu said. "Maybe one inspired by a girlfriend, something like that. Besides, lots of Marines get tattoos having to do with their pride in the Corps."

"Another interesting point, Tetu," Pack said. "He mentioned that girls asked him to the prom, but he didn't accept. And he mentioned his mother, but only to say she meant nothing to him. Other than that, no mention of females. I dismissed the notion he might be gay, on the grounds that probably would've surfaced during his time in the virtually all-male worlds he's operated in. Maybe he's asexual, although other than knowing the definition of the word, I know nothing about what it truly means. He also never mentioned killing a woman or girl, now that you raise the point."

They took a break from talking as they stopped somewhere in Wyoming for gas and a snack. Pack sat in the Lariat a few extra minutes to hear a haunting Nick Cave song moan to its conclusion. As he got out, he noted how stiff and painful his shoulders remained.

+++

The full-service Rest Areas and extravagantly large truck stops were rich boons to Blaise Paschal. The latter had showers and sometimes both had legions of closed-door toilet stalls. Behind the stalls he could work magical transformations.

Before embarking on some deep cover operations, an Agency anaplastologist would spend hours, sometimes days, endowing Paschal with a new physical identity. These anaplastologists could turn women

197

into men, make a young man an old man, create a deformity where before there was none. Print a body with realistic looking moles and scars. And it goes without saying they could cover existing blemishes as if they'd never existed. The new appearance would last a very long time. The talent and the process fascinated the inquisitive Paschal. But what to do when you needed to change appearance during the course of an operation in hostile territory? The operative couldn't take the anaplastologist with him.

The Boy Scouts have merit badges. Most professions, from engineering to medicine to the military, have available additional credentials that the enterprising among them may achieve through time and study. The Agency is no different. An enterprising agent may study to earn the credential titled 'Master of Disguise.' For the people thus awarded, changing appearance is not a simple matter of applying makeup and donning a mask. It is a skill rigorously learned which, when applied with equal rigor, will produce a result rivaling that which a professional anaplastologist could produce. The 'kit', affectionately called the "Dagger", would fit into a small paper bag and enable the individual to garner the desired effect in a matter of minutes. Blaise Paschal was never without the "Dagger."

Before ditching his most recent vehicle at a truck stop, Blaise went into the merchandise shop and bought a cheap tee shirt and cargo shorts. He changed in the toilet stall in the men's room and stowed his current clothes in the shopping bag. With handheld mirror, he began his personal transformation, an activity he had undergone many times.

The physical transformation alone usually isn't sufficient to carry the day. The agent was taught constantly to be aware of his new appearance, and to act in accordance with it at all times. If you affect a stoop, for example, or walk with a limp, you'd better be certain to remember the appropriate movements associated with the change. If you made yourself old, you had to act old. Acting was a prerequisite to success. The acting extended to voice tone, timbre, pacing, and employment of slang as well. He felt as if he knew the character whose identity he'd just assumed. He was Karl R. Farris, from California, and the face he'd created was a striking match to the face shown on the driver's license in his hand. He had formed this face and used this identity a half-dozen times without incident.

He left the stall and walked around the merchandise area a second time. None of the eight counter people seemed to recognize him from mere minutes earlier. He saw flyers for taxi services and ordered one, a standard Yellow Cab. Because this was a great place to buy burners, he purchased three more for later use. He went outside and waited for the taxi, dumping his old clothes in two separate and widely spaced dumpsters.

The cab would take 30 minutes to arrive from 15 miles away. He returned to his former vehicle and rubbed every surface free of prints. He searched for any speck of lint, any dirt, any evidence of footprints. He covered everything. Now he was back in full-undercover mode. He wanted to be recognized up in Montana, but not so here.

The lady taxi driver wanted to chat. They generally could be counted on to talk. Getting the fare to talk made drivers more comfortable, less nervous about being robbed or mugged. Blaise didn't want to be heard. He gave a faint smile she could see from her rearview, and in answer to why he needed the taxi at a truck stop, he said, "Car's being fixed there. Got to get into town for a meeting."

"Where's the meeting?" she asked.

"First Union Bank, center of town," he said. He'd just looked up the location of the bank. Believable destination, but near the bus station, his actual destination. He said no more to the lady. From the backseat, he paid her thirty-five on a twenty-five fare, and expressed a brief sincere thank you for her prompt arrival and comfortable ride. He added that last thought to expunge any reservations she might have had about the danger he presented. On the tiny chance she were questioned by some lawman.

In Memphis he bought a one-way to Washington, DC. Didn't care whether he'd gotten the last seat, but in fact every seat was taken before they drove away from the bus terminal. All but three aboard were dark-skinned. He liked that. Probably less likely to recall a Caucasian face. The black kid seated beside him near the back was content to listen to his tunes the entire way.

For a while he thought of his next moves. Didn't matter, he'd figure something out, as he always did. Identify the target: DONE. He'd had face-to-faces with the top three dudes in the outfit he'd worked for in Iraq. Couple times, come to think of it. International Anchor, they'd named their company. Self-righteous one-time Generals now out to turn big bucks. One of them, Paschal believed, was a straight-up guy who believed the business served the national interest.

Paschal also regarded that man as the smartest of the three. The other two were aggressively greedy, in his opinion. He had replayed his short discussions with them many times in his mind. And in his mind's eye he had replayed their facial expressions and overall body language. He translated their greed to three deaths that day in Fallujah, and if he hadn't been quick-witted, there would have been four. They looked down their noses at him. They should've known better.

Fix the target: he'd do his usual thing, scope them out closely, note their patterns of movement, who they spoke with, the quality of their security denial systems, when they were most vulnerable. Blaise didn't know if he'd kill them immediately or make them suffer. He smiled, thinking not many people on earth had killed in as many different ways as he. Yes, he was good at his job.

Remove the target: If you did the second step well, the third step was easy. He was on the way to their world, about to lay some hurt on them.

PART III

MASTER OF DISGUISE

CHAPTER THIRTEEN

Paschal sat in a poorly lighted alehouse for two days before he found his mark. Not exactly a mark, but at least a broad-browed man who looked honest but dim as his surroundings. He arranged for Paschal to purchase a hooptie for the grand sum of $500. Blaise personally checked it out. Wouldn't last another 50,000 miles, but would for the no-more-than 5,000 he had in mind.

He claimed another acquisition as well: three rooms in Alexandria in a place slightly superior to a flophouse, but only slightly. There were burn marks on every piece of furniture, an acrid odor of baked-in cigarette smoke, a poor seal on the mini-fridge door, dripping faucets, and water stains in the basin. But it was cheap, and Paschal/Farris was happily living beneath his means.

He developed a plan to insinuate himself into the life of his first target, former General Mike Monticule. Information on the man wasn't listed, but he had no problem finding him. He lived in Annandale, near the city's Community Park.

Paschal began by driving past the home, slowly. Figured he should do so one time only, because his almost-disreputable vehicle attracted attention he did not desire. As he passed Monticule's home, he saw a handsome Cape Cod likely built around the midpoint of the last century. No fence along front or sides. Home sat among tall trees all around the property. He could see five mulched beds of evergreen trees and flowers, all curved in shapes akin to golf bunkers, or maybe golf greens. Paschal couldn't form a strong opinion about whether

Monticule was living beneath or above his means. Large sloping lawn sitting on roughly three acres. Looked to be 4000-4500 square feet. The kind of place that would appear warm and cheery at Christmastime. It would be cold then certainly, snow likely. But it wasn't winter. At least two strong summer months left. Three-car garage. Driveway leading to the garage was the width of a two-lane highway. Pavers, not asphalt.

He drove over to the Annandale Community Park and found a parking slot. He got out and walked his way back toward Monticule's home. As Karl Farris, Paschal had adopted a leonine look, with a few well-placed moles dotting his face and upper arms, with faux tats showing on his neck and forearms. His light brown hair fell in a bushy heap to his shoulders. He could be mistaken for a man at least ten years younger than his actual mid-thirties. Today he wore the cheap cargo shorts, sneakers, and a cut-off tee, arms open to the top of the delts.

He found a common area nearby from which he could scope out the home. It was eight A.M. Monticule was probably already at work, but Paschal didn't care. He would take his time. At nine-thirty he ran over to a rest room at the park, hoping he'd miss nothing. Tomorrow, he reminded himself, bring a bottle to pee in. At around ten-thirty he saw a fit woman, mid-fifties or so, exit the house to get into a late model SUV. She wore tights and carried a gym bag, which meant she probably was going to a gym. These kinds of ladies, he thought, probably had a coffee klatch afterward, where they talked about how tough and draining their lives are. On some coming day, he might follow her. But he was getting ahead of himself. One small step at a time.

The lady of the house got back around one P.M. She came out once to look at a flowerbed, had scissors in hand, seemed to be doing some deadheading, but he couldn't see clearly. She didn't come out, to the front of the house anyway, the rest of the day. Monticule turned into the driveway at a few minutes after six. He raised the garage door remotely, and drove on in. Paschal had seen enough for the first day.

The next day he watched a lawn maintenance crew of two guys do the mowing, trimming, edging, and blowing of the Monticule place. As they were ramping their mowers onto their trailers, he stepped over to ask whether they could use another man on the crew. The older Hispanic fellow said, "Hey, man, he's always hiring day labor. New people come and go all the time." He motioned for Paschal to step a distance away from the second worker. "This guy working here with me? He might not show up tomorrow. You needin' work, man?"

"You bet, but here's the deal. I can be a steady hand, on time every day, if you start me a week from today. Just moved here and gotta get me some shelter and a ride. After that, I'm with you far into the future as you can see. What're you payin'?"

"How's, um, seven fifty a week? On a five-day week gotta do, um, about eight or nine houses a day. I do things right, and expect you will too. If you don't, man, I'll cut bait quick. You OK with that? And by the way, what's your name?"

"Name's Karl Farris." He proffered the Cali license with his name and photo. "Your offer? Good deal. What time you want me and where?" Paschal asked.

They set it up and that was that. Paschal had interest in only one job, and that was at this house. Contrary to the views he'd just expressed, he'd be gone the day after working at this house, maybe the same afternoon. He didn't like forfeiting the $150 day's pay, but he could deal with it. Hell, maybe he'd ask for the pay that day, on the grounds he had down payments and security fees to pay up front. Yeah, that's what he'd do.

He hadn't forgotten to keep an eye on the Monticule woman. She'd followed the same routine as the day before, on the same schedule. The timing of her coming and going suggested she was involved in a class at the gym. He'd know in another day or two, because he was now about to follow her, tomorrow.

+++

They left the gas station in Wyoming, continuing their return to Montana. Tetu said, "You think he'll be back after you, Matai?"

"Very, very unlikely, Tetu," Pack said. "I don't think there's room to doubt that he released me. He fed me some concoction that knocked me out for most of the day. Yeah, it's possible he did it to keep me quiet until he returned, but I'd say he did it to gain time to put distance between us. I'm sure he is capable of opening a car door and hotwiring it in, oh, under a minute. They ought to be looking for stolen cars within a couple mile radius of that motel. What business would he have had in Fort Collins? None is my answer."

"Why did he let you go?" Tetu said.

"You'd have to ask him to know for sure. But we're in the surmising business here, aren't we?" Pack replied. "Given that we get nowhere unless we make educated guesses at this point, I surmise it has something to do with my being a fellow Marine. Much as man tries to sever that bond of Marine-hood, it's awfully hard to do come nutcracking time. Maybe he didn't consciously consider that, but at some level I believe it was a factor. A second factor may have been that he respected me. I didn't kowtow to him. He had the power—and I hate admitting that—in our brief relationship on the road, but I didn't hesitate to disagree with him. I'm not sure he anticipated that. A third factor perhaps was his wish for me to spread the word about him. Has he crossed over from avenger to fame-seeker? I'm thinking all of these played a role in his releasing me. Further, I suspect he wants me to be grateful that he let me go unharmed. More than grateful…indebted…yeah, as I ponder this, I do think he wants to believe I'm in his debt."

"How do you feel, Matai? Do you feel indebted?" Tetu asked.

"For sure I do not. Absolutely not. He zapped the wrong man, Tetu. Somehow, I aim to get him, and I believe, in some way I can't explain at the moment, I'll bring him down before any law enforcement agency.

"Look, Tetu, for a long time I'll question whether I should have resisted him physically. Maybe I'll wake up one day and in a blinding flash see a moment when an opportunity presented itself, but right now I think I played it right. He should be concerned, maybe worried, that I'll figure out a way to stop him. If I can't do it, who can?"

"I believe you can, Matai," Tetu said, "and I tell you Tetu is volunteering to help. We are a team. Do you know another man like me, Matai?"

Pack grinned broadly, turning toward Tetu. "Nobody has a better right-hand man than you, Tetu. Not Tonto to the Lone Ranger, not Festus to Marshall Dillon, not Nora to Nick Charles."

"Thank you, Matai, although I do not know the Charles people."

They were about a hundred miles from the cabin when Pack's phone chimed. He fished it out, answering "Pack here."

"Hello, General. This is Juan Martino, FBI, Kalispell office."

"Sure, Juan. How could I forget being detained at your facility?" Pack said, making little effort to sound amicable.

"Sorry about that, but my recall is it turned out well. Anyway, my reason for calling is to tell you I've received an Interrogatory, a list of questions, from my higher ups. They'd like a reply yesterday, of course. Can you help a poor agent out?" Martino said.

Pack said, "Juan, I respect how you handled that situation with Governor Dahl and me and Sheriff Mollison. You're right about it turning out well. But I have to say, your FBI hasn't treated me right, in my opinion. My days of being pushed around are over. I threatened those—pardon me, jerk agents—in Denver with having a lawyer speak for me. Should I have a lawyer, Juan?"

"That's up to you, General. But honestly, do you genuinely believe I'm hostile to anything you say or stand for? I can assure you, I am not. The deepest part of me respects you a great deal, although as long as we're doing business I shouldn't have said that."

"All right, Juan, my skin is just overly tender from meeting with those Denver people. Thanks for hearing me vent. I also know deep down you're one of the good guys. So, with that out of the way, what can I do for you?"

"Back to the Interrogatory they plunked on me: I can come to your place or you can come to Kalispell," Martino said.

"Come to my place then. Tomorrow?"

"Good, no later than mid-morning. I'll phone when I'm thirty minutes out," Martino said.

"I have an idea, Matai," Tetu said.

"I'm listening," Pack said.

"Tetu heard Matai say he will meet Agent Martino tomorrow morning. My proposal: I stay at the cabin tonight, I go out when Agent Martino comes, then I return to cabin. Then I help you organize cabin as you want it. After that we drive both vehicles to my Lodge. You stay with me a little while. We have room, you know. Swan would enjoy your company. You could come and go as you please. Maybe we could talk and plan."

"You're a wily fellow, Tetu. Usually you're a step ahead of me. I accept your offer," Pack said.

+++

Juan Martino arrived on schedule. Tetu drove into town to kill time as Pack and Martino conducted private business. In truth, however, nothing would be said that Tetu had not heard during the drive from Denver.

Tetu decided to see if Sheriff Mollison was in. Mollison saw Tetu first. "Hey, big man, get on over here. It's always a special event when you show up. How're you doin'?"

"I'm good, Sheriff Joe," Tetu said, "maybe better than the General. He's up at the cabin meeting with Agent Martino now. Hope it turns out better than his meeting with the FBI in Denver. General says they treated him like a criminal, and boy, Sheriff, he was not pleased with them. Threatened to have a lawyer speak for him. You know they had to anger him bad for him to say that. Boss of Denver FBI tried to smooth things over, but General still wasn't happy. Guess they didn't get what they needed, so they sent questions to Agent Martino to go over with General. Anyway, Sheriff, once Agent is gone, I'm taking General to Lodge for a while. Would you keep an eye on cabin while he's away?"

"Sure will, Tetu. I'll personally go by up there different times every day. How long'll he be at your place?"

"Don't know, Sheriff. I tell you in confidential, he wants to get this man himself. Wonder if he'll tell FBI all he knows? We will maybe make plan to trap him," Tetu said.

"How you gonna do that?" Mollison asked.

"We don't know yet, but the General wins fights, doesn't he?" Tetu said.

"He does that," Mollison muttered with admiration. "But you better not leave me outta the equation, you hear me, Tetu?"

"The General never forgets Sheriff Mollison," Tetu concluded.

+++

Agent Martino was saying, "The man in charge somewhere, whether Denver or higher I don't know, thinks they got good facts from you, but not much of value about *who* Paschal is. How did you size him up? What do you think his next steps will be? By the way, General, I'm required to tape this conversation, which I'm now informing you of, for the record." He went on, for the record, to establish the location of the meeting, the full names of the subjects involved, and so forth. Boilerplate stuff.

"As I understand your question, Agent Martino,' Pack said, being sure to speak into the recorder, "you're asking me to voice opinions, albeit opinions based on my several days with Blaise Paschal, as well as on my previous association with him as a member of my Division. I'm willing to do this, with the perfect understanding these are indeed opinions. I know what he recited to me, information about people, places, and events he claimed to be true. I cannot, of course, attest to the truth of any bit of information he presented.

"I'll begin with the assertion he's a complicated person. We all are, I guess, but he's more complicated than most. To structure my analysis of Paschal the person, I will use a framework of the Seven

Cardinal Sins. In case you're a bit rusty, they are Lust, Gluttony, Sloth, Wrath, Envy, Greed, and Pride.

"By Lust I mean unbridled sexual desire, some kind of disordered love for other individuals. He seemed to me to be without any form of sexual desire. I thought of him as asexual, not genuinely understanding what that means. As I told my friend Tetu, I do not see him as homosexual, in that I believe that would have come out in the virtually all-male world he's existed in most of his life. Similarly, his failure to speak of females in any meaningful fashion, excepting an expression of loathing for his mother, causes me to conclude he is no predator of women. Further, he spoke of no violence directed toward women or girls.

"Gluttony and Greed are both sins of desire, so I'll address them together. He spoke of himself as being guided by a desire to live beneath his means. He mentioned nothing that led me to think he overindulges or overconsumes anything to the point of waste. With respect to Greed, I noted no rapacious desire or pursuit of material possessions. He lives a nomadic life, and has, I would imagine, what he carries with him and nothing more. As he reminded me, he turned down two million dollars belonging to me, and he was confident he could've pulled off the caper.

"Sloth means to me a habitual disinclination to exertion. He is most affirmatively not guilty of this sin. He stays highly active in both mind and body. To the contrary, he is a model of the rigorous lifestyle.

"We all understand the sin of Wrath, I think. Anger, rage, hatred, self-destructive behavior. He does carry heavy baggage relative to this sin. From his earliest years he was resentful of the hellhole he lived in. Through his own will and intelligence, though, he escaped that life and found a measure of solace in the Marine Corps. But he was as much of a loner as a man in the Corps can be. I saw that he had no long-term future as a Marine, and it was I who put the CIA on his scent. They took him, and according to his testimony to me, and I believe him, he was a natural deep cover agent. They awarded him several times, he says, for perilous duty performed well."

Marino interrupted Pack to feign surprise that the Company would not admit he worked for them. And also genuine surprise that it was Pack who alerted them to Paschal.

"Of course they won't admit it," Pack said. "We both know that's their M.O., and to deviate from standard practice would be scandalous in this case. So I'm not expecting them to cooperate with anyone in this matter.

"Envy is an interesting one," Pack went on. "Is he covetous of traits or possessions of others? I don't see it. He believes he's already at the top of the heap. I told Tetu he thinks of himself as an Emperor, which is why he's never lonely. His empire is made up of some real people, and some fictitious people, and he rules them all. For a time he was my ruler, in his mind, and I did his bidding. Living in his empire is dangerous, because the people in it never know when he's going to give them an arbitrary thumbs-down.

"The one I've saved for last is the one most systems of theology consider the most serious. That is Pride. In part, it entails failing to recognize the accomplishments of others. In part, it entails putting one's own wants, desires, and whims ahead of the welfare of the general population. I think all I've averred to this point paints the picture of a man consumed with Pride. I actually wanted him out of the Corps because he was incapable of placing the welfare of his men ahead of his own desires. Yes, he is guilty of the sin of Pride, in my opinion. At this point, sir, we have to hope there is truth in the expression 'pride goeth before a fall.'"

"Thanks for the analysis, General. Nice job," Marino added. "Now what do you speculate he'll do next?"

"I think he thinks he's finished overseas. If anything remains for him to do over there, he'd see it as mopping up. So, um, I expect he thinks he has business in America. If I were the Bureau, I'd be looking at the greater DC area. Find out the outfit he worked for, find the execs who might've had direct contact with him, and tell them to be careful. I'd ask if any of them who did meet him can recall anything in his body language that indicated he didn't like them."

After saying this taped interview had concluded, Martino flipped off his recorder.

"And one more thing, Juan. After thinking this through, I believe it's time to expose him to the public."

Juan Martino looked sheepish, like maybe he was embarrassed to disagree. "I'll pass your view up the chain, General, but from what I hear the Director is much opposed to the idea."

"Why?" Pack asked, figuring he already knew the answer.

"You'd have to ask the Director to know for certain, but those guys up in DC take protecting one another damn seriously. The CIA and FBI Directors are more or less on an even plane, and they take pains to avoid criticizing one another."

"Well, Juan, let's hope protecting American citizens is regarded as more important than an interagency food fight."

CHAPTER FOURTEEN

The next morning, pee bottle in his daypack, Paschal took up a vantage spot among the shrubs across from the Monticule residence. Knowing he would follow the Missus today, he wore a long-sleeved shirt and long trousers, presenting a more decent appearance. It was six A.M. At six-fifteen retired General Mike Monticule backed his Porsche Boxster out of the driveway. He carried a briefcase. Paschal thought he might follow him to work within the next day or two. The thought swept through his mind that he might have trouble maintaining the speed to keep pace with the Boxster. Maybe he ought to just be ready at the entrance to his work lot, and follow him in from that point.

He waited for Monticule's wife to appear. She came out on schedule at ten-thirty. As he saw the garage door lift, he ran to his old vehicle and waited to tail her. As she intersected with the main road, he fell in behind her. She drove cautiously. To the apparent consternation of some behind her, she never exceeded the posted speed. Fortunately, the gym was no more than two miles from her home. *"These things,"* *Farris/Paschal was thinking, "need renaming. A gym is grimy, a* *rundown building where hardcore training for combat sports takes* *place. This place looks how an Apple Headquarters is supposed to."* It had four floors and was probably forty thousand square feet. He had to get closer than he'd hoped in order to spot her when she came out of whichever of the countless rooms she was headed for. He saw her link up with four other ladies who seemed to be going to the same place. They'd seen each other just yesterday but acted as if it'd been years.

They waited outside a big room until another class wound up. At least fifty women between twenty and fifty filed out, still wiping perspiration from their bodies. Many men would've found their appearance lascivious, but Blaise Paschal had no reaction to them. Instead, from a safe distance he observed the next horde enter to go through whatever paces were required inside. Two heavy doors opened to the matted room. Each door had a narrow rectangular window cut into it. The instructor was on an elevated platform with a wireless mic draping her neck, and presently began hopping around as if she were headlining a show in Vegas. The ladies fell into their assigned positions and began doing what appeared to Paschal to be a combination of yoga and Pilates, Piyo he'd heard the new fad called.

They probably had cameras in here, he thought, and he didn't want to appear to be a stalker that would draw the attention of security, so he set off, trying to move with purpose, as if he knew where he was going. He found a sign indicating the direction of the juice bar. Reckoned he'd be safe if he hung out there for forty or forty-five minutes, the minimum length of Mrs. Monticule's class. Then he would wait behind a column for them to spill out of the class and follow her again.

The juice bar had a wall full of offerings, most healthy but some not so. He settled for a coffee and bagel. He found a table and flipped through one of the numerous fitness magazines lying around. The requisite time passed and he ventured back up. His wait wasn't long. One class followed immediately after another, so the rule was no dawdling inside the exercise room. They streamed out swiftly, chatting madly, talking about the strenuousness of the workout, the brilliance of the exercise leader, blah blah. A number of them headed in the direction of the juice bar. Mrs. Monticule was among them. Luckily for Paschal, this was a coed emporium, so he wasn't totally out of place. The group of ladies he was interested in got in line to place their bar orders. Paschal followed suit. He could overhear them talking about their husbands.

Presently, one of the ladies said to Mrs. Monticule, "Hey, Trish, Jim hasn't seen Mike in ages, and he enjoys his company so much. He made me promise to send Mike a message. Said to tell him he has a tee time for a foursome on Saturday, and is holding one of the places for Mike. Tee time is nine, so he could be home by one or two."

Mrs. Trish Monticule replied, "Gosh, Pammy, he enjoys Jim so much too, and he'll be sorry he missed out, but he's flying out Friday and won't return till the following Wednesday."

Paschal dropped out of the queue. He didn't want another coffee and bagel, and he'd gotten what he came for. Now he had to decide which direction he'd go. This was working out well. No need to take that lawn job.

+++

Tetu arrived back at Pack's cabin around mid-afternoon, well after Agent Juan Martino had finished the interrogation. He found Pack downstairs in his office. "How did it work out, Matai?"

"I answered the questions he asked, fully I believe, and I therefore am satisfied," Pack said. "Don't know what more I could've done."

"Did you ask him to, ah, bring the man to the public attention?" Tetu said.

"I did, but he doesn't think that will happen. I'm sure he'll do his part, which is to forward my opinion, but whether they'll accept the advice is their call. That said, I tend to agree with Martino that they won't see it my way. Covering for one another is more important."

"Tell me, Matai, is there another way to expose this man?"

"Of course, Tetu. I can think of two. One, I do it myself. I tell the press I have a major announcement, and I believe they'd show up with their notebooks and cameras. Two, I speak to General Green about it. He's a helluva good man, and might press the issue in Washington on my behalf, but I hate to put him in that position. I'll have to chew it over a while longer."

"When will we go to the Lodge, Matai? I'll go now if you will say you'll come in the morning."

"That's good with me, Tetu. Go on up, partner. I promise I'll be up tomorrow no later than ten," Pack said. "Thanks for the help. For picking me up, for helping me think through this situation, for offering great advice. You've been invaluable these five or six years, and I thank you."

"Aw, Matai, you give Tetu too much credit. He doesn't do much, but he does agree with the part about always being available to help the Matai he loves," Tetu said. "Tetu is happy to see Matai safe at home. This man might come around again. Remember that. Tighten your doors tonight and sleep with a good rifle. Miss Keeley would insist on it."

"Will do, Tetu. Drive safely."

+++

Swan wasn't expecting Tetu back until tomorrow. She'd stayed late working at the church. Preparing her message for Sunday. Swan had irons in many fires around the Upper Yaak. She and a few ladies had resuscitated the dingy old wooden structure the Kootenai Tribe had ceded to the church. It wasn't being used for anything by the tribe. Now it was mildly inviting, and Swan had future plans for the building as funds became available. Thanks to volunteers its interior sported a fresh coat of paint and chairs sufficient to accommodate a hundred people. Not much, but a start. She had plans to install a second wood stove at the back of the church before the bitter winter cold arrived. The parking area wasn't paved, but a large natural open area meant there was no problem finding a parking space. Getting to it could be a challenge, but enough people had four wheelers, and were willing to pick up neighbors, that if one wanted to attend church in this rocky, rooted, rutted place, there was a way to get there. The *unum necessarium* was will. It could be sloughy and boggy, though, when the rare warm winter day partially melted the snow and ice. They liked Swan, and word about her excellent presentations had spread. More came to hear her, and to participate in the singing and general fellowship, with each passing week. In particular, more members of the Kootenai tribe were showing up.

The attraction for the Kootenai was twofold: one, her messages were Bible-based and uplifting. She presented a wholesome, lovely, and loving countenance, and she spoke eloquently. For many of the younger tribal members, she was an example of the benefits that could accrue when one received a good education and was motivated by strong moral values. The second attraction for the Kootenai youth was her social work with young members. She gave hope to abused young girls, of whom there were too many. Swan knew of all the studies showing that no ethnic category in America suffered as high an incidence of abuse as Native American girls. She had seen it all too often in her own Blackfoot upbringing. Her personal mission was to do her small part to overturn that problem. If she could make a demonstrable difference here in Kootenai territory, who knew, maybe she could export her solutions to other tribes. So, because she dealt with so many Kootenai youth, they translated their support for her social work over into her church.

Tetu had been concerned that Swan wasn't at home when he got to the Lodge at seven P.M. He was about to go up to the church to find her when he heard a car pulling up outside. It was Swan in her reliable Subaru Forester. Tetu embraced her for longer than he needed to, relieved to find her OK. "What's the matter, Tetu?" Swan asked. "I was just working on my message in the quiet of the church. Look at me. I'm fine."

"I am on edge, Swan, I guess because Matai was kidnapped, and the man who did it remains free. I am happy to see you. Now I am good, seeing you are home."

The following morning Tetu was up earlier than normal, eager to get the Lodge up and running. He checked on the three Kootenai men to be sure the hunters' breakfast was being prepared to standard, the tables set properly, everything was clean, and the larders were full. Young Tommy, the kid from up the road at Georgann's General Store, came before school three days a week to update stock levels on food and fuel, and occasionally on replacement parts required. From Tommy's records replenishment lists were drawn up and an adult made resupply runs. Tetu was satisfied with all he saw, and took a moment to hug the fatherless Tommy and compliment him on an important job well done. Tetu was indeed happy this morning, the more so because in a few more hours Matai would be on the grounds.

Swan came into the kitchen, gave Tetu a hug and kiss, and told him she had an appointment at nine.

"Who's it with?" he asked. He was aware she would not violate confidentiality, but might let him in on the topic.

"Sixteen-year-old female, her thirteen-year-old sister is missing. Been gone a week, and my client is deeply shaken. Thinks she knows the abductors, and fears what they may have done to her."

Tetu said, "But you're a social worker, Swan. What she reports is the business of the law. What can you do to help?"

"I can visit the res police on her behalf. I can seek representation for the poor child. You know, Tetu, everywhere in

America we keep missing persons records on females. Everywhere but on Native American reservations. It is a disgrace, but no one seems to care. I care, and I will fight for these girls. It is my duty," Swan said.

"Tetu hopes," he said, shifting seamlessly to his use of third person to refer to himself, "it is a mistake, that she will appear today at her home."

"And so do I, Tetu. You are a fine man. I love you. Now I must go. See you about three, I hope, but maybe an hour or so later."

+++

Pack's Lariat pulled in shortly before ten. He'd toted a couple of heavy bags with him. Tetu was in the office and watched Pack's vehicle. He hustled out to help Pack with the bags. "Great, Matai is here!" Tetu fairly screamed. "Let me help with the bags and show you to your room. This is the first time you will stay in my home."

Pack rendered a sharp salute and told Tetu he was glad to join him and Swan for a few days. Tetu's home sat off to the left rear of the Lodge not far from the swift-flowing Yaak River. It was a comfortable two-story log home. Tetu said, "Follow me upstairs, Matai. You will be the first honored guest to sleep upstairs."

"Thanks, Taits," Pack said, calling him by a rarely-deployed hypocorism. "This is a beautiful home. I see why you wanted me to come here. My humble cabin wasn't good enough for you."

"Come on, Matai," Tetu laughed. "Your cabin to me is a palace."

Pack convinced Tetu to go about his business for the day, and said they could get together at the home or the Lodge bar later in the day. He also offered to buy dinner for Tetu and Swan at Tetu's own Lodge, which happened to be about the only place in Yaak where one might order a meal off a menu.

+++

At around four-thirty, from the kitchen Tetu could hear the sounds of a familiar voice yelling above the outdoorsmen at the bar: "Where's Tetu?" he intoned insistently. Tetu came running from the back. The man was Craig Wood, the mountain man and local medicine man, known to everyone in the valley.

Tetu's heart was thumping madly. Craig was a man accustomed to dealing with exigent circumstances, so something serious must be underway. Before he could speak, Craig said, "You better get up to the church. I was delivering flowers from Judith for the Sunday service. There was a Kootenai girl cowering in the corner, as afraid as I believe I've ever seen anyone. Didn't want me near her. Said only Tetu she will speak with. I think something's happened to Swan, that maybe somebody took her away. She was mumbling and crying, hard to understand, but I think it was something about Swan being taken."

Tetu thwopped Craig on the shoulder, his way under the circumstances of saying thanks, as he ran past him toward the door. "Mr. Wood, please follow us back up there," he said over his shoulder.

He ran into his house to grab a weapon as he yelled for Pack to appear. No answer from Pack. He ran outside, calling for Pack in his loudest voice. From below, walking near the stream, Pack heard, and yelled back. "On my way, Tetu," Pack yelled back, feeling a bilious rumble in his stomach. Pack scrambled up the hillside as swiftly as his feet could.

"Matai, I think somebody has taken Swan. We have to go to the church immediately. Let's go."

"My vehicle, Tetu. I have a bag of weapons inside. Get in and let's go." Tetu noticed Craig Wood was already in his vehicle with the engine running.

Once in the Lariat, Pack handed his smartphone to Tetu, saying, "Martino's personal number is in the Contacts. Call him and tell him to stand by for a later call. We might need him. Don't go into detail." Tetu complied.

It was ten miles to the church, the last two up the rocks and stumps and roots. Pack drove with single-minded focus, jostling them furiously even while belted in. As they neared the church, Tetu said, "Inside is a frightened girl. No weapons yet. Let me go in alone first. She asked for me."

Pack got out as Tetu went in. Pack pulled from his bag a Marlin Model 1895 SBC lever-action rifle. Stainless finish with ag ray laminated wood stock. Sitting atop it was a Leopold Optics FX-II Scout IER, 2.5 x 28mm scope with stainless finish. A weapon with knockdown power. Tetu had left a Glock 19 resting on his seat. Both men were thinking of a showdown with Blaise Paschal.

Tetu collected himself before he entered, willing himself to appear calm in front of the girl. He suspected it was the sixteen-year-old female Swan had spoken of this morning.

She was still curled tight into herself in the manner Craig Wood had described. It was dim in the building at this hour. Craig himself installed lighting several months ago, but it was not enough to illuminate the room brightly. Tetu stayed a respectful distance from the girl, maybe fifteen feet, to give her a chance to trust him. "I am Tetu, Swan's husband," Tetu said gently. "No one can hurt you. Please let me take you home. And I would like you to explain everything that happened to my wife. We must save her."

"I have seen you, Mr. Tetu." She stopped as she sobbed more. Tetu could observe her begin to uncoil. She put out a hand to be helped up. Tetu approached with care, and lifted her off the floor as if she weighed nothing. Don't press too hard, he told himself.

"Swan was working with me. She is so good. She helps me. Three men came in with guns. They handled her roughly, told her they are holding her accountable. They shoved me down and pointed their guns at me, saying if I moved they would shoot me." She sobbed more.

"Do you know these men?" Tetu asked.

"All I know is they are Kootenai, not from around the Yaak, but farther down in the Reservation seat of government. They have come up here before, speaking for the res government, they say, ordering us to do things their way. They are dictators, Mr. Tetu."

"Do you think they have taken her to Pablo?" Tetu asked. Pablo was the seat of the Kootenai reservation.

"Yes, sir, I believe they have taken her there," the girl stammered.

"What is your name, young lady?" Tetu asked politely.

"It is Little Deer, Mr. Tetu."

"Do you trust me, Little Deer?"

"Yes, I do."

"Then may I ask you to go with Mr. Craig Wood? He will drive you home. I would trust him with my life, and I have. He will treat you with kindness and total respect, Little Deer."

"Thank you. I will go with him." She reached out to the giant and squeezed his hand.

+++

Pack ignored the speed limit signs. It was a four-hour drive to Pablo. They would get there around nine if all went well. The abductors had about an hour head start on them. They drove in silence for a while before Tetu spoke: "Maybe this will be awkward, Matai. You were Governor. You have met these people. You have sat with them, talked with them, eaten with them. You can't go in there with a weapon. Maybe you stay outside, I go in and find her. Swan is my wife, my responsibility. What do you think?"

"I know Pablo well, Tetu. They have a law enforcement center. One building houses police, courtroom, meeting rooms, jail, all of it. That's most likely where they have taken her. They have a police force of five, I think, or did a few years ago.

"Now, if I were you I'd be thinking the same as you. I'd see it as my responsibility to get her. But see, I'm not sure your position is the correct one. I was in fact the Governor. That might carry a little weight still. Not sure about that. They have received me well in the past, is all I'm saying, so maybe the better approach is for me to go in alone. Let's think on this thing a little more."

"Do you think Paschal is behind this, Matai? If he is, that changes everything, in my mind," Tetu said.

"I don't think so. What leverage would he have over these people? None that comes to mind. To be honest, Tetu, this situation isn't good, but it's a bit of a relief to believe Paschal has nothing to do with it."

"Then let's do as Matai says and think about what we do in Pablo," Tetu said.

CHAPTER FIFTEEN

On this Thursday morning, Paschal got out early. At 3:30 A.M. he went into the extended stay motel's business center. Even he was surprised when the day before he'd looked to see if they had a computer and printer available. A chair and table in a shallow alcove off to the side of the reception desk made up the 'business centre.' Yes, 'center' was spelled in British style to imbue it with a cachet it manifestly did not merit, Paschal supposed. The clerk was in a back room, presumably snoozing on a cot as Paschal did his business. He typed out in size 18 font, bold, the words of a brief message he would leave for the Piyo-sculpted Trish Monticule.

Then he fondled an object he'd picked up at the Salvation Army store the day before. He drove his hooptie on over to the International Anchor offices in Fairfax. The company did not have its own mega-headquarters. By the standards of a Northrop Grumman or Raytheon, it was a small operation—in terms of capital, that was true, but not necessarily in terms of global influence. He was looking now at a twelve-story brick building that housed a number of companies. International Anchor occupied less than one floor of the building.

Paschal had been here before, during his initial job interview with the top dogs of the organization. Their bank of parking slots was in the location he remembered. He took one of the Visitor spots a couple of hundred feet away and waited. Mostly it was the people who regarded themselves as mission essential who arrived this early. Perhaps one in ten spots were occupied at this hour.

He needed to get near Monticule, chest to chest with the man if he could. Cameras attached to the building probably couldn't get a clear shot of him, but he assumed the worst. If the camera captured his appearance, no one would recognize him as Blaise Paschal. He would remain Karl Farris for a few more hours.

Right on time, Monticule showed up. Farris/Paschal acted as if he'd just exited an eye-catching sports car not far down the line. In a friendly, cheerful voice he called out, "I'll be damned, is that you, Mike Monticule? It's been forever and a day!"

Monticule himself was no dummy. He had achieved high enough status to understand there were many people he'd worked with over the years for whom he potentially was a target. He always carried. His hand almost unconsciously felt in his jacket pocket for the Ruger .380 it contained. He stood unspeaking next to his Boxster as the stranger approached. "Do I know you?" he said finally.

"Well, inspect me, sir. We went to the War College together. I'll give you my initials and you tell me if you can come up with a name," Paschal said as he kept walking in Monticule's direction.

"We've changed a lot since then, which was a long time ago," Monticule said. For a reason he couldn't explain, he was growing a bit nervous about this person. His view of the fellow was not quite distinct, but he certainly looked too young to have been a War College classmate. But he didn't take decisive action. He simply stood there waiting for something to happen.

Paschal closed to within three feet when he saw the Ruger begin to come out of the jacket. Paschal was faster with his Glock. He plugged Monticule with three rounds before the Ruger was fully out of the pocket. "Damn you, Monticule," Paschal said to himself. He scanned the lot the full 360 degrees. Someone may have seen it, but if they had he couldn't see them. He had intended to beat the man to death, not shoot him. Self-defense, he told himself, as he made for his shabby vehicle.

He had driven five miles away from Monticule's building and no one was tailing him. He was enroute back to the Annandale Community Park. He took up his spot in the shrubs across from the Monticule home. He suspected the sculpted Trish would be upset at missing her Piyo today.

At a few minutes before eight-thirty the garage door climbed up its track. Trish backed her SUV out and sped away. Not disguising his Karl Farris self, he walked deliberately toward the home. From the moment he pulled the paper from the printer, he'd handled it with another sheet. He tucked his folded sheet of plain white typing paper into the mailbox. It said: "IF YOU HADN'T TOLD ME MIKE COULDN'T PLAY GOLF WITH MY JIM THIS SAT., HE WOULD STILL BE ALIVE. LOOSE LIPS SINK SHIPS, TRISH. CAREFUL WHAT YOU SAY AT OUR GYM. BE REAL CAREFUL, SISTER. YOU COULD BE NEXT. I MIGHT COME FOR YOU. YOUR FORMER FRIEND, PAMMY."

+++

Pack's phone rang as he and Tetu sped toward Pablo. He handed it to Tetu, asking him to take a message. "This is Tetu answering for General Pack."

It was Agent Martino. "Tetu, I need to speak with the General."

Tetu said, "He is driving now, pretty fast. Can't take his eyes off road."

"This is pretty important," Martino said. "Can't he pull over to take it?"

"Sorry, no. Does this concern what I called about this afternoon? If it is, we won't need your help yet. Matai will call when he can. This is emergency we have now."

"OK, Tetu. Please tell him this has to do with Paschal. I think it's very important. As soon as he can, have him call me," Martino said. Then he added, frustrated, "What in hell's goin' on that's so important he can't talk about Paschal?"

"My wife Swan is in danger, maybe bad danger. We are going for her. We will call if we need you. Sorry, must go now," Tetu said, switching the line off.

"Good job, Tetu," Pack said. "Paschal can wait. Swan is number one right now."

+++

They had decided, with Tetu concurring reluctantly, that Pack would enter the Law Enforcement Center alone. Although no time limit had been established, they further agreed that if he did not come out with

Swan after a reasonable period of time, Tetu was coming in. No doubt he would enter in a high state of rage.

A Kootenai woman, eaten up with ennui, if her posture offered a clue, sat at a desk just inside the main entrance. Pack nodded politely, and said, "Ma'am, I'm looking for Swan Palaita. I believe she was brought here within the last hour. Where is she?"

The woman looked nonplussed. "You are Governor Pack. We know you. I'm not supposed to let anyone enter, but I suppose you are different. Everyone knows you. They are in the courtroom."

"Thank you, ma'am. I'm going to have a look in," Pack said.

Pack turned the handle, straightening himself into his most erect posture. At a glance, he saw Swan sitting in a witness chair flanked by two armed men. Half-dozen Kootenai men occupied seats in a front row. A man appeared to be questioning her, but froze when Pack entered. This man observed Pack stride deliberately toward the front of the room. When Swan saw Pack she attempted to escape her chair and run to him, but was thrown back roughly by the armed men at her side.

"I am here," Pack said, "to walk away with this woman. She has done you no harm, and what you are doing is unconscionable in a civil society. You cannot believe this is what your noble tribe stands for."

"Governor Pack, you have no authority here. You do not know why we have brought this woman before this court."

"I am all ears. Explain yourself," Pack said.

233

"We owe you no explanation, but because you were the Governor of this state and treated us respectfully, I will return the good turn. There are five hundred sixty-five nations of Native American peoples recognized by your Bureau of Indian Affairs. Some take no money and are not indebted to the federal government. Some of us feel we must, and so we do. But always there are strings attached, and we remain the pawns of Washington in the same ways we were in the early nineteen hundreds. They rob us of our dignity. They put us in boarding schools run by whites against our will. They try to tell us what we can and cannot teach in our schools. They say, 'you cannot build that road. You cannot harvest the petroleum that lies beneath your land. You can use this water but not that water,' and so on. We are serfs. Our braves are emasculated. We have a police force of five for an immense territory."

Pack interrupted. "I have heard these arguments before, and have fought Washington on your behalf. I got many concessions. But you cannot live in the past. Would your warrior ancestors approve your taking a young woman at gunpoint, a Blackfoot woman who loves your tribe as much as her own? Would they have approved your men terrifying an innocent young Kootenai girl called Little Deer at gunpoint? Men of any race must act like men; they do not treat women in such a fashion. How do you expect me to respect you if you do not respect your own women and children? Surely you have a stronger argument than you have presented, do you not?"

"You speak the truth, Pack, when you say we surely have stronger arguments. We do. This woman," he said, pointing at Swan, "is guilty of attempting to destroy the values of this tribe. She has a church, the white man's church, which she is using to steal Kootenai away from our native beliefs. Who gave her this right? Our tribal council rejects her teachings. And we have our own college, where the Psychology Department rejects as heretical her private teachings to some of our young people who go to her for answers. It is our right to ban her from Kootenai land, and to close down the church she uses."

Pack said, "Have you spoken with any of the youth she has helped? She is doing much more than giving them hope. She is inspiring them to work, to learn, to help your braves from attacking your young females. Her husband, my friend, employs three of the young men at his business. You cannot deny that many of your girls have gone missing, many beaten, and an alarming number raped by young men who feel trapped in the dead-end world of the res. I know Swan Threemoons, now Swan Palaita, and she emphatically does not want them to become white, nor does she want them to leave this reservation. She wants the Kootenai society to function to its full potential. She comes with love. And this is how you treat her? You ought to feel shame."

The man was struggling to counter Pack. He said, without passion, "You know you have no jurisdiction here. We could physically escort you out of here, and we might. And, because she is Native but not Kootenai, we could do much worse to Threemoons."

"Yes, you could do that, and if you did, I promise that before the daylight shines, my FBI contacts will be here to assume control of this matter. I have the means to make life more difficult for your people. I don't wish to do so, but I would and I will if you do not meet several conditions."

The oldest man in the front row stood, and said with authority, raising his hand: "This Governor has been respectful of our people. Let us hear his conditions."

Pack said, "Thank you, Chief. One, Swan Palaita must be released now, with me, not an hour later, not tomorrow. Two, you are far removed in space and time from the northern branch of your tribe that has developed confidence in Swan and supported her magnificently, so I ask you to consult with them, and let their voices be heard. If they wish to continue allowing her to use the building for her church, let it be so. Three, hard as it might be, apologize to Little Deer. That young woman would take that as a sign that real men, the genuine leaders of this nation, are concerned about her. Four, I ask both you and Swan to meet on a schedule, perhaps once per quarter. In such meetings she would present to you the kinds of issues she has been involved with and inform you of the recommendations and suggestions she has made. There need be no secrets between you. She will take part willingly and respectfully, I can assure you. Last, I will ask Swan to speak on her own behalf, and to tell you—and me—if anything I have said about her is untrue."

The old Chief pondered, then replied, "You and Swan Threemoons will step outside while I discuss this with the council. You will not leave. We will call you to return."

Appearing relieved, Swan moved toward Pack. The moment they were in the hallway, Swan said, "Where is Tetu, Simon? Is Tetu safe and does he know what has happened?"

"Tetu is outside, at the truck waiting. Let him stay there until this is finished. This is a delicate situation, Swan. Tetu wanted to barge in here and start ripping faces off. No one is taking his Swan. I have dealt with these people before, and think I understand how to speak with them. Let's settle this peacefully, even if it was started violently. I'll take you to Tetu when this is done, but you must trust me a little longer. I have to step outside for a minute to explain you're OK. Above all, I've got to stop him from coming in right now. Wait here. I'll be right back."

Swan trusted Pack, and saw the wisdom of his advice, so she waited outside the courtroom for this to be over. Pack was back with Swan when the man came to tell them to reenter.

The Chief said, "There will be no need for Swan Threemoons to defend herself. It is good to know Pack understands what this woman is doing, and that she does not intend to threaten our customs. We will give her a chance. It may be that we do not stand in her way, or it may be, six months in the future, that we do consider her a threat. But between now and then, we will accept your conditions. We will speak with our northern branch and ask for their assurances about Threemoons. We will hear Threemoons' report to us three months from today, at noon, at this place. And I, the Chief of the Kootenai, will personally go to the Yaak to speak with young Little Deer. I take responsibility. We are finished. You may go."

A few of the braves were visibly disappointed. Pack embraced the old man and thanked him for his understanding. Swan stood proud, and with head raised nodded to the Chief, but did not speak. Tetu was anxious, still waiting.

+++

Pack let Tetu drive back to his Lodge in Yaak. Swan sat in the front with him, Pack in the back. Tetu drove one-handed much of the time as he held Swan's hand atop the center console. "Tetu was coming for you, but Matai had a different plan, and it was probably better," Tetu said. Pack knew what was going on: Tetu remained a bit embarrassed that it wasn't he who had made a dramatic rescue.

It was dark and Tetu had his eyes on the road and didn't see Swan smile as she said, "Tetu, don't be ridiculous. You could have beaten up every one of them without sweating, and I know that. Yes, Governor Pack did have a better idea. He solved the problem without violence, something you could not have done. Tetu loves Swan, doesn't he? And he wanted to fight for her. And I know that, so let that be the end of your concern, OK?"

"Tetu is happy then," the big fellow said. Then, as if suddenly remembering, he said, "Matai, Agent Martino wanted you to call him about Paschal."

"Thanks, Tetu, but I remember. I was, uh, just delaying a bit....All right, I'll call him now."

It was well past working hours, but Martino was still in his office. "Sorry, Governor, did your emergency turn out OK?"

"Yep, Tetu's wife is with Tetu and me as we speak. What's up?" Pack said to the FBI man.

"You unfortunately pegged Paschal correctly. Or at least the Bureau thinks so. Someone murdered a General Mike Monticule outside his office building in Fairfax. He was a co-founder of an outfit called International Anchor, the company that formerly employed Paschal. The only thing we've got is that someone in the parking area saw a white male drive off shortly after he heard gunshots fired. Said the vehicle was, using his word, disreputable. Monticule was shot three times. He was armed himself, and apparently trying to pull his own Ruger .380 at the time. All this happened this morning, early. Mrs. Monticule was called to the hospital, where her husband had already been pronounced dead. When she returned home, she found a curious note in her mailbox." He told Pack it'd been typed, then read it to him. "Any thoughts?"

"Did your people warn International Anchor?" Pack asked.

"I can't say," Martino said.

"Can't or won't?"

"General, I do my best, but I'm so far down the chain they don't worry about informing me of details," Martino said.

"Then tell them if they expect me to continue to cooperate with you, they keep you informed. I believe I hold a card or two here, Agent. I do have some thoughts, and I'll share them—this time. But you let them know I'm not kidding. They tell you what's going on, or I start

freelancing. Am I clear? I rather like you, Martino. Stand up for
yourself."

"I'll do that," Martino said, not sure whether to feel more
complimented or scolded.

"First, the note. That was Paschal, no doubt about it. He's
playing, having his sick fun, by facetiously pinning blame on one of
Mrs. Monticule's friends. He doesn't expect anyone will believe that. If
you'll recall, I mentioned a word he used with me. *Insinuate.* He said
he burrows himself into the innards of his victims and gnaws them to
death. Of course he didn't mean that literally, but what he meant was
that he plans thoroughly. He doesn't typically strike randomly or
spontaneously. I hypothesize that Paschal had observed the Monticule
home, and knew when they came and went, and probably where they
were going. He might even have worked around their house. He clearly
followed Mrs. Monticule to her gym, and got so near her that he
overheard a conversation about her husband—admittedly, I'm
assuming she actually said words similar to those in the note. Maybe
he's actually telling her he knew when to hit her husband. Adding salt
to her wound by making her an accessory to the killing. Look, I give
the Bureau a ton of credit, and think it likely you guys have already
reached generally the same conclusions. I'm not a professionally
trained investigator, but I'd surmise that while getting trace evidence
might help you convict in court, it won't help you find him. You've got
to understand how he thinks."

Martino started to say something, but Pack cut him off. "Look,
Agent Martino, I'm seeing a pattern here. I make a suggestion, and

somebody somewhere laughs it off and disregards. Then you ask me for another opinion, I give it, and it's shrugged off. What am I doing? I don't give a damn about a DC turf battle between agencies. I say again, I believe it's time to put together a report for the media for dissemination to the public. Since I was a victim of this guy Paschal, I might decide to do it myself if no one else does. I didn't know General Monticule, really knew nothing about him. But he didn't deserve to die at Paschal's hand. More will die unless you make a plan to draw him out. See what your people can do to effectuate such a plan. The direct approach doesn't work with Paschal. Think indirect. Think B.H. Liddell-Hart."

"Who?" Martino said.

"Forget that reference," Pack said. "Just think indirect approach."

"Thanks, General. I'll carry your water to my boss," Martino said.

CHAPTER SIXTEEN

Tetu, Swan, and Pack hadn't got back to the cabin until two-thirty A.M. Tetu was the first out of bed. He went directly over to the Lodge to check on the breakfast meal prep. He didn't want to erase the memory of the day before, but he also didn't want to dwell on the anxiety he had experienced. It would take some time before he got over feeling he hadn't been Swan's Protector. Those were Kootenai men who had done that to his wife. And those were Kootenai men, albeit young men, working right there in his kitchen. Yesterday morning he greeted them amicably, with good cheer. This morning, he looked at them differently. He wouldn't try to fake cheeriness. So he simply asked them soberly whether things were on or off track.

They hadn't heard about what went down with Swan and Little Deer yesterday. There hadn't been time for word to percolate through the Yaak Kootenai. The one working over three skillets said, "What's wrong, Tetu? Tell us straight up if you ain't happy with me, or is it all of us you ain't happy with? If it's me, say so, and tell me what I need to do to make it right. I been workin' here what, three months, and thought I was doin' good."

The boy's speaking up was a relief. Tetu could tell he didn't know about Swan's abduction. "Some Kootenai men stormed into the church yesterday, handled Swan roughly, took her to Pablo for some kind of trial. There was a Native girl at the church with Swan. Her name is Little Deer. They scared her bad. Matai Pack and I followed them to Pablo and brought her back. Tetu was angry, wanted to kill them. How do you feel about that?" He was testing the loyalty of this youth.

The young man laid his spatula aside. He looked Tetu in the eye and said, "Every Kootenai I know, Mr. Palaita, will be saddened. They're not the same as the people in Pablo, who don't understand what Swan and you have done for us. We'll make this right, OK?"

"Nah, it's not your problem and Tetu isn't asking for help. I think Governor Pack worked something out with Pablo last night. No one hurts Swan again, you can tell your people that for me....Now, let us do our work and not talk of this again."

Pack slept until eight. Swan had left a note that she'd left coffee and breakfast makings on the kitchen counter. He took the coffee, ignored the rest. He felt like a long river walk. As he turned down the path toward the river, a wolf stared him down. Had to be a member of the Yaak Pack, as Ranger Ranklin Shiningfish called it. Beautiful animal, intended no harm to humans, so Pack just admired him until he jogged back upriver, no doubt to rejoin his pack. Then Pack continued the walk, stepping gingerly over the sharp upcroppings of rock all along this stretch. Securing Swan seemed a thing of the distant past. He was thinking of Paschal.

The wolf he'd encountered followed a code. He killed when threatened or when he needed food. Was Paschal really different from the wolf? What threat was Mike Monticule to him? What threat was the Iraqi in whose head he planted the bullet in order to take his clothing? He might've killed Pack, who was no threat to him. When would he kill again? Who would it be? When and where? Paschal had shown that he

243

could vaporize himself. Between jobs he remade himself, became someone unrecognizable from any earlier personal identity. Or so it seemed to Pack.

Pack tried in his mind to turn this into a military problem. He thought if he could identify Paschal's center of gravity, he could then set up a plan to attack it. Clausewitz wrote that the center of gravity is "the hub of all power and movement, on which everything depends." For Pack, that was the most useful concept the great theorist ever conceived. If you successfully attacked the opponent's unique center of gravity, you were effectively pushing a pin through his brain. It had the effect of conserving the attacking force's resources: time, money, energy, and troops.

So as Pack proceeded on the trek, he would put the ferreting out of Paschal's center of gravity *out of his mind.* Just let the idea, floating around somewhere in there, marinate until tomorrow or the next day. Something would come to him.

+++

Paschal had only a few hours until he would shed his Karl Farris identity. First, he needed to sell his car. He returned to the bar, saw a man he'd seen chatting up the dim broad-browed innocent he'd purchased the car from, asked how he might find him this time of day. The fellow replied, "Works steady as a mechanic over at Peroni's Body Shop two blocks over. That'd be Spring Hill Ave, you'll have to look for the number."

"Many thanks, man," Paschal said.

He found the seller, thanked him, said he had to go home to Cali permanently, and thought another form of transportation would be wiser. "Great wheels, really, man, but I don't want to chance a cross-country trip in it. Wanna buy it back? Good deal for you."

"Three hundred's all I can afford right now, but if that'll work for you, we can do it," the original seller, now potential buyer, said.

Paschal would've accepted any offer. All he wanted was to legally sign the car back over. By the end of the afternoon, the title had been transferred and Paschal was in a restroom shifting his identity to one Spencer Hutchins. When he came out, Karl Farris would have vanished.

+++

The next day Pack woke up with center of gravity on his mind. Seemed to him that before attempting to apply the concept in a non-military situation, he needed to be fully clear on what it meant in the instant case. Clausewitz hadn't used it in the same way physical scientists used it, but he had indeed taken clues from them. It wasn't akin to the idea of center of mass.

In terms of a military operation, center of gravity is employed to describe where, if the enemy were struck there, would the effect emanate the furthest? It could be, for example, public support for the war effort, or the capital city, or a charismatic commander, or the lines of communication.

Pack began to ponder what about Paschal he could strike that would knock him badly off balance, and cause him to crash. So then Pack asked himself, What gives Paschal purpose and direction? What holds everything together for him?

At that point he recalled his lecture to the FBI Agent. He had applied the framework of the Seven Deadly Sins. He had claimed Paschal is not avaricious in the classical sense, not envious, definitely not lazy, not lustful (as far as he had the means to know), and not gluttonous.

Wrath and Pride, those were the two forces motivating Paschal. Pack considered, however, that he could throw out Wrath. Paschal's anger was controlled, some breed of cold rage that sat on ice until he wanted to use it. So Pride was the key. His was an overweening Pride that bordered on Hubris. But it wasn't quite to the level of Hubris, in Pack's estimation, because if he were truly hubristic he would have made more mistakes, the outcome of which would have been his death or capture.

So Paschal's center of gravity rested somewhere in his Pride. Of what was he proud, Pack asked himself? A better question might be, what aspect of his life was Blaise Paschal not proud of? He clearly was proud of his native intelligence, his ability to grasp whatever he took up with an ease that had to have made many comrades envious. He was a savage physically, yes, but he couldn't have developed his prodigious physical talents without abundant intelligence. Pack reckoned that Paschal's greatest strength, and therefore greatest vulnerability, was his mind. Pack gave it a name, *cerebral savagery.*

Simon Pack determined that the surest path to stopping Blaise Paschal from continuing to kill was to divert his attention to Pack himself. *The indirect approach, Keeley had cautioned Simon, might be the preferred option more often than you think.* Or, should a law enforcement agency take the lead in trying to flush him out? Pack had given them the clues to settle on this solution. But, if they did it, Paschal would see through the ploy immediately, or so Pack thought. Nobody knew Paschal better than Pack, certainly no one in a position to stop him. If the Bureau belittled Paschal, the killer would see a formless, featureless, anonymous group of people…he would flip them off without a thought. If Pack, the man who had had actual conversations with him, and drilled into his psyche a bit, belittled him, he would be furious. He would regard Pack as a serf not only standing up to, but provoking the Emperor himself. He could not permit that kind of uprising in his empire.

It was the only solution Pack thought had a chance of success. Paschal was a vaporous figure, one virtually impossible to snare. He had the advantage of shape-shifting like few in the world can. He had physical gifts, and was in his prime years. And he had killed for the bulk of his adult life. In simple point of fact, Blaise Paschal had honed his savage skills to the highest level. Now Pack had to decide whether he would act unilaterally or with the support of his federal government. Were he to act alone, he would ignite another firestorm, something he had been known to do too many times in his furious, curious life.

Because he imagined Tetu's mind remained on the events of the day before, he didn't think it was a good time to share his thoughts.

Instead, he called Agent Juan Martino, who wasn't available. Wherever he was, when notified Pack had called, he returned it immediately. Martino said, "What've you got, General?"

"Wrong question, Agent. I should be asking what you've got. We have maybe a week, I'd say, until we have another victim. Are your highers talking with you yet?"

There was a long pause. Pack believed it probably meant Martino was embarrassed to admit he was still being kept out of the info loop. "What can I do? I can't force them to talk with me," the Agent said.

"OK, Juan, let me ask it this way: Have you been forceful with them? I am totally serious, and need an honest answer," Pack said.

"Then I'll put it this way: How I spoke with my boss in Salt Lake might've gotten me fired a year ago, and that's the God's honest truth. I told him this case had its American antecedents right here in my territory, yet I'm still a toadstool, and I by damn don't like it. I told—not asked—him to show some confidence in me or fire me. He apologized, but to this point hasn't taken any action to show he took me seriously."

"All right, Juan. Good going. Look around, you'll observe that the milquetoasts seldom get promoted. Look, I'm hatching a plan, still just hatching it mind you, but within two days I'll have fleshed it out enough to bring you in. If I do, I don't want to imagine you'd betray me. It would probably, I'm telling you in advance, be risky for both of us," Pack said.

"I'm ready to stand up, General. Call me whenever," Martino said.

+++

Blaise Paschal had shucked the well-placed moles, the shaggy hair, and every other vestige of Karl Farris. He was Spencer Hutchins and he had the documents to support the identity. He had a buzz cut of ginger hair and in two days would see that his facial hair became an in-fashion semi-permanent stubble of the same tint. He had treated his skin to make it appear fair, about the polar opposite of his natural skin. With this new skin, he would have to show an effort to stay out of the sun to avoid burning. This is a man who doesn't tan, just burns, people would think at a glance. And, as always, he removed any trace of the vitiligo that plagued him.

He went to Salvation Army again. Bought a couple of sets of clothing that would make him a star on Casual Fridays at the office. Sharp permanent press slacks, argyle socks (if he chose to wear any at all), multi-colored sports shirts (one long- and one short-sleeved), and a pair of relaxed fit Skechers suitable for both dark and light outfits. To top off the appearance he was going for, he added a North Face rainproof windbreaker, a nautical-themed baseball cap, and a middling quality pair of sunshades. Then he returned his old clothes to Salvation Army in what he thought of as an exchange.

Next step: catch a bus to North Carolina to hang out a few days until he had researched his next victim.

+++

Army General Royce Pseud retired four years prior with four stars. A native Louisianan, he always held great love for his native state, a love that only deepened because he was unable ever to finagle an assignment to the Joint Readiness Training Center at Fort Polk, the lone Army Active Duty post in Louisiana. He had sired seven children, and all had migrated to Louisiana; his only explanation was that they had grown up hearing him proclaim its virtues. His children had children of their own now, and most of them also lived in the state. It was only natural then for General Pseud to have begun to re-claim his roots there.

Royce Pseud planned to remain as Managing General Partner of International Anchor for just one more year before going home. He wasn't disclosing his plan to the other two partners until he had everything in place…and until he'd made the money he'd calculated he needed to live in style. He was sick of the DC lifestyle. He eschewed the parties, at which most present spoke of themselves as essential to the lives of ordinary Americans. And, he thought ruefully, he was more than a little ashamed of himself for succumbing to the lure of the money that dripped from the DC trees. Nonetheless, he had to confront the reality that he was at heart no different from his fellow money-grubbers.

Immediately upon retirement from the Army, Pseud went to Louisiana looking for a permanent landing spot. He had grown up in a middle-class environment in Covington, part of the North Shore of Lake Pontchartrain. Mandeville and Covington were places well-to-do New Orleanians had come for more than a century to escape the blistering summer months. Pseud had seen few locales in America that seemed less homogenized than the area north of the Big Easy. The French and Cajun influence was writ large wherever one turned, from storefronts to billboards to language. He loved the local color that suffused this still moderately populated section of the country.

There were a number of grand old homes still available in Covington and Mandeville, but he recalled as a kid the strange allure of Madisonville. So he went to Madisonville, a town west of Mandeville. Property taxes would be low there, and his construction dollar would go at least three times further than in northern Virginia. He fell in love with a piece of land on the western edge of the broad Tchefuncte River, where he had a home built to specifications he'd developed for years. It was his retirement dream home, with five fireplaces, three floors, boat dock, gazebo, personal study, and not far from one of the finest seafood restaurants in the world. He would get himself a boat, and when he tired of fishing on the Tchefuncte, he'd float on out to Pontchartrain.

He couldn't have known it, but he was the vanguard of others with the same idea. Within six months after his place was completely built, four extremely prominent country singers were erecting their own mansions along the same section of river. Two of them formed the most famous husband and wife team in Nashville history. The latter had recently rented an island estate for two weeks at $200,000 per week. Pseud expected it wouldn't take the gawkers long to begin their parade up and down the small road to have a look at the rich and famous neighbors. Had he been able to foresee what he was moving into, he might've chosen differently.

Today, Royce Pseud's taste for northern Virginia had grown more acidic still. One of International Anchor's Big Three, his friend and partner Mike Monticule, had been murdered in their parking lot. He rose and peered out his window to the very spot, shaking his head in dismay at the mayhem in contemporary America. We're becoming Afghanistan ourselves, he thought bitterly. He dismissed the idea that a disgruntled employee of his own company had killed Mike. There were just too many other possible explanations. And so many companies housed in this building…could have been someone disgruntled from their outfits. Or it could've been a random act of crazy violence seen throughout the country these days. Who the hell could tell? He'd heard the hallway rumors that some government agency had advised every company in the building to heighten security. But that was common sense, not news. He, after all, was managing general partner, and he'd had no official notice. What he and the remaining partner had decided, however, is that after Monticule's funeral they would take turns taking a week off, meaning a week off out of town. Pseud would take the second week. The plan fit nicely with their typical late-summer vacation schedule anyway.

+++

Spencer Hutchins/Paschal blended in with the millennials in the Triangle, that confluence of major universities in the Piedmont region of North Carolina. Spencer could sit sipping a costly beverage in Starbucks passing himself off as a junior prof at Duke, as he did today, or tomorrow he might be researching his next target at one of the last remaining Internet cafes. He was the picture of radiant health, scrubbed and muscular and bright-looking. As Spencer, he didn't hesitate to turn his high-wattage smile on one of the ladies sneaking a look in his direction. He was even lodging decently on this trip in order to keep up his image. He attempted a modest extroversion that didn't fit his character Karl Farris in Fairfax.

He had selected this area of North Carolina chiefly because if he needed to return to DC, he could get there in a hurry. But also because he wanted to be an entirely different person from the Karl Farris who was foraging for lawn maintenance jobs. In truth, this was but a waypoint. He would say farewell when he felt he had enough information to make his next move.

After a few days he figured he could have gone to work for Ancestry.com. There's an idea, he thought. If needed, I can say I'm doing genealogical research for them. He'd taken apart the Pseud lineage. Happily, they all lived within a tight radius—maybe 30 miles separated them all. He found a Twitter entry from son Trevor posted more than a year ago. It said, "Hurrah! Mom and Dad are building home near us. Can't wait till they're here!" Then he found records of building permits issued in the name of Royce T. Pseud for a place in Madisonville. Spencer's instinct was pulling him toward Louisiana.

He took a bus from Durham to New Orleans. He would stay
overnight a day or two somewhere on the North Shore, from which he
could continue to be Spencer Hutchins, Mr. Clean Cut. Although he
couldn't yet know for sure, he suspected that at some point he'd assume
a new identity as he blended into anonymity in New Orleans.

He took the newly operational water taxi from NOLA to
Mandeville. Within walking distance he found a comfortable motel.
Next stop: Trevor Pseud. Much as he didn't like it, he'd have to rent a
car.

+++

Hutchins'/Paschal's research had informed him that Trevor Pseud
practiced law in Mandeville. He didn't have a clear picture of how
successful Trevor was. Could be he ran a fly-by-night operation,
although he had graduated from a reputable law school.

His website portrayed Trevor as a full-service country lawyer.
It said, in general, that Trevor "continued the tradition of offering
experienced and dedicated legal service in several practice areas,
including personal injury, auto accidents, Social Security Disability and
SSI, criminal law, wills, estates, probate, family law, and real estate
law. My firm has received an AV rating from Martindale-Hubbell,
which signifies that the firm has attained the height of professional
excellence. No matter what your legal issues are, we work tirelessly to
protect your best interests." Subsequent pages broke down the details of

services available in each category. All in all, it was an impressive website for a one-man operation in a small town.

Hutchins was pleased to see real estate law mentioned. Even if he had not, he would've gone in on some pretext.

So here Hutchins was, in the parking lot of Trevor B. Pseud, Esquire, Attorney-at-Law. His place was a simple concrete building that sat just off the heavily traveled US 190. The parking lot was ample but unpaved. The nearest business was a coin-operated laundry about 50 meters away, on one side, and a diner on the other, about the same distance away. At mid-morning, the waiting area was jammed up with people. Hutchins signed in, saw he had quite a wait, so he went outside waiting for a seat to come open. He peered through the ample front window to see people who appeared to represent a broad range of the socio-economic spectrum. No doubt this man kept busy. Had to employ several paralegals to keep pace with this workload.

A seat or two came open, so he went back in to claim one. He listened to the people talking. Good old Trevor had a great reputation, that was clear. "My cousin went to a couple places up here, they said they couldn't help her, so she went to NOLA, got the same story there. Then someone told her about Mr. Pseud, and he did help her. She swears by him," a middle-aged woman said. Others bestowed similar compliments on Trevor Pseud. Hutchins thought he liked this guy before he met him. Couldn't let that interfere with his mission, though.

Sometime past noon, he got in to see Trevor. The lawyer was eating a sandwich and drinking a Diet soda. He apologized, saying, "I don't go out for lunch, so please pardon my manners. Just trying to fit everyone in. So, Mr. Hutchins, how may I help you?"

"Spencer's fine, sir. I'm about to move down from the upper Midwest, and am interested in purchasing a piece of property over on the Tchefuncte in Madisonville. All the ads on radio and TV tell us we ought to have a real estate attorney to protect our interests, so consider this a preliminary query to ascertain your ability and availability to help me," Hutchins/Paschal said.

"Hmm," Pseud muttered, "your timing is fortuitous, Spencer. I'll explain why in a moment, but first, understand I'm not looking for business. You've been out there," he said, pointing toward the waiting room, "a while, I assume, and you see the workload I'm carrying. But...to your point, a couple of things about your question are interesting. First, most homebuyers and builders do not need a real estate attorney, in my experience. Those ads are from firms with questionable ethics trying to spin up business. On the other hand, I think yes, anyone purchasing over on the Tchefuncte should have one. Why? Well, because it's on the river, and most of that area's in a flood zone. If you have lawyerly advice on how high above water level your property should be, that's a good thing. But, beyond that, we've found the EPA is bad about framing environmental impact statements in ways unnecessarily detrimental to the buyer. A lawyer can file counters to statements that often are patently ridiculous. I've taken some of these cases to court, with great success, I might add. To be honest, Spencer, there are suddenly loads of high-end buyers vying for that property, and whenever that's the case you're going to find a herd of shysters trying to get a cut of that money. Some of those shysters are in the real estate biz as well. A good real estate attorney will review every transaction before his client signs off on it. Any appraisal or inspection, for example, I'd review for errors of omission and commission.

"So, in reply to your question, my answer is yes, given that the river section of Madisonville is the place you're considering, I'll represent you if you want. So when you have something firm in mind, come on back. If you'll make an appointment, you won't have to wait as long, OK?"

Then Spencer Hutchins hit the mother lode. "One more thing, Spencer, kinda personal in nature, but you look like a sharp, clean-cut guy, so let me ask you: would you be interested in coming to a party right there in the area where you're looking to buy? Next Friday, around seven, at my Dad's place. He's coming down for a week—I mean, he lives in Virginia now, but bought this as a retirement home. Hasn't had a chance to enjoy it much yet, and won't be down full time for some months away. Anyhow, our family—and it's big—will all be there to help him christen the place. You can get a few minutes with him, let him explain some of the pitfalls to avoid, and there have been a few, I know that. Didn't want his son defending him, though, so he kept me out of it. Bet you didn't expect an invitation when you walked in here, did you?"

"Nope, for sure, I didn't expect it, Mr. Pseud. Look, I have a pretty tight schedule myself at the moment, so would it be all right if I call your secretary later this afternoon to RSVP? Sounds like it could be immensely helpful, plus I'm sure I'd enjoy meeting your dad. I truly appreciate the offer, and want to take you up on it, if I can make it fit," Spencer said.

"OK, then, Spencer, Velma will await your call," Trevor said.

"Thanks for the time, Mr. Pseud, and farewell."

A tight schedule indeed. Right, Spencer thought. *My schedule will consist of planning what I do after I waste your old man. Wouldn't miss your party for the world.*

CHAPTER SEVENTEEN

Pack would work from the inside out. He wanted to sit down with Tetu and Swan. They were involved, possibly in a way that would put them in danger, so he had to start with them. Then he would move outward, maybe even go to Helena to speak with Governor Dahl, and it would be useful if Martino were present at the same time. And he couldn't neglect Sheriff Mollison either, although he didn't anticipate his involvement.

And so it was, two evenings after he had secured Swan's release, Pack sat down with Swan and Tetu in their living room. The Palaita couple was especially relaxed, settling into the ease of their sofa, ready to converse cordially with Simon.

"Glad to see we're getting back to normal," Pack said. "I understand the Chief spoke in apology to Little Deer already, today in fact, showing he was true to his word. I think from this point onward you'll be able to continue your work, Swan, unimpeded and in peace. Those men from Pablo made a bad mistake, a tremendous error in judgment."

"Yes, thank you, Governor, for taking the prudent action. And Tetu, who I know was ready to blast his way in. Both of you took care of me in your own ways. I'll see Little Deer tomorrow, I hope. We'll help her get over that awful experience. That girl has been through a lot."

"OK," Pack began deliberately, "I need to speak with you about something I've been thinking concerning the man who abducted me. If you—either of you—has the least reservation with anything I say, I ask you to stop me right away. If you object to anything I propose, I'll go back to the drawing board to try to make a new plan. And I must tell you he's been on my mind not because he took advantage of me, but because I'm totally certain he will continue to kill unless he's stopped. I have a duty to stand in his path. I do that by having him come after me. I believe it's within my power of ingenuity to make him do that. I know him better than any person still alive."

Tetu was already a step ahead of Pack. He would've wanted to be involved under any circumstances, but also because he believed he had failed Swan several days ago. He could regain his status in her eyes, as he saw it. Swan, of course, saw the matter differently, but that didn't matter. Tetu perked up, but felt sure he would concur with whatever Pack proposed.

Pack continued. "Now, understand that to my knowledge—and I'm highly confident of the truth of this—is that Paschal sets out to kill only his targets, not their spouses or friends or family. He seeks vengeance on those he believes have either demeaned him or failed to support him. I don't know of one instance where he has done bodily harm to an associate or spouse. His last victim was a man who headed up a company he recently worked as part of.

"If I prompt him to come after me, it'll be me and only me he tries to kill. His vulnerability is his pride, particularly his pride in his animal cunning and native intelligence. The man has moxie, we have to credit him for that. If I can get a large enough audience and besmirch him in front of it, he will come after me. He told me he's a master of disguises, and about that I have no doubt. He has the ability to appear to be someone who looks, acts, and speaks differently from who he actually is. My going after him would be an exercise in futility. I wouldn't even be able to identify him, I feel certain. I have to strike indirectly. Keeley cautioned me to fight more with my brain than with my fists." Pack paused, looking at Swan and Tetu for reaction. Then he added, "This whole mess is rotten. I believe he's got great good inside him. If only he would direct his energy and talents toward ends that would serve humanity. But we could say the same of many evil men, and it's not my job to rehabilitate him. He elected not to speak about redemption when I gave him the chance."

Sensing that Pack wanted feedback, Tetu said, "Matai, make a role for me. I must be part of your plan. Swan, speak plainly whether you agree or disagree."

Swan said, "Tetu, you are my husband, and you are wise. You do what you have to and I will support you fully."

Tetu scooted forward on the sofa, eyes open wide, propping his forearms on his knees, saying, "Matai, whatever you ask, Tetu will do. Now I ask, where will we do this?"

"My cabin is the first choice. It's remote, he's been there, and I wouldn't be putting any other lives in danger," Pack said. "I'm almost ashamed to tell you I considered Yaak also, given this was the site of several of our battles that turned out well."

Swan said, "But wouldn't he know you're trying to lure him in, Governor, and therefore be smart enough to stay away?"

"I've thought of that, and after mulling it over, I always come to the same conclusion. He might perceive what I'm doing, yes, but he won't be able to stop himself. Wounded pride is the most severe wound for him, and whoever caused the injury he will attack. The way I see it happening is, he'll get into the area I live in, he'll recon to see that I'm around, he'll monitor my comings and goings, and he'll strike when he thinks my guard is low. He'll burrow closer and closer until he has me in a corner. I intend to show him I'm unaware both that he's around and that he has me in a corner."

"Matai," Tetu said, "have we ever failed as a team? No. If we are a team again, we cannot lose."

"I know you're right, Tetu, but let's not get ahead of ourselves. I've got some obstacles to overcome first. I want to speak with Jim Dahl at his place, and will ask Martino to go with me. You're welcome to go to Helena with me, but it's not necessary, and I'd feel better with you making sure your business is in good shape. I also want to speak with Harris Green, make him aware of what I'm about to do. Finally, I have to get on television, and maybe on radio too. You know, Tetu, when you don't talk much as a politician, people are more willing to listen when you have something to say."

Tetu was already thinking of swearing in his Kootenai employees to be prepared to take up arms in defense of Swan during his absence. "When will we go to your cabin, Matai?"

"Let me get these tasks done in sequence, then I'll call you to come down. Stay here until then. I'm going back home now and get this party started. Swan, thanks for your great hospitality. I'll be back, and in not too long I think we'll get this wrapped up," Pack said. But privately he knew this vague plan had many weaknesses, and might not get off the ground.

+++

Pack and Martino got the appointment with Governor Jim Dahl. Martino needed the flexibility of having his own transportation, so they travelled to Helena separately. Pack hadn't wanted to have these discussions over the phone, only face to face. He rehashed the thinking he'd expressed to Tetu and Swan. Once he'd finished, he said, "Look, gentlemen, I know you can poke countless holes in this plan, which is actually little more than a sketch map. But that's just the way this is. I'm going to have to be a defensive lineman on this one, or maybe a better analogy is an inside linebacker, in that maybe I can pick up a clue from the way the offense is deployed, but I won't be in position to commit myself until the offense executes the play. Success will depend chiefly on my reflexes and read of the situation. It's risky, but understand this has been my kind of work pretty much throughout my military life. It's *fingerspitzengefuhl,* fingertip feel, and you either have it or you don't. My biggest selling point is that neither the military nor any of the federal law enforcement agencies stands to lose anything in this…I'm the one who'd do the dying…but that won't happen. Is Blaise Paschal better at this than I am? He is not. Period."

"You're wrong about the lawdogs having nothing to lose, though," Martino said jokingly, laughing as he spoke. "The truth is Salt

Lake will be the lawnmower that shreds my ass to tiny bits for knowingly allowing you to do this. Naw, you've taught me an important truth, General. We always have to earn our respect, but sometimes, if it's our due, we also must demand it. I've done good work as an agent at an important outpost, but sorry to say, my regional chief is so wrapped up in his own work he doesn't pay much attention to my people in Kalispell. So I'll face whatever consequences are in store for me personally. Said another way, I don't much give a flip. Go for it."

Then a somber Governor Jim Dahl spoke: "Correct me if I'm wrong, Juan, but I think I'm about to speak for both of us. I hope, General, that you'll find a way for my agents and the Kalispell FBI agents, to back you up." Agent Martino nodded his concurrence. "I know they can't be front and center in ways that would give your operation away, but if we can lurk in the background and appear at a crucial moment, let us know. We'd like to take him alive, and to have no one hurt."

"Thanks for that, Jim. I'll keep that in mind. And believe me, taking him alive is my wish too. Now, if you don't mind, I'd like to place a secure call to General Harris Green."

Eventually they connected with Harris Green, Chairman of the Joint Chiefs. Pack delivered the abbreviated version of his sketch. Pack then said, "My formulation is simple, Chief. I could tell you out of courtesy or not tell you and appear disloyal. Obviously I chose the latter. I'm fine with your denying we ever had this conversation."

Green replied, "You're my favorite General Officer of this century, Simon. You know that. If asked, I won't deny we spoke. I won't go further than that. Just that we spoke about Blaise Paschal. And remember, I started this. I called you first, so let's just end it there. The President likes the job I'm doing, so I'm not worried. The Agency's the problem here for not admitting their guy has been on a murderous spree, and for not releasing details about who he is and what he's done. I can't speak for them or otherwise do their jobs for them. OK?"

"Good to go, then. Thanks, Harris." Pack signed off, and the confab in Helena concluded.

+++

Wilkie Buffer was accustomed to television and radio appearances. The biggest names interviewed him as a featured guest about once a quarter, on average. He possessed certifiable clout among those people in New York and Washington. Sometimes he discussed his latest written work, but most often it was to get his take on a current event of national moment. Pack could've easily arranged his own interviews, but opted to have Buffer run interference. Buffer had in fact lined up interviews on the most-watched cable news shows and on three of the most-listened to radio shows. The interviewers could not, of course, do a creditable job without knowing the general nature of the reason for inviting their guest, Simon Pack. Buffer and Pack had not wanted to appear to be doing the hosts' jobs, however, so they gave the producers sufficient 'tease' material from which to draw up questions. They could do the rest on the fly.

Most Americans knew Pack by sight and name, and most trusted him, according to polls. He might've even run for President, but was not temperamentally inclined to do so.

Pack got to his point quickly in every interview. There is among the public a man with the highest-level martial skills. He has killed numerous national leaders, military men, and fellow Americans overseas, and now he is following a similar path in his country of birth. His name officially is Blaise Paschal, but he uses many aliases. Pack gave Paschal's actual height and weight, but emphasized that he has the skills of a Hollywood special effects expert, thereby enabling him to alter his appearance into someone unrecognizable as Blaise Paschal. Explained his proficiency in languages.

Pack told viewers and listeners that Paschal had abducted him and held him prisoner for several days. This appearance, however, was not about Pack but about those yet to die at Paschal's hand. Anyone who has ever known this man should be on high alert. His last known victim was General Mike Monticule of Fairfax, Virginia. There surely would be others.

"I'm not a denizen of DC," Pack said, "but I can tell you if all our investigative and intelligence agencies would come clean, the public might be aware of the various aliases and identities he employs." When interviewers pressed, Pack would reply, "I can only say I have first-hand knowledge he worked for years overseas as a deep-cover agent and subsequently performed quasi-military duties for a DC-based company called International Anchor."

"Why is he doing this?" they all would ask.

Hedging a bit, Pack then hammered at Paschal's essential cowardice, how he saw everyone as his subjects and himself as emperor, and if he sensed a rebellious spirit among his subjects, he ruthlessly quelled it. Pack said, "I am a genuine Marine, along with hundreds of thousands of others. Paschal is a fake Marine, a coward, a blusterer, a man who exaggerates his prowess, and who cannot survive a fair fight with men like me, and he knows it." As he listened to a replay of his first interview, Pack identified areas of improvement, but on balance thought he'd succeeded in hitting Paschal where it hurt most.

By Thursday, newspapers and talk radio were addressing the story from multiple angles, the most troubling with blaring headlines such as "*PACK HINTS AT CONSTITUTIONAL CRISIS!*" and "Feds Shielding Killer from Public Eye" and "BOLO: Blaise Paschal". Others, more cautious, penned stories like "What's Behind Pack's Alarmism?" and "CIA Rogue at Large in America". Another large newspaper saw a chance to perpetuate its decades-long campaign against private soldier/agent-for-hire companies sanctioned by the US Government. Pack cared only that one person heard his message, and he prayed that Paschal would act on it.

+++

Spencer Hutchins was getting the message. Anger smoldered as he sat watching Simon Pack in front of some obsequious interviewer. He had a lot of time to kill, and for the time being his motel room was the logical place to be. No sense tempting fate on the one in a million chance anyone could connect Spencer Hutchins to Blaise Paschal. But, Paschal continued to ruminate, that means that theoretically there are 310 people in America who might be able to make the Hutchins-Paschal connection. And when you're talking about life and death, one in three hundred ten aren't great odds.

But this watching Pack attempt to destroy who he actually was, Blaise Paschal, was already stale. One part of Paschal was telling him to shut it off, do anything but listen to Pack's crap. *There's only one letter standing between you and crap, Pack.* Another part, one he couldn't manage to control, was telling him to watch all of it, get the picture of Pack indelibly inked onto his brain. Watch him writhe when I remind him of the vulgarities he spoke about me.

Yeah, Paschal thought more, Pack has stepped way out of line. I outsmarted him, I dominated him, I laughed in his face, I put him in chains, so the big impressive man is so embarrassed he resorts to lying about me, tries to shift the attention to me because he can't face the reality that by comparison he's inferior, deficient in every way.

No way he's dealt with a man like me before. '*The General*,' he thought sneeringly, is accustomed to telling compliant Marines what to do, say, think. But Simon, I'm not compliant. You DO…NOT…tell Blaise Paschal what to do or say or think. I'll bitchslap you back into compliance with MY wishes. You're next, mister. And you won't know what hit you. You can't watch that rundown rickety ugly old cabin all day every day. You're tired, man, and I'm fueled by rage, and when your guard drops, I'm gonna hammer the hell outta your stupid flat-nosed face. Shouldn't have let you live, after all. What on earth did I see in you worth admiring?

You called me a coward? No man alive says that to Blaise Paschal and stays alive for long. You haven't faced a hundredth of the danger I have. You haven't killed a hundredth of the men I have. I have the power to subjugate to my will any person I choose. The only question I have about your life is the method by which you'll die an unnatural death. Then let's see how much you have to say about Blaise Paschal, the man whose mastery over you will have been final.

CHAPTER EIGHTEEN

Friday had finally arrived. As Spencer Hutchins, Paschal had finished preparations for the evening. He checked out of the slightly upscale motel. He gave the female behind the Reception counter a toothy smile and said a humble farewell. As she continued to type into her computer she said, in the friendliest of fashions, "And where are you off to now, Mr. Hutchins?"

Spencer answered, as if his work subjected him to unimaginable stresses, "Dearborn, Michigan, I'm afraid. Annual meeting of our General Managers. They get less interesting year by year. Anyway, I prefer New Orleans any day of the week, but duty calls," he said with a shrug. *What can I do?*

He had coordinated with the rental car agency to park in spot A-18 after hours and simply drop the key in the office door slot.

All his gear was packed neatly, as always, in his rucksack, each item in its appointed place so he could remove what he wanted quickly, by feel. He would wear an unzipped windbreaker to the Pseud riverside home in Madisonville. Two items he withheld from the ruck; he'd insert them into his back pockets once he exited the vehicle. Once on the road after leaving Pseud's place, he'd call for a taxi and have it waiting at the car agency.

+++

It was five P.M., and most of the Pseud family would not arrive until nearly seven, after work hours. Many would spend the night in the spacious quarters. Trevor the workaholic lawyer, however, had given himself a break on what was a special day for him. For too many years his dad had worked unaccompanied tours overseas, and five years might have passed in which he saw his dad five or six months total. Putting his arm around his old man would be awfully nice, Trevor thought.

So, at four that afternoon, he found his dad puttering around the yard. He hugged him and told him how much he'd looked forward to this visit from him and his mom.

"This was kind of sudden, Trev," Royce Pseud said, "but it sure is good to get away from DC. I've had all I can take. I'll be counting down the days until I can come to this heaven. We can fish, hunt, maybe get some gator tags, cook some crawdads and jambalaya, sit around a fire, enjoy all those years we missed out. Less than nine months left. I'll give the partners six months' notice."

Trevor looked solemn. "Dad, I guess you don't want to think about it, but with the loss of General Monticule, you now have only one partner to inform."

"You're right…on both counts. I still can't believe it. He was just trying to get to the building from his car. If you've seen the news lately, you've heard Simon Pack asserting that this killer was most likely a former employee of International Anchor. I just don't know. Nobody except Pack has warned us to stay vigilant. I'm here now out of caution. Maybe it's unwarranted, maybe not." Then he appeared to cheer up a bit. "Anyway, what matters is that I'm here about to enjoy the company of family."

"That's right, dad, let's just have a good reunion tonight. Forget about Washington and everything in it," Trevor said.

Then Royce seemed to think of something else. He raised a brow as he said to Trevor, "Your mom says you've invited someone outside the family tonight. Apropos of Pack's warning, do you think this guest of yours is clean? I'm trying hard not to act paranoid, son, but at the same time I do want to be careful. Tell me about this fellow."

"Dad, I don't expect you to brag about your oldest son, but let me tell you I work like the devil. I'm essentially a one-man shop, and I work so much I'd make a decent living if I paid myself five dollars an hour. I see all kinds of people with all kinds of weird problems. If the potential case has to do with the law, I take it. My point is, I see people who lie to me remorselessly, sometimes several times a day. I have a pretty keen eye and ear for bullshit. So, this nice-looking fellow in bespoke—you like that word?—attire walks in and discusses what he perceives as a need for a real estate lawyer. Wants to move over here on this stretch of the Tchefuncte, he says. Now that's as much as he knows. I don't live here, and he doesn't know you do, so anyway, the thought strikes me that maybe you could inform him of the roadblocks you ran into in making your deal. So I ask him to come over this evening. *I ask him, he doesn't ask me.* His name is Spencer Hutchins, and he looked totally surprised when I made the invitation. In my mind, he is a no-BS guy. I'd stake my reputation on it, dad."

Royce placed his hand on his son's shoulder. He said, "That's all I needed to hear, son. I was being paranoid. I'll be happy to speak with him. How old is he?"

"He looks to be mid-thirties, about my age," Trevor said.

"OK, if he's not family, he'll be easy to spot," Royce said with a smile. "Let's have a beer a few hours early." Royce drank a few more beers before the family assembled.

+++

The Pseud family was having a grand time, most drinking but not to a point of inebriation. A horde of children ran around with cupcake icing smeared across their mouths, drinking Kool-Aid, with mothers chasing behind admonishing them not to spill anything and to sit at the table when eating. Spencer Hutchins could smell the burgers and hot dogs on the grill dockside. Trevor was his escort for a short time, but made no move to introduce him to his father.

Royce Pseud, he could overhear, said, "I'm not driving anywhere, am I? I think I'm entitled to be a happy drunk on my own property," which drew a round of laughter and agreement from those outside. Trevor noticed that Spencer seemed to be hitting it off well with everyone. There was no pressure to fit in here, he observed. *Just be yourself, unless you're a jerk,* was the prevailing attitude.

At around nine, Royce appeared in the living room, where Spencer/Blaise mingled with more than a dozen adults. Most of the talk was idle chitchat, just people basking in the buzz. Royce tapped

Spencer on the shoulder. "Enjoying the party, young man?" the General asked.

"I assuredly am, sir," Spencer said, sticking out his hand to an unsteady Royce. "You without question are the General who heads up this fine family. Honored to meet you, and I'd like to thank your son— Trevor, in case there's any confusion about which son—for asking me to drop in."

Royce began to speak again, but Spencer feigned an inability to make out his words clearly. There truly was so much chatter that hearing the *paterfamilias* was a strain. The older man motioned for them to move, apparently to a place of quiet. Spencer followed as the man doddered his way through the front door and out among the cars on the driveway. Spencer said, once they were in open air, "Shouldn't you tell them you've gone outside for a bit, sir?"

"Hell, no," Royce Pseud replied, his voice as shaky as his gait. "I look like an invalid gotta be looked after ever' step?"

"Of course not, General." Spencer angled himself so that he could see back toward the windows of the Pseud house that faced in his direction. He also had a view of the sides of the house in case anyone should appear in that way.

"Now let me tell you about this neighborhood," Royce began, but Spencer, seeing his main chance, let him proceed no further. He whipped the bear spray from his left back pocket and directed the jet stream directly into Royce's eyes.

A full stream of bear spray in one's face is akin to a severe, unexpected jolt of electricity: the receiver is so badly stunned he is momentarily incapacitated, unable to draw a breath to speak or scream. Royce fell to his knees, between two cars, as Spencer drew out his titanium nightstick and beat him roundly…to death. Just lethal body blows, no blood trail.

Spencer estimated the distance to his car at twenty feet. He had to move quickly before anyone appeared before a window. He took the risk, fireman-carrying the middle-sized man to his, Spencer's car. He brought out a rope from his trunk and tied it to the belt of Royce's trousers. He drove away down the street of houses under construction, dragging Royce behind as if he were wedding bells. Then Spencer stopped, untied the rope, and flung the body inside the shell of a new home.

And then, mightily pleased with himself, he sped away toward the car rental agency. The taxi, the man on the phone said, would be waiting.

+++

"Where's dad?" one of his kids asked.

"I saw him leading whatshisname, Spencer, out the front door around fifteen minutes ago. Maybe they walked down the street, looking at the houses going up," Trevor said. "Spencer's interested in buying here along the Tchefuncte." But inside Spencer instantly felt so sick he felt as if he might vomit. Oh, my God, he thought helplessly and hopelessly, I am responsible for this. Grasping this awful possibility, he yelled, "Somebody stay here with the children, everybody else outside to search for dad! Now!"

Some ten minutes later, Trevor heard a sibling scream, "NONONONO! Call 911. Dad is hurt bad, but I believe he's alive."

Trevor went in the ambulance with Royce as it careened toward St. Tammany Parish Hospital in Covington. Royce was clinging to life ever so weakly. In his haste Blaise Paschal had screwed up.

Trevor was a man of reason, not governed by passion. His heart was rent for setting in motion the force that had prematurely ended this ill-fated visit. Much as the sight of his broken father plagued him, he wanted to hold it together in order to pass every detail of his information on Spencer Hutchins to the investigators.

+++

FBI Agent Martino called Pack. "General, we need to talk. I need you to come to my office. Doesn't involve questioning you. Just a conversation about new information. When can you make it?"

It was Saturday, and if Martino was on duty in his office it probably was important. "Say in five hours from now," Pack said.

He called Tetu. "This is sudden, Tetu, but do you think you can come down today? This is kickoff, if you understand me."

"Thirty minutes, Matai, to brief my people, then I'm on my way."

"I won't be at home, Tetu. Going down to Kalispell to visit our favorite guy. You've got a key. Go on in and make yourself at home. And be careful," Pack said.

"You be careful too, Matai," Tetu said. "Tetu will make your cabin a fort."

The dependable Tetu was in the cabin by noon. At around three a delivery truck pulled down into the gravel driveway. Tetu watched from a window, cradling a shotgun. He watched as the ferret-like fellow skipped to the door. He opened the door, but kept the shotgun in his shooting hand.

The deliveryman was doubly shocked. First by Tetu's immense stature, and second by the sight of the shotgun. "Whoa, sir, I have a delivery for the former Governor, Simon Pack. That's all. Nothin' more than that, I promise."

Tetu didn't speak at first, just pointed the shotgun for the man to lead him to the cargo. "Show me," he said, adding, "and raise that cargo door real slow."

"No problem," the slight fellow said, noting that Tetu trained his weapon on the cargo area, as if he were expecting an enemy force to leap out. And that is precisely what Tetu had in mind.

As the door slid up, Tetu relaxed. He saw the cargo.

Tetu said, "You sure you're at the right place. Who sent this stuff?"

"I can cover it all, mister. First, it's all paid for by Mrs. Keeley Pack. She included a letter to be delivered with the goods. In addition to the two BMW 1200GS cycles, there are leathers to fit each, meaning husband and wife. Also, there are custom helmets for each with their initials emblazoned in gold leaf. I've brought this all the way from Denver. I thought you'd be happy to have it."

Tetu had mixed emotions. Pack would feel joy that they came from Keeley, and Pack would be disconsolate at being reminded of her. "OK, mister, let's roll them down the ramp and stow them in the garage. I'll go inside and lift the garage door."

"I had specific directions from the BMW dealer in Denver. I'm not to leave until you sign off the vehicles are in operationally good condition. Seems Mrs. Pack was meticulous with her instructions. I've brought gasoline and oil and am supposed to fire them up for you. OK if I do that now? And can you sign off for Mr. Pack?"

"Sure, mister," Tetu said. "Sorry for the shotgun and all. The General's not here right now, and I'm taking care of things for him. You can check me out if you need to. I worked for him when he was Governor."

"Not a problem." The man filled the gas tanks and left the remainder of the cans, and did the same with the oil. As he went about the filling, the man explained that this model was good for both on- and off-road driving. He started them up, Tetu watching carefully his every move. He thought Matai probably knew motorcycles, but in case he didn't Tetu wanted to be prepared to show him.

The deliveryman's final act was to hand over the handwritten note from Keeley. It was tucked into a clear plastic document protector. When the man left, Tetu read the note: "*Dear Simon, this is my wedding gift to you. We can ride together, free as the wind. Beautiful,*

aren't they? His and Hers. Hope you like them. Love always, Keel."
And a PS: "Sorry if they're a little late. I ordered the package weeks
ago, but wanted everything (especially the leathers and helmets) to be
perfect before delivery."

+++

"I know you weren't obligated to come down, General, so I appreciate it. Thought it's time we talked in a secure facility. There's been some news. Before I forget to mention it, I'm happy to report this meeting is sanctioned from the top. They want me communicating with you. Better late than never, right? Anyway, one of the two surviving partners of International Anchor was beaten to within an inch of his life last night," Martino said.

"Damn, Juan, I've been doing everything within my power to persuade the Bureau to keep an eye on those people. There's no excuse for this, in my opinion," Pack said.

"No, I agree with you, sincerely I do, but it seems now at last you have the attention of the top dogs in my agency. They finally see you were right all along. I assure you the last of the three partners will get blanket security. But they guesstimate that you're the next target. The way you belittled him got his attention. At the same time, I think Washington in general is so agitated by you their prime objective is not to protect you but to get him. The CIA Director in particular is ticked at you enough he's ready to have one of *his* guys do you in," Martino said.

"I don't give a tinker's damn about any of them, Juan. I've said before I'm no investigative genius, but I did have direct access to Paschal, access that no one in the FBI had or will have. I have a sense of the man none in your agency has." Pack was huffing in frustration. "And as far as the CIA is concerned, all I have to do is point out—as I have, indirectly—that I perceive it hasn't provided the FBI with critical information which, had it been available, might have brought Paschal's rampage to an end already. I've worked with them on black ops a number of times, and I'm pissed but not shocked they used me when it suited them, but are ready to dump on me now. Look here, Agent Martino, once I decided to disregard all the counsel not to go public, one thing bothered me most. My worst fear is that now—when, not if, Paschal comes after me—the FBI will botch it. He has tiny but powerful antenna on every inch of his body, and I know for sure he'll sense an FBI presence and fail to act. My deal to you today is a win-win for the Bureau: stay away and let him come after me. If he wins, what the hell, no loss to the FBI but you have a pretty good fix on him. If I win, I've done the job we all want done. And, Juan, I don't need the credit and am not looking for any. I'll get him, one way or another. Take that back to your people."

"Roger, General, got it. Now would you like to hear more?" Martino said.

"Yeah, go ahead," Pack said.

"This second partner was another Army General, retired, name of Royce Pseud." Pack placed his palms up and shook his head, indicating he didn't know the man. "The attack happened in Louisiana, not northern Virginia. We are speaking with people in the motel he stayed in as Spencer Hutchins. All we got is that he claimed he was leaving for Dearborn, Michigan, for a Regional Managers meeting, presumably something related to the auto industry. We also identified a taxi driver who took him from Mandeville, Louisiana, to New Orleans last night. He did not take him to the airport. We have a pretty good description of 'Spencer Hutchins' from several people, and they match. Reddish-ginger hair, trimmed short, with a short growth of facial hair, about six-three, no tats or piercings observable.

"General Pseud's son—actually one of his sons—Trevor, a lawyer in that area, is distraught, seeing himself as absolutely responsible for his dad's fate. He invited 'Spencer' to a Pseud reunion," Martino said, speaking from notes.

"And why did he invite him?" Pack asked.

"Because 'Spencer' had come to his office seeking assistance in making a real estate purchase on a pricey home in the same area where his father Royce has built his retirement home," Martino said.

"Bingo," Pack said. "I believe I stressed that Paschal does his homework. He *insinuates* himself into the milieu of his victims, which is what he did in this case. He gnaws his way in, then attacks. If this was a reunion, and others were present, how did he pull this off?"

"I guess Royce was two or three sheets to the wind, and invited 'Spencer' outdoors where they could be heard above the din inside the house," Martino said. "And what's worse is, Trevor said he explicitly told his dad he'd serve as a character reference for 'Spencer.'"

"Bingo again, Juan. He is a convincing character, I assured you. It'll be harder for him to do in trying to get to me. I know his tactics, techniques, and procedures, so to speak. You've been to my place, and are aware of its remoteness. What you might not know is that aside from Joe Mollison and one or two others down in town, I don't have friends. I go into town to buy groceries, for an occasional breakfast with the Sheriff, and to pick up mail…that's about it. Unfortunately for me, now that I think of it, the funeral up there at the cabin awoke many locals to the fact that I even live relatively near them. Nonetheless, my greater point stands: it'll be harder for him to insinuate himself into my milieu than for any of the others. So, let him come, I'll be ready."

"The Bureau is accumulating a lot of information on him pretty rapidly, and starting to fit the pieces together, General. I can't promise they won't spook Paschal, but I'll be passionate in conveying your druthers. The FBI has careerists just like every large organization, and it only takes one who's out to put another notch on his holster to blow up your intentions," Martino said in summation.

CHAPTER NINETEEN

'Spencer Hutchins' existed no longer. In the bus station restroom, Paschal made himself into Alan Thomas, a native of the Sunflower State, Kansas. To narrow it down, he was a native of Gardner, a town of roughly 20,000 situated southwest of Overland Park. He operated a complex of grain elevators in that area. He ruminated pompously that one of the benefits of his line of work lay in becoming smart in numerous areas of commerce.

He would not follow a direct route to Missoula, Montana, preferring instead to make it deliberately circuitous. He wasn't sure how many changes of bus this would entail, but he didn't care. Whether it took three or four days he didn't care, other than that he'd have to put up with the crappy conditions of these bus lines.

Stealing a vehicle no longer made sense. Too chancy, given his certain "Most Wanted, Be on the Lookout For" status. He needed to be nimble and quick this time, couldn't drive up in a Transit van. He had time to find a cheap motorcycle, and remembered seeing a place in downtown Missoula that carried a few. But there were other options as well. Maybe once he got to a computer he could find a place to buy direct.

His new persona, Alan Thomas, was a sixty-ish man, looking weathered as a man from Kansas his age might be expected to. He returned his skin to a tint roughly its natural color, but he gave himself furrows and creases that were not natural to him. His eyes bore crow's feet and his eyelids were thicker and droopier than they should've been.

He was careful to conceal the vitiligo that had afflicted him for a decade or more. His hair was a moppy, unkempt salt-and-pepper mess. The alteration he liked most was the slight hump he added to his back. To heighten the effect of an ailing back he might add a cane at some point. In any case, this new identity would demand more acting skill than his earlier incarnations. He'd have to slow the cadence of his speech, flatten his accent, employ more age-appropriate patois, and move much more slowly, as he affected a pronounced stoop. Again, he reflected pompously that he'd have made a fine stage and screen actor. A visit to a bargain store would let him acquire the attire fitting the new character. There he was, falling in love with himself again. *I am the Master of Disguises.*

+++

Pack returned to the cabin. He'd called on the way to let Tetu know when to expect him. He found his friend in the kitchen preparing their dinner. With Tetu the meal wouldn't be fancy, but it'd damn well be filling.

Pack said hi, went to the bathroom, then came out to sit at the kitchen table as Tetu worked. "So, Matai, tell me about it. How did the FBI man treat you?"

"It went about as I expected. Mostly, anyway. He told me Paschal struck again last night, in Louisiana. The man was a partner, originally one of three, at International Anchor. His name is Royce Pseud, and he's still alive, or was a few hours ago. But he's not in shape to talk. Not yet. I guess he incurred so many injuries there's little point in ticking them off. One of the sons invited Paschal to a family gathering. In any case, it was definitely Paschal. The FBI believes they're starting to fit a number of shards of evidence together. I didn't say this to Martino, but my overall reaction is, so what? I know in my bones he's coming for me next. I've been right so far, Tetu, and I'm right in claiming he'll be here next. No doubt about it. I tell you, Tetu, I've had a few—so few I could count them on one hand—occasions in combat where I knew with apodictic certitude what the enemy would do next. The person who's never experienced such a thing will find it in-credible, literally not credible, but I swear to you it has happened to me. I am acutely aware when it happens. And it has happened now. He is coming here. And this is what I've wanted from the start. The killing will stop when he comes for me.

"I'm sure there were people who watched me on TV and said to themselves, 'That Simon Pack is like all the others, looking for his moment in the sun. He was out of the camera's eye for several months, and because he couldn't abide not being the center of attention, he had to get himself back in the picture.'"

Tetu himself couldn't take Pack saying such things. "It's not true, Matai. I know you. You do not try to get attention."

"Thanks for saying that, Tetu. I know that's not true too, but I'm just saying a lot of people looked at me that way, I'm sure. But it doesn't matter. When I stop Paschal, some of the same people will also say 'There goes Pack again, trying to be the martyr.' Well, I'm not a martyr either, but I do have a strong desire to be the one to put myself between him and the others he would want to kill."

It was time to eat. As always at Pack's table, they gave thanks for their meals and every other blessing in their lives. Then Pack raised another topic related to Paschal. "Tetu, let's clean up, then go down to the office to wargame this situation, OK?"

"Good. But after cleaning up, could we do one other thing before we go down?" Tetu asked.

"Sure, Tetu. Will I be surprised?"

Tetu still wasn't sure how to handle this, so he simply nodded affirmatively, not giving away his view about whether Pack would be positively or negatively affected by the surprise.

When every dish and piece of cookware was spic and span and put away, Pack turned to Tetu and said, "OK, tell me what you want to say."

They finished. Before taking Pack to the garage, Tetu said, "First, please read this, Matai." He stepped back and observed as Pack read Keeley's message. Tetu was gratified to see a smile. Pack slowly pivoted his head side to side, saying, "She was a wonder, wasn't she, my friend?"

The mountainous Tetu, himself acting as out of character as Pack just had, clapped Pack on the back and added, "Yes, she was, Matai. We were all lucky, I think."

Tetu had tucked both bikes up into a corner of the garage, with the helmets and cans placed neatly beside them. The first time Tetu saw Pack's garage, he stopped and stared openly at the precision and cleanliness that defined the place. He had tried to copy that practice in putting the new items in their places.

Pack walked over to them, began lifting lids, unscrewing this and that, inspecting the tires, checking the feel of his butt on the seat, looking at the gauges, getting the feel of his hands on the bars. "Tetu, this is a popular motorcycle. Popular because it is good quality. Dependable and fast. On or off road. Wish I could've gotten inside Keel's head to determine how she made this choice. And you know what else? You and I are going for a ride, Tetu. Not this minute, but tomorrow. We're going to put them on the road, in Keel's honor. Are you up for it?"

"Matai," Tetu said without much conviction, "I am not built for the motorcycle, as anyone would know from looking at me, but in honor of the giver, I am going to do it. When the man delivered them, he tested them, he said, because Keeley directed his company to do so. I watched him do every step, so I could show you if I had to."

Pack laughed. "Oh, yeah, that Keeley was on top of everything. I can see her telling them that delivery wouldn't be complete until the test was done. She was a stickler for detail. So tomorrow we try them out. Weather forecast is good, so be prepared big fella. Now let's go to the basement." Tetu thought this event he had half dreaded had gone quite smoothly.

In the basement office Pack said, "Let's get comfortable, Taits. Get something from the refrigerator if you want. I'm going to have a glass of Knob Creek and kick back."

Pack took a sip, then pressed his chair back, his feet sprawled in front of him. "Wargame. That's what we came down here to do, wasn't it? So, Tetu, if you were Paschal and had just nearly murdered a man in Louisiana and were coming here, how would you go about it?"

Tetu always had gotten profound pleasure from these sorts of talks with Pack. It wasn't unusual. Pack called on Tetu in this fashion when he was Governor. Tetu took pleasure because Pack not simply treated him, but genuinely looked at him, as an equal in the transaction. "OK, Matai, I would stay close to the ground. I would not take the airplane. If I rent a car, it means paperwork, which I do not want right now. I will pretend to be someone different from who I was in Louisiana."

"I agree," Pack said. "So how would he travel? Would he hitchhike, try to thumb rides from strangers? Or maybe hitch from one truck stop to the next?"

"That's a good idea, Matai. It is a real possibility. But the disadvantage is that he would be inside a vehicle for a long time, and the driver probably would want to talk to him. Truck drivers listen to radio much of the time, so they probably know about him, and if Paschal makes one slip of the tongue, he is maybe in trouble of being reported. The same goes if he is in a private car with someone. Also, people in Louisiana especially will know about the beating, so getting out of the state could be a big problem."

"All right, so if these aren't optimal means of transport, what else is there?" Pack queried.

"If he is as good as his reputation, he could steal a vehicle." Tetu had performed this drill with Pack many times, so he knew what was going on: Pack was searching for the most likely enemy course of action. "But I would say a stolen car would have been less of a problem, not as great a risk, at the beginning as now. I think he will not steal a vehicle this time."

"Right again…in my opinion, Tetu. So what does that leave us with?"

Tetu smiled, understanding that now was the time to disclose the grand prize that lay behind the door. "He will take a bus, Matai."

"I believe he will too. But before I go too far, could he take the train?" Pack pushed.

"Yes, he could, but…how should I say this?" Tetu said.

"I am reading your mind, Tetu," Pack interjected. "It goes something like this: people aboard a train are more leisurely about their travel. They get up and walk around. They go to the lounge car. They go to their cabins. They go up to the observation deck. They pay more attention to their fellow passengers. They chat with fellow travelers. That behavior doesn't generally pertain on a bus, does it? And one other point, though not a major one in the case of Paschal: making an AMTRAK connection from Louisiana to Montana takes you over half the country. It's both expensive and time-consuming."

"Matai was reading Tetu's mind," Tetu said, again reverting to the third person.

"All right, Taits, we agree Paschal most likely will use bus transport. So how long will it take him?"

"I would have to look up the distance, Matai," Tetu said.

"Well, I already have, and the answer is…about twenty-four hundred miles. There are too many permutations and combinations of connections he might make for us to know reliably how long such a trip would take, but best case guess is three days. Let's assume today is day one. That means Paschal could be somewhere in our area by Monday. Don't get me wrong: I don't think we'll see him that soon. He'll want to do his usual *insinuation* routine. But we must be prepared for worst case, which is to say, Monday. Now, let's go to the next phase. What does 'being prepared' mean in our case?"

"You tell me, Matai. I just say we are a team, we sort of know where the other will be and when and what to do in every situation," Tetu said.

"I always warm up inside when you say that, Tetu, and it ain't just this," Pack said, taking another sip of Knob Creek, "making me say that. We're battle buddies, pardner, that's for sure. Yep, we work well together. Anyway, here's how I see it. You're my insurance. Above all, we don't want Paschal to escape our noose. I want to take him down myself. I want you going back to the Yaak as good as you are now. But, if anything happens that takes me out of the fight, I want you to hammer him by whatever means you deem appropriate. More specifically, starting Monday morning, I'd prefer that you not leave the cabin. So, if you need to buy anything, let's do it as part of our ride tomorrow morning. OK, why don't I want you out of the cabin? Because I don't want him to know you're around. The only person who ought to know you're here is Sheriff Mollison, and I'll be sure he keeps it quiet. Even if we reach the point he enters this cabin, you keep out of sight until needed, but ready to act. A second reason I don't want you out is that I need you to cover the cabin while I'm out…and I do intend to go out on my normal runs to town. I don't want him to think I'm nervous or in hiding. At the same time, I'll be looking for him in all directions. I don't care what appearance he presents, I believe I'll smell him. From time to time it'd be helpful if you surreptitiously gaze out the windows all around the cabin to see if he's lurking, or maybe if you see or sense anything out of the ordinary. How we doin' so far?"

Tetu had absorbed every word, and he was excited. "Your plan is now our plan, Matai. It will be three against one." He paused, and looked soberly at Pack. "Matai, it will be you, me, and Keeley against Paschal."

Pack raised his glass and said in a voice barely audible, "That's right. You, me, and Keeley versus Paschal."

CHAPTER TWENTY

Governor Jim Dahl called Sheriff Joe Mollison. "Joe," the Governor began, "I've been thinking about the General, and I'm concerned for his safety. I know how good he is in desperate situations, brave, tough, and smart, but this guy Paschal is something different. I'm not saying the General is in over his head, but I have this feeling I'm not supporting him as I ought to. Your thoughts?"

"I've had the identical thoughts, Governor. I'll speak with him, but am pretty sure he'll want to keep us out of the way. Paschal, from what I understand, can sniff out lawmen from miles away. We'd have to be careful. But here's what my real answer is: even if he declines our support, let me slap together some ideas to support from some distance away, maybe in the woodline leading up to his cabin. That's a wild play, so let me think on it and I'll get back to you."

It didn't take Mollison long to call Governor Dahl. He had an idea, something short of a plan…no direct action, just surveillance.

+++

It was a Wednesday when Alan Thomas checked himself into a low-rent motel that abutted the University of Montana campus in Missoula. It was a short walk to the university media center, where rows of computers were available to use at no charge. Although he had all the information on Pack he needed, he wanted particularly to examine news photos that included Pack. His other prime objective was to locate motorcycles for sale by owner.

First things first. In many of the photos of Pack the Governor there was near him a gigantic man identified as Tetu Palaita. Paschal quickly began to see Palaita as an avenue to Pack, a kind of back door approach. His next search found several stories in which Palaita was prominently mentioned. One story was actually about Tetu himself. Tetu, however, had not been interviewed for the story, nor had he corroborated anything written about him. The author believed Tetu Palaita had been with Pack on several occasions involving gunplay and other forms of physical violence. "Tetu Palaita is an extension of Pack himself," the author wrote. "He is devoted to his boss unfathomably." The author concluded his human-interest piece by stating that Palaita was, after more than five years, 'breaking up' with Pack to take over as proprietor of an outdoorsman lodge in the community of Yaak, a hamlet in the far northwestern corner of the state.

The thought occurred to him, as he looked at the news stories on Pack, that before continuing to look for motorcycles available online, he ought to check out student bulletin boards first. From experience, he knew these boards usually were situated somewhere near the entrance of major buildings on campus. Presently, he found what he was looking for. There were hundreds of 3 x 5 cards and sticky notes pinned and pasted in a more or less jumbled fashion. In a few minutes he found a couple of motorcycles for sale. Students had gotten good use of the motorcycles for the summer. Now the coming winter weather would obviate their utility until late spring or early summer. Further, most students probably needed the money with the new school year in front of them. A good deal could be had, Paschal figured.

Mr. Alan Thomas had no interest in buying insurance, just as he had had none after buying the hooptie in DC. He told the kid he was just a visitor from Kansas and wanted to see the sights in this part of the country. The kid looked at him quizzically, then said, "Hey, mister, how about you just lease it from me for a couple weeks, then return it when you're done? You use it, I keep it long term. This bike's been good to me. But understand, I'm going to have to ask full sale price up front, but we'll put the bulk of it in escrow, for you to re-claim when you return. You're responsible for damage or loss."

Alan Thomas wheedled and bargained with the student until both were satisfied. A deal got done, but he doubted he'd ever see the kid again.

+++

Sheriff Mollison invited Pack to the Sundance for breakfast. "Any signs yet he's around?" Mollison said.

"No, but you might know better than me. Seen any new faces in town?" Pack answered.

Mollison chuckled. "Simon, my friend, you really don't get around town much, do ya? Every day there're tourists littering the town. From all over the country. That said, you're right, my people and I can do a better job of looking out for him. First off, we can rule out women. Second, we're looking for a guy of a certain size. That'll help some, but if he's as good at disguises as you think he is, we still face a tall task. But you're right, we can whittle the possibilities down quite a bit." He added facetiously, "I'll talk to the thousands of men and women on my force about refining the search."

"OK, Joe, now let me tell you Tetu's up in the cabin. He's staying inside. I don't want anyone to know he's there except you. He's protecting the property, but if and when Paschal shows up, I've told Tetu he's backup only. This fight is mine, and only mine."

"Simon, you're hitting on a point I wanted to bring up. Listen, Governor Dahl and I are real worried about you…now before you say anything, let me point out that we don't have any reservations about your ability to handle yourself against anyone, but this guy is a stone-cold killer who's been exercising his skills on a regular basis. Jim Dahl and I want to help," Mollison said.

Pack said, "Joe, I want all you people out of the picture. If he senses you're around, the situation will just be worse for all of us. He doesn't normally go after what you might call 'assistants, or assistors' but I'm telling you if they're within his sight, he'll make a point of killing them too. Same goes for Jim's people, of course."

"You've put me in a tricky position, Simon," Mollison said. "I've already made certain 'arrangements' with the Governor."

Pack frowned. "Shit, Joe, don't do this to me. What're you thinking?"

"There's only one route up to your cabin," Mollison said. "The pavement runs out, then two sections of dirt and gravel road. I want to put a man far off the dirt road way up in the trees. He'd be dropped off

295

so there'd be no vehicles in the area to give himself away. He's just a spotter who could call you if he sees the guy. And the Governor— because you've used the word *insinuation* with us so often—wants to put a man in Yaak, maybe have him staying at the Lodge. We think it's possible he knows about Tetu and might try to get info on you from him."

Pack thought before speaking. "I don't like it, but I'm not responsible for the public safety any longer, so in the end it's your call. But," he added sternly, "no rookies. I don't want some junior guy perched up on a hill, even if he is camouflaged well, to do something stupid like having his firearm or binoculars glint in the sun and be picked up by Paschal. And no pre-emptive strikes on him. Attention to detail, OK, Joe?"

"I hear you," Mollison said, "and I'll have a good deputy on the job." Deputy Janice Tare, who had been in Pack's cabin investigating after Pack's abduction, was Mollison's choice. The young woman was courageous, she could shoot, and she most definitely paid attention to detail.

"All right, Joe," Pack said, "we've never had a cross word with one another, right? So let's end breakfast with my telling you about something good that happened to me last Friday night. I came back after seeing Martino in Kalispell, and Tetu gave me a little letter from Keeley. She'd given me a His and Hers set of motorcycles, with accessories, delivered from Denver, as a wedding gift. Beautiful BMWs, the Adventurer model if you're familiar. It was quite a moment, giving thanks for her all over again, although truly I never stop doing so. So, Saturday morning, Tetu and I took them out for a maiden run. Glad we weren't seen by your guys, 'cause we'd have been pulled over for speeding and various other unspoken crimes. Anyway, you should've seen the big man. Never ridden before is my guess, though he never admitted it. He looked apprehensive, to say the least. You ever been on that new motorcycle and ATV trail system the Forest Service just opened? It runs less than a mile from my cabin, and I wasn't happy when that thing went in. I remember the National Forest Service literature said the trails will be open to 'all sorts of off-road vehicles and be closed during big-game hunting season.' I recall that press release so well because I found the wording odd…you know, 'to all sorts of off-road vehicles.' Anyway, I took Tetu on it, told him these bikes are off-road as well as on-road, so the test ride wouldn't be complete until we took it on the trail. Damn, Joe, we jounced and bounced like you wouldn't believe. Beat the hell out of our kidneys. Gotta admit, it was a thrill, especially the off-road part. By the time we were finished, though, he was riding like a pro, actually said he loved it. Keeley would've been happy for us."

+++

Alan Thomas kept his room reservation in Missoula, but left it for what he calculated would be two or three nights. He got a room for two nights in the Sportsman Lodge, which was also the only place to stay in Yaak. When he drove past the Montana's Armpit saloon, he observed with satisfaction that around a dozen motorcycles were parked in the dirt lot around it. Outside the Lodge the overwhelmingly favorite vehicles were four-wheelers, mostly trucks, but he also saw three motorcycles. He was glad to know his ride wouldn't stand out. He'd managed to strap his full ruck to the kid's bike, which had made the five-and-a-half-hour trip without incident. He saw a General Store just across from the saloon with a sign proclaiming its two pumps carried the only gasoline in the area. He tanked up.

A boy of about eleven came out of the General Store and said, "Hi, sir, my mom owns the store and I work here some. Can I help you? My name's Tommy."

Alan Thomas tried to be Kansas-friendly. "Well, son, I'm just takin' in the views up here. I'm from Kansas. I'cn pump my own gas, if that's allowed. This little bugger only holds about six gallons, so won't take long. Cash only, huh?"

"Yessir," Tommy said, "mom doesn't make much as it is, and the card company charge is just too much, she says."

"Smart woman," Alan Thomas said. "Everybody's out to take your last dime, that's for sure."

"Whadda ya do in Kansas?"

"I run grain elevators. You know what they are?" Alan asked to make small talk, even as he hoped for a swift end to the chitchat.

"I believe I do. We have them in Montana too," Tommy said. "But probably not as many or as big as in Kansas." Then, thinking out loud, Tommy added, "We always get people coming through here, but they're usually going someplace else. Lots of people from California and Washington pass through on their way east. Then back again. You on the way east too?"

"Nope, reckon I'll stay here a couple days."

"Doesn't look like you're gonna fish or hunt, reasons most come here," Tommy observed, waving his hand over the bike as if to say, 'I don't see fishing or hunting gear.'

"Well, son, people hike too, don't they? I might look old and have a bad back, but my doctor says walkin's the best thing in the world for it."

"Oh," Tommy said, and walked back into the store.

When the man walked inside to pay, he met Tommy's mom, Georgann. She called him Mr. Thomas, so he knew Tommy had already told her his name. On the spur of the moment, Alan said, "Ma'am, would you know Mr. Tetu Palaita? Apologize if I butchered the pronunciation. Only reason I ask is I came upon a news story about him, and it said he lives in Yaak."

Georgann said, "Tommy said you're staying at the Sportsman Lodge. That's where you'd find him. He owns the place. Tommy and I think he's worth his weight in gold, and lemme tell you that'd be an awful lot of gold, Mr. Thomas. You can't miss Tetu. He's one of the largest men you'll ever see."

Tommy couldn't resist joining in. He said proudly, "Tetu hires me to work down there a few days a week."

"Good for you, son. Maybe we'll cross paths. So long." Paschal came away from the General Store regretting he'd talked so much. He resolved not to bring up Tetu's name for the remainder of the day. He'd wait until tomorrow afternoon.

That evening he ate dinner in the Lodge dining room, but didn't see Tetu. After dinner he went up to the saloon. Sat at a table, nursed a few beers, listened to the honkytonk, furtively watched the patrons. Nearly everyone in there interacted as if they knew one another, except one big guy. The big guy had failed in his effort to blend in. His clothes spoke cowboy, but something was off, or maybe he wasn't wearing them right. Haircut said military or state trooper. All of the male patrons had headgear, either cowboy hats or baseball caps, but that man had none. His scanning of the crowd was too obvious, like he was looking for someone. Paschal believed that someone was Paschal himself.

He left seven on a five, and rose as if leaving for the night. Once on the porch, he walked off to the right swiftly, where he could peer out from behind a large tree. He saw the big guy come out not even a minute later. From the darkness, Paschal could see the man highlighted by the lights of the saloon. The man was scanning in every direction, searching up and down the road. "He's looking for me," Paschal said to himself. "And if he's in Yaak looking for me he's most likely bunking at the Lodge."

This was still the summer season of thunder, lightning, and slashing rains. Thunder cracked like sonic booms, and the sky suddenly shone bright for a moment, then dark again. On and off, on and off the cycle went. Curiously, the rain that began to fall was scrimpy, barely more than a mist.

Paschal hung in the shadows until the man left the saloon. From a safe distance he followed as the man drove away in the direction of the Lodge. Alan Thomas continued down the road past the lodge, then circled back and returned to the saloon. He snooped around the lot full of trucks until he found an exposed tire iron/lug wrench, which he lifted and drove back to the Lodge. He went to the man's Ford Taurus, used his Leatherman tool to cut the front and rear brake lines, loosened the muffler bearings, and loosened the lug nuts on the rear tires. Then he turned in for the night.

+++

The next morning at breakfast, Alan Thomas pretended not to notice his pursuer. The man was a couple of tables over. When one of the Kootenai men arrived to take his order, Alan Thomas said conspicuously, "Say, can you tell me the rough distance to Libby? I need to pick up some fishing gear, and I've heard there's a great little shop down there."

The waiter answered, and Thomas seemed satisfied. He was certain the man had heard and would follow him.

The road that runs through Yaak goes northeast or southwest. Libby lies southwest, a hard downhill most of the way. He counted on the man to track him to Libby, or at least in the direction of Libby. He hoped he and the man wouldn't get that far.

He went to his room after breakfast, fetched his helmet and a daypack, and proceeded in casual leisure to his bike. He mounted, kick started and commenced down the mountain. When he didn't immediately see the Taurus in his rearview, he pulled off and settled a short way up a logging trail. Finally, he saw it. The man's vehicle was careening madly down the steep mountain road. As Alan Thomas made his way back onto the hard surface, he picked up speed and observed the man frantically trying to slow or halt his car, which now he drove like a luge sled. And then it happened: the man jerked his emergency hand brake upward, causing the Taurus to spin like a top on the rain-slicked road before it went airborne, only to be stopped thirty meters down by the yellow brick road splendor of tamarack forest. The car was splintered from first striking a craggy spine of rock that formed a sharp narrow ridge. Alan Thomas believed there could be no life inside, but he waited a few minutes to be sure. After a time, Alan approached cautiously, keeping three points of contact as he shimmied down the grossly uneven terrain. He saw the man gurgling inside. "You won't be needing this anymore," he said as he ripped away a section of the man's shirt. Then he stuffed the shirt rag into the gas tank and lighted it. He skittered back up the cliffside as rapidly as he could. Not a vehicle had passed for the duration of the event. Alan Thomas wound his way back up the road to the Lodge. He deliberately retained his room key, swiftly packed his ruck, locked the door, and stole away on his motorcycle. He knew there was now only one direction of travel.

As he roared northeast on the empty road he could not hear the bellow of a loudspeaker down at the Lodge. Outside, Tetu's friend, Forest Ranger Ranklin Shiningfish, spoke urgently into the megaphone: "Everyone, everyone must form up outside immediately. This is a

MANDATORY EVACUATION. Fire is approaching rapidly. If you are not out within five minutes, we will open your doors and bring you out. We will escort you to a safe area and shelter."

Last year the fires were especially destructive, and the Forest Service evacuated the town of Eureka, 35 miles to the east of Yaak as the crow flies. Shiningfish told Swan he was sorry, but there was no choice. He would lead them out to a camp the Forest Service had set up for such eventualities. "Can I check to be sure everything is locked tight, Ranklin?" Swan asked.

"Of course, but you must hurry. The fire is not far away." Smoke was thickening by the minute.

Everyone, including Ranger Shiningfish, had no reason to suspect this was anything but a lightning fire. Investigation would later bring out the truth, but not yet. Firefighters from the Rexford and Fortine District and the Three Rivers District were already at work, with more resources on the way.

Before scurrying away from Shiningfish, Swan asked, "How far away from our Lodge is it, Ranger?"

"Less than a mile. Now move," Shiningfish commanded.

The road southwest was already blocked. In a matter of minutes, the Ranger had his convoy moving northeast toward the relative safety of a camp adjacent to the command post for the firefighting teams. It had not been possible to determine if anyone staying at the Lodge was missing. Once in the camp—temporarily, they all hoped—Swan would begin to.... Then she replaced that thought with, "*What does it matter? The Kootenai boys and I checked all the rooms to be sure everyone was out, and that's all I could do. Those not present in their rooms could be anywhere. Out hunting, fishing, hiking. Or maybe, like that Alan Thomas fellow, they needed to go shopping."*

+++

Governor Dahl walked over to his Chief of Staff's office. "Any calls from our trooper in Yaak?"

"No, sir. Last call was when he checked in over there," the Chief said.

"Try him again, right now," Dahl said. "I expected more of him than this. He has an obligation to keep me informed. That's his entire reason for being right now, damnit."

The Chief of Staff made the call. He held the phone up for Dahl to hear it ringing. They stopped counting at eight.

"Then try Tetu's Lodge, talk to Tetu or Swan and report back." Dahl turned on his heels and returned to his office.

The Chief at last ascertained that the Lodge had been evac'd, and the occupants moved to a holding area. He further gleaned information from the Forest Service Command Post that the trooper was not among those in the camp. Dahl could not yet confirm his eyes on Paschal was missing, but he was growing more apprehensive by the minute.

+++

Alan Thomas was by necessity taking the alternate way around to Pack's cabin. There weren't many businesses out here. He saw a billboard advertising "Granny's Diner" two miles ahead. He pulled in there to adjust his plan. *Whoever the big man in Yaak was, he was some sort of officer of the law. Won't be long before they know something's happened to him. And once they get control of the fire, they'll find his car, and once they start taking the scene apart, they'll know it wasn't a simple accident. They'll know lightning didn't start the fire and they'll know someone's responsible for the law officer's death. Yeah, won't take long for them to put Alan Thomas on their Prime Suspects list. Alan Thomas can't live much longer, but it's I who must kill him off. Alan Thomas will live for no more than thirty-six hours. In that small window of time he must dispatch Simon Pack. Hold that thought: Alan Thomas will die after I check out of the student motel in Missoula. I want Pack to see me as Blaise Paschal. I want him to see himself dying by the hand of Blaise Paschal. My original plan was to let the people in Pack's area see Alan Thomas riding oafishly on his motorcycle, get them accustomed to the backward Kansas farmer ogling the mountain vistas. Sit in an adjacent booth at the Sundance and listen to him and that Sheriff talk about Paschal.*

    Now, I guess you could say Alan Thomas is compressing his schedule. Might be better to take Pack tomorrow night or after midnight. I therefore will return to the student motel in Missoula for a long rest before going to Pack's place tomorrow. Alan Thomas needs his strength.

+++

Swan Palaita had been able to connect with Tetu. She told him she was just fine, that the latest word from the Command Post was that their tactics were getting results. They were highly confident the firebreaks they'd established would hold the blaze at bay, not allow it reach the Lodge or the other two businesses near it. The thunder and lightning had continued, but thankfully the rain began to match them in intensity. It promised to be "a gullywasher" the firefighter said.

She told Tetu proudly that none of the three Kootenai youth was going home. They wanted to be there to help Swan the instant the Lodge reopened. So, when Tetu invited her to come stay at Pack's cabin, she happily declined, saying, "Honestly, Tetu, look at this situation. Maybe you think I'm crazy, but I'm bursting with joy. I don't know why exactly, but I think God is blessing us. I can't leave here now. We will reopen soon, and I know there will be no damage. And if some of these guests leave, others will take their places. I tell you, Tetu, these Kootenai boys staying is a breakthrough, a major one, and I cannot wait to tell our worshipers how proud I am of them. They are turning from their bitter, cruel ways, forsaking the destructive path they followed, and I thank God."

And then, more jocularly, "Hey, Tetu, I know for certain now that moving to Yaak and mortgaging our futures for our Lodge was God's plan. You and the Governor stay safe, mister! Take care of each other."

306

CHAPTER TWENTY-ONE

Neither Mollison nor Dahl had provided Pack the particulars of their surveillance coverage. Pack knew nothing of the man Governor Dahl assigned to Yaak. It had been a good idea, Dahl believed still, but today he was sadly confident his man in Yaak had been compromised…or worse. All attempts to contact him had failed.

"Joe, you were the architect of this plan," the Governor began with the Sheriff, then cut himself off. "Let me start over, because that sounds to my ear to be accusatory, and I don't mean that at all. I think your idea to have a man in Yaak was a good call, but I might have bad news. Not sure if you're aware the hamlet was evacuated because of a fire nearby, but the Lodge's guests got moved to a Forest Service sanctuary, so the situation's more chaotic than it would be ordinarily. He's not at the sanctuary camp either, and no one saw him as the guests formed up at the Lodge to make the move. I don't have evidence to say he's missing, injured, or dead, but the signs at this point suggest foul play. And if the foul play was directed toward my trooper, the culprit very likely is Blaise Paschal. Maybe you should fill the General in on what's occurred, tell him to go on higher alert."

"Sorry about your man, Governor. We can still hope there's a logical explanation for his failure to keep you apprised, and that the most severe injury he suffers is an ass chewing from you," Mollison lamented. "At the same time, we have to assume Paschal is behind this. And, yes, I'm going to bring the General in on this personally. Thanks, Governor."

Mollison phoned Pack. "Simon, be cautious. Don't want to say too much on the phone, but he might be closer than we think. Understand?"

"Sure do," Pack said. "Just remember, the rules we agreed to still apply. Keep your designee at a good distance. My fight, OK?"

"I don't like it, but our agreement's still in place," Mollison said.

+++

It was a little past mid-afternoon. Pack had reviewed the ground rules with Tetu: "You are reserve. You do not get involved until I can no longer carry on the fight. If at that point you wanna use the Marlin on him, fine. Don't let him get away. If he comes tonight, and I think he will, I'll be waiting for him here in the garage. Somewhere between unconsciously and subconsciously, when he thinks of me he thinks 'Marine', which he'll connect with prior training, which he'll connect with a post-midnight attack. A time he thinks I'll be groggy, less alert, with balky reflexes. So, Tetu, I don't care where you watch from, but I don't want him to see you. From down the hill, up the hill, from a window, any place's OK as long as you stay out of sight." Tetu acknowledged.

"No offense, Tetu, but I'd like to be alone a little while to think through how this game might play out," Pack said. Tetu complied.

Pack walked around the area outside the garage. He looked around the entire property, but came back to the garage area. He considered 'what if?' the battle starts here or over there? Who will make the first move? How close to him do I want to get?

The gravel driveway led into the garage. It was flat and broad at the base, before it rolled into the garage. From the base the driveway sloped upward to a dirt road. Telephone poles squared off the base of the driveway. If the telephone poles weren't there, one could drive straight downhill for most of five acres. Two large men fighting out in that area could roll quite a ways down the hill. Pack looked at the woodpile wedged between two trees perhaps ten meters down the hill. Those 18" cuts of wood would make excellent weapons, Pack knew, if either was so inclined to resort to them. Then again, so would the rocks—because truly the driveway was more properly called rock than gravel—if one decided to use them.

Then he thought: *I don't want to overthink this either. I think I already have overthought. What's most important is that I've gotten the feel of the stage we'll perform on. This won't be a ballet. It'd be impossible to choreograph the fight. Violence is often active, but it's primarily reactive. I've been in fights before, and each has its own rhythm. I have to get in the rhythm and go with the flow.*

And I have to be prepared for the pain. Real fights hurt. The adrenaline rush never keeps up with the pain. You have to know you'll feel the pain. But you fight through it.

Mixed martial arts training is better than no training, but it does not mean he's a street fighter. I can't allow him to execute spinning kicks and fancy flips. I'll test the depth of his commitment to real violence. I can't play into his strengths. I have to capitalize on my own strengths.

What are my strengths? One, although our body types are similar, I'm bigger and maybe stronger. I was good enough to be a college All-American lineman, the best at my position, and had talent enough to play in the National Football League. I pancaked many nose tackles who went on to star in the pro's. I need to hit him like I've done to blocking sleds thousands of times. Use my elbows and knees. Go for his nose, eyes, genitals. Get in close, don't give him the advantage of stand-off fighting.

Paschal's comfortable with doing horrific things to people, but I'd wager most of those have been weaker or unable to fight back effectively.

All right, I'm comfortable now. Just sit in my camp chair and wait.

+++

Sometime after midnight, Tetu snuck out the back door. He carried the Marlin lever-action rifle, with scope, as well as a Glock 17 in his cargo pocket. He found a spot up the hill behind a tree. He sat in Buddha-like silence.

There was no Sheriff's Deputy spotter out at night.

Pack had removed his watch and wedding ring. His pockets were empty. He didn't know the time; it was immaterial, did not bear on the situation in any way relevant to him. He heard the sound of a small engine, just barely, from down below on the road. As the whine grew keener, Pack swallowed three three-ounce energy drinks and walked the empty containers over to his recycle bin. Then he walked to the edge of the garage and stood there in the darkness.

He tried to imagine how Paschal would've played this if Pack hadn't been waiting for him. Stealthily entered through a window? Kicked in a door? Don't waste brain cells thinking about it, Pack told himself. That, too, is immaterial at this point.

Paschal dismounted his cycle up on the dirt road and walked down the gravel drive. It was too dark to see the garage door raised. Pack's voice clearly startled him, as he said, "Cabin's closed to you, Paschal. Better for you to get on your little bike and move off the property. You said you didn't care for the place anyway. A common intruder could get himself shot rolling in like you have."

Paschal drew some kind of handgun from his waistband and pointed it at Pack. A lamppost at the top of the driveway furnished low-wattage illumination. "And I could shoot you."

"I guess you *could* shoot an unarmed man, Paschal. You've told me you've done it before. But I know you won't tonight. This is a special case. I'm the man who called you a coward before an audience of millions. You'll put the gun down. You'll remember that you're younger, you think you're smarter, you believe all your dojo training has prepared you well, so all in all this oughta be a cakewalk for you, right?" Pack was reasonably sure he was giving Paschal pause. How long had it been since someone, anyone, had stood up to him this way?

They were twenty feet apart.

Pack's F-150 Lariat still rested like a metal monument in the driveway.

"You know, Generalissimo, I…am…going…to kill…you…with only the tools available on my body."

"Like you zapped me in the back of neck. Like you shackled me like a dog. Yeah, you're a real man, Blaise. Now drop your pistol and let's get this over with."

Paschal peered for a long while at the pistol, considering, it seemed to Pack, whether he really ought to cast it aside. At last, he flicked it off to his right. Maybe it landed in a flowerbed. At the moment it left his hand, Pack charged low like a raging bull. As he had done countless times to blocking sleds. Aiming for the beltline, driving upward and back, continuing after contact to pump the legs hard. Wrap up his arms if you can. Don't give him room to get leverage with a strike from hands, arms, elbows. Think *brutality*.

But this couldn't be choreographed just so. His bull rush was part success, part failure. Pack's momentum hurled the two of them hard into a side door of the Lariat. Now it was dented. They ricocheted off onto the gravel, with Pack on top. That was the success. The failure was that Paschal had reacted swiftly enough to drive his knee into the charging Pack. Pack's chest caught most of the knee. It did not knock out his wind.

Some of the knee caught his face. Blood spurted from Pack's nose. He knew it broke his nose. It hurt. It blurred his vision.

Pack had Paschal's arms pinned. Paschal struggled to free them. Pack tucked his head in tight next to Paschal's left rib cage.

Paschal flailed his head up and down, trying to reach Pack's head for a butt, but he couldn't reach that far.

Paschal freed his right leg and brought his heel down hard on Pack's left Achilles, just below his calf. Pack winced, knowing he couldn't let that happen over and over.

Pack had no choice but to release his prone position bear hug. He couldn't make his next moves as quickly as he'd like because his hands were trapped under Paschal's weight as well as his own.

Paschal emitted a foul odor, up close, as if days of sweat from exertion and nerves had permeated his clothes as well as skin.

The noise coming from the combatants roused the unseen world of nocturnal creatures whose claws and paws could now be heard scuttling across the forest floor.

With a loud growl, Pack ripped his hands free. His left hand tore at Paschal's face. Two fingernails raked across Paschal's eye sockets, then on a second pass found purchase in his nostrils. Paschal's hands tried to protect his face. Pack felt sure he had separated the base of a nostril from Paschal's face. Paschal wailed in pain, but hammered the back of Pack's head and neck with a clubbed hand.

The blows to the head were slowly causing Pack to lose consciousness, but he told himself to remain stalwart. He told himself he was impervious to the wicked blows. But the laws of human physiology are themselves impervious to the affects of mind games.

With his right hand, Pack struggled to grasp Paschal's genitals. But the writhing, jerking Paschal kept shifting the target. Finally Pack felt his target and squeezed Paschal's scrotum with a vise grip, twisting and tugging as he did so.

In the midst of his awful, sickening pain Paschal managed to connect on a wild fist strike into the soft area of the temple. He worked a fist into the same area a second time, then a third and fourth. Pack had suffered football concussions, and thought these could be added to that total. But he fought on. Momentarily stunned, Pack had allowed Paschal to get to his feet.

Both men were in bad shape, neither capable of mounting an immediate assault. So here was Paschal, experiencing that indescribable pain of getting his balls squeezed and twisted. A man may never know the pain of childbirth, but a woman will never know the deep throbbing pain of a nut-kick. It lingers. You have a log in your bladder, you want to vomit your guts out. Paschal had those feelings.

And across from him was Pack, whose world was spinning. Paschal appeared in the weak light like four men stumbling and wobbling. He wasn't sure he could hit Paschal if he lunged for him. But he did risk stepping in toward Paschal and from down deep he drove his hip and shoulder into a textbook uppercut that carried the maximum force Pack could summon. It struck Paschal under his left jaw. Having luck at the right moment is a godsend. Pack had gotten lucky. Nine times out of ten he wouldn't have been able to hit Paschal that solidly.

Paschal was hurting in too many places to track, and couldn't tell what part of his body was most painful. He felt for his jaw. It was broken. Shards of teeth rattled inside his mouth. He had bitten his lip, and his tongue, from which blood poured down his shirt. His saliva, mixed with the blood, tasted like kerosene. One of his nostrils flapped in a loose fold across his face. He could see, but his eyeballs throbbed from the scratches.

Pack collapsed to a knee, not from weariness, but from a sudden jolting pain that felt like a gunshot into his left Achilles. It must have been a product of the damage inflicted by Paschal's heel strikes on it. He was able to rise again, but the stabbing pain reduced his movement to a slow stiff-legged limp.

Paschal stumbled away, bobbing up the hill awkwardly, in great pain, in search of his motorcycle. His legs were the least damaged area of his person, but his groin pain tugged him downward. He did not have the luxury of curling into a fetal position right now. He had scanned for his pistol for a few seconds, but gave up. He needed to get back to Missoula, somehow, to establish a new identity, and be gone from the state of Montana.

Had a passerby observed Paschal in full sunlight, he might've said, "No need to establish a new identity, mister. Nobody could tell what you looked like a half-hour ago anyway."

Tetu emerged from up the hill. "I waited, as you ordered, Matai. Now do you want me to treat your wounds or go after him?"

"Go, Tetu," is all Pack had to say.

"Will you be OK?" Tetu followed up.

"Yes, go now," Pack said again, as he lay back, letting air out in a slow exhale.

Tetu fired up one of the BMW 1200s and set out after Paschal, who had no more than a thirty-second headstart. Because the BMW was much quieter, he could follow the sounds of Paschal's bike. Within a mile he spotted the light from Paschal's machine. Still on a dirt surface, Tetu sped up to forty. Then fifty.

Then Paschal saw the BMW headlight wrapping around his leg. He sped up as he moved onto an asphalt surface. With Tetu still on the dirt path, Paschal sped up to sixty on the pavement, then seventy. Paschal silently calculated that keeping this motorcycle on the road was among the two or three, if not the, most challenging tasks he'd ever undertaken. His pain and impaired sense of sight required the sustained focus of every cell in his body. If he yielded even a nanosecond to his desire to seek relief, the momentary loss of control would spell disaster.

Tetu's bike could easily exceed 120 mph, so when he entered the paved road, he sped up to close within a few bike lengths of Paschal. He roared above the din of engines. "Stop, Paschal!"

Paschal paid him no attention. He thought it was Pack, but he couldn't have cared less who it was. He knew only what he felt—pain. With every thump of his heart, the pain increased and his will to resist waned. He lacked the energy to sustain this escape attempt. He could no longer control the weaving motorcycle. His hand felt so weak it involuntarily eased off the throttle. His bike slowed to fifty, then forty. He couldn't go on. He ached awfully and everywhere.

Tetu looked on, watching the slow motion denouement of Paschal's mad odyssey.

Paschal was virtually lying on the handlebars of his bike. As the machine slowed to under 10 mph, it tottered off the road and fell on its side into a ditch. Paschal was done, but Tetu took no chance.

He got off his bike, shucked the helmet, and approached Paschal with the Glock pointed at his back. Paschal had not worn his helmet. Tetu shone his TacLite onto the battered face of Pack's opponent. Paschal wasn't dead, but he wasn't moving. Pack had broken him. In the end, Blaise Paschal was *not as:* Not as smart as Pack. Not as tough as Pack. Not as noble as Pack. And Paschal had not had Keeley Eliopoulous on his side. Pack's guardian angel had made sure of the outcome.

Deputy Janice Tare was there first, another cruiser close behind. Then an ambulance. Tetu told them to call another aid team to Pack's cabin right away. It wasn't daylight yet, but the first weak glow of the day announced dawn was but minutes away.

Tetu watched with a full heart as Deputy Tare hooked the cuffs tight behind Paschal's back.

Tetu had an inspiration. During the combat he and Matai had been involved in up in the Yaak about six months back, Pack had had him call Agent Martino a few times. He had retained the number in his contacts. Martino was still in bed when he answered. Tetu spit out the words, in a voice cold and hard: "Agent Martino, this is Tetu Palaita. Matai Pack has defeated Paschal, broken him, beaten him through and through. Paschal has been cuffed and is on the way to Sheriff Mollison's jail. Thank you, and goodbye." He did not wait for a reply. Now he could turn around and return to Pack's side.

Tetu was as happy as he'd ever been, truly ever, in his life. Before mounting the Beamer 1200 Adventurer, he stood to his fullest height, puffed out his chest, seeing himself as one of his warrior ancestors, looked out toward the forest, and bellowed something in his native tongue, a primal giving of thanks that he had teamed with Matai Pack again to defeat a force of evil. He would be a complete man again in the eyes of Swan.

CHAPTER TWENTY-TWO

Before the medics arrived, Pack meditated. His first thought was that Tetu had been prescient in saying he, Pack, *and Keeley* would subdue Paschal. Indeed Keeley had been there throughout. She had planted ideas about how to entrap Paschal. She had planted the motorcycles. It was as if God Himself had directed their delivery. Yes, he or Tetu may have tracked Paschal in a truck, but who knew Paschal would arrive on a vehicle nimble enough to shake them on a logging trail? He felt Keeley's presence as he lay there, and thanked her for the help as a smile creased his face and tears rolled involuntarily from the pain of the shattered nose.

As he'd prepared for the fight, he forgot about the lingering pain in his shoulders. The pain in his nose and head and Achilles overtook the former shoulder pain, which he could now relegate to discomfort status. *Guess I can be thankful for that,* he mused. But he wasn't worried. Tetu never failed; he would bag Paschal one way or another. And he knew from the big-picture perspective he'd be just fine…that was one benefit of having been hurt before. You knew how seriously you ought to take various injuries.

And he thought about how the big guys in Washington had failed, and he'd done their work for them. So many times he'd gotten stuck cleaning up the messes bigshots had made. But when others shirk their responsibilities, Pack knew, someone had to step up and repair the situation. He was sorry many people had died at Paschal's hand, and he himself certainly could not exult in stopping the man before he could kill others. He was simply satisfied that he had done his duty. Trying to make his miniscule speck of the universe a more respectable place to live. A more decent place.

Pack believed he was what he seemed: a simple man who tried to do his duty, a man who tried to stay out of the way of his fellow men, to be more kind than unkind, more understanding than seeking to be understood. But he also reckoned that most things and most people are not what they seem. Who indeed was Blaise Paschal? He lived and loved the life of a guisard, and probably forgot who he really was somewhere along the line. It was supremely unfortunate, Pack imagined, that a human being as gifted as Paschal had turned those gifts in the wrong direction. All he had accomplished amounted to the heap of debris he'd left behind: scores dead overseas; a Montana State Trooper, he would learn in a few days, burned alive; Mike Monticule shot to death; Royce Pseud beaten to a point where his chance of reclaiming a life was dim; and distraught family members.

Blaise Paschal's had not been a life well lived. His life, in the main, had not served his fellow man.

But Simon Pack had again sought to drive out the pernicious forces of disorder, because, and simply because, his sense of duty in some inscrutable fashion called him to leave his barely perceptible speck of the cosmos a better place than he found it.

A NOTE FROM THE AUTHOR

The character I cast as the Bad Guy, Blaise Paschal, is based on a man I knew personally. His real name was not Blaise Paschal. He possessed all of Paschal's virtues but, to my knowledge, none of his character defects. Al-Qaeda murdered him on that bridge in Fallujah in 2004, his body hanged and set ablaze. He was every bit the supersoldier I portrayed, a man indescribably talented physically and intellectually. Most of the details of his life comport with reality. I witnessed him demonstrate most of the skills attributed to him through Paschal. I have thought of him often in the years since his death, always according his memory the utmost respect.

I thank Dr. James Patrick Sullivan for opening my mind to Karl Jung. I sat at the feet of a master in each telephone conversation with Dr. Sullivan. He read my earlier books and himself made the connection between Pack and trains. A strong argument can be made that he is the pre-eminent Jungian in America today.

I received essential information about trains in general and Amtrak in particular from two men with encyclopedic knowledge on both subjects. Judge John Lenderman and Mr. Phillip Sturgill stopped me from making glaring errors. Perhaps, despite their counsel, I made other errors—if I did, the fault is not theirs.

And there are several others, no less important, who are long-term steady influences in a general sense: Coach Hugh Wyatt, whose scintillating website I read faithfully...Coach Wyatt, a Yale man, gave me access to Coach Carmen Cozza's statement on the value of Work as a means of negotiating rough spots. James A. Larson, my lifetime friend and confidant, who is the inspiration for the character of Governor James Dahl. Simon Pack, wherever he is. And to Keeley Eliopoulous.

ABOUT THE AUTHOR

John M. Vermillion graduated from the US Military Academy at West Point and retired from the US Army as an Infantry Colonel after almost 25 years. For the next 10 years he worked overseas (Germany, Kuwait, Saudi Arabia, Croatia, Bosnia, and Iraq) in a variety of quasi-military positions. In addition to a long slate of military schools, including the Airborne and Ranger programs, he also graduated from the School of Advanced Military Studies and the National War College. Along the path of military assignments he served as a platoon leader in Vietnam and as instructor of English at West Point.

Author Page:

https/www.amazon.com/John-M.-Vermillion/e/B00JGC4FSG

Made in the USA
Columbia, SC
09 March 2018